Elaine considered the advisability of discussing her personal problems with Myra. After all, they were coworkers. She tried not to notice when Myra crossed her shapely legs. In a moment of flitting curiosity, she wondered what she would be like in bed. Horrified by the thought, she sat forward in her chair and began to play with the pen on her desk again. "No, everything is actually rather quiet here today. I'm a little concerned about Laurel."

"Did something happen?" Myra leaned forward, a worried look on her face.

Elaine was touched that she cared. "I don't know. It's . . ." She wavered. Laurel would have a cow if she ever found out that she was telling anyone about the store's problems, but Elaine needed to talk to someone. She was tired of not being able to confide her worries. "You know that Laurel owns the Lavender Page and it's having financial difficulties."

"It's those horrible chain stores," Myra said and waved her hand.

"Precisely. Small businesses like Laurel's can't compete, but she is so stubborn. She'll never give up."

"What can I do to help, darling? I'm ashamed to say I don't read much, but I could go over and buy gift certificates for all my friends."

Elaine felt a sudden rush of warmth for this woman's generous heart.

Also by Megan Carter:

Passionate Kisses
When Love Finds a Home
On The Wings Of Love

Writing as Frankie J. Jones:

Voices of the Heart
Whispers In The Wind
For Every Season
Survival of Love
Rhythm Tide
Midas Touch
Room for Love
Captive Heart

Please Forgive Me

Megan Carter

Bella
BOOKS

2007

Bella Books, Inc.
P.O. Box 10543
Tallahassee, FL 32302

Printed in the United States of America on acid-free paper
First Edition

Editor: Christi Cassidy
Cover designer: LA Callaghan

ISBN-10: 1-59493-091-0
ISBN-13: 978-1-59493-091-1

For Martha
You make it all possible

ACKNOWLEDGMENTS

Martha Cabrera—My first reader. You always keep me honest. Thanks for all you do.

Peggy J. Herring—My second reader. Don't give up. One of these days I may surprise you and learn where those funny commas really go.

Carol Poynor—Thanks for double-checking my double-checking.

Christi Cassidy—My editor extraordinaire. When God passed out patience you must have gotten in line twice. You always make it better.

About the Author

Megan Carter is a pen name for Frankie J. Jones. She enjoys hanging out with friends at the coast and taking long, romantic road trips with her partner. Previous Megan Carter titles include *On the Wings of Love*, *When Love Finds a Home* and *Passionate Kisses*. You may e-mail the author at mcarterbooks@aol.com.

CHAPTER ONE

Laurel Becker pushed away from the computer and rubbed her tired eyes. The muscles in her neck and back cramped from the long hours of sitting. She leaned back into the chair and focused her attention on the Halloween mobile that hung over her desk. The holiday was still almost a week away, but Allie had insisted on putting the decorations up early. Laurel didn't find dancing goblins and gaping skulls nearly as scary as the financial data that she had spent the evening reviewing. She might be able to con herself in moments of weakness, but the glaring red numbers on the electronic income statement couldn't be disputed. Profits for the Lavender Page bookstore were down for the third consecutive quarter. The store's customer base had started on a steady downward spiral eighteen months ago when one of the mega-chain bookstores opened less than eight blocks away. Her small store was no match for their well-stocked women's studies and lesbian fiction sections and the hefty discounts they offered.

In a desperate attempt to challenge the bigger store, she'd given the Lavender Page a fresh look by repainting the interior and revamping displays. When that failed she offered special repeat shopping incentives and increased the number of store events, but sales continued to slip. Last year, in an attempt to capitalize on the holiday sales, she had emptied out her personal savings account to pay for the printing of a full-color brochure. She used it in the largest advertising blitz of the store's history and then cried herself to sleep for a week after the meager increase in sales failed to recoup her expenses. Even with all the extra efforts, end-of-year totals showed sales down by thirty percent.

For the first time in its nearly twenty-five-year history, the Lavender Page teetered on the brink of failure. The only hope of recovery was the rapidly approaching holiday season. Unfortunately, in order to capitalize on it the store needed another infusion of cash, something she no longer possessed.

Tired of the never-ending vicious cycle, she wrenched open the bottom drawer of Chris's battered old oak desk. From the back of the drawer she removed a nearly empty bottle of amaretto. The bottle had been a birthday present from her friend Lou, who also happened to be one of her best customers. Laurel poured a splash of the amber liquid into a ceramic cup that was missing its handle. The simple act brought with it a host of memories of her and Chris sharing a drink after closing the store for the day—back when women still supported the store, before the chain stores bulldozed their way into the market. Now a two-dollar discount was all that was necessary to lure the customers away.

"Stop it," she scolded herself. Times were hard for everyone. Books were outrageously expensive. Customers should go where they could get the best deals. Why should she blame them for her ineptitude? If Chris had lived, she would know exactly what to do to save the store. Laurel sipped her drink and welcomed the slight burn that it left behind. With Chris in charge, the Lavender Page would never have gotten into this position.

She glanced around the modest office. Additional furniture

included a plastic-topped work table, two gray metal file cabinets, a scruffy-looking brown tweed sofa, a couple of straight-backed chairs and a small bookcase filled with catalogs. Nothing much had changed from when Chris had used this room. In fact, the only real change Laurel had made was the computer now sitting on the desk. It was connected to the computer on the sales counter. She had added it six years ago, along with modern point-of-sale software, which allowed her to replace the cantankerous old cash register. The tedious chore of the physical inventory virtually disappeared, thanks to the new computerized system that tracked inventory and sales.

Her gaze drifted back to the monitor and the damning income statement. With some careful planning and a little luck, she would be able to make the payroll through the end of the year, but there wouldn't be enough left to pay down the current balances to her creditors. Since all of the accounts carried past-due balances, requesting an increase on her credit limits didn't seem like a viable option. The only remaining option was to use her second line of distributors. She rarely used these accounts. They offered much smaller discounts and charged more for shipping. The additional costs led to smaller profits and on and on and on. Frustrated to the point of screaming, she punched the power button on the computer without properly closing out of the documents. Instantly, she regretted her rash decision. She couldn't afford the time it would take to rebuild the data. She considered turning the machine back on to ensure that her childish impulse hadn't caused any damage, but she lacked the willpower to do so. Instead, she closed her eyes.

"Chris, I really need to have a good holiday season," she whispered. The thought of possibly having to declare bankruptcy caused a shiver to crawl down her back. To chase away the thought she opened her eyes and sipped her drink again before reaching farther back into the drawer and removing a framed photo. Time dulled the wave of pain that washed through her. Chris had been dead for almost ten years. The image of the short, sturdy woman with the pale blue eyes and sandy-colored hair was the complete opposite of Laurel's current lover, Elaine Alexander, who had long muscled legs, warm green eyes and short auburn hair.

Chris had possessed an extraordinary memory and could talk to customers about any book in the store. There had been a natural warmth and calmness about her that drew people to her. She loved being in the thick of things, whether it was something to do with the lesbian community or her homeowner's association.

Elaine, on the other hand, loved the outdoors. She spent her free time hiking in one of the local parks, or she would head to the coast. She loved to fish almost as much as Laurel did.

Laurel ran her thumb over the photo. *Chris, I need you. I don't know what to do to save your store.* Chris's talents as a businesswoman far exceeded her own, and she'd possessed an almost uncanny ability to read people. She'd always known what to say or do to help the women who came to the store seeking information.

After starting to work at the Lavender Page, Laurel had quickly discovered that sixty percent of the job of running a bookstore was being a psychologist of sorts. Many of the women who drifted in were searching for answers on how to start a relationship, maintain a relationship, end one or recover from one gone sour. They were looking for answers on how to deal with God, family and coworkers. Some came seeking information on health issues that they didn't feel comfortable discussing with their doctors. Over the years, books dealing with adoption, artificial insemination and other child-related issues found their way into the store. Smiling couples came in asking for help with planning their commitment ceremonies. Young women and occasionally not-so-young women inched their way around the shelves and tried to blend in with the wall while they searched through the books dealing with sexuality.

Chris had known exactly what to do to help all these women. She'd listened to their stories, made more cups of tea and held more hands than Laurel cared to remember. In the years since Chris's death, Laurel had tried brewing tea and handholding, but she never felt comfortable with it. For years after Chris died, Laurel would have nightmares that the women would stop coming to the store when they discovered that her own life was a bigger mess than theirs was.

She didn't date anyone for three years after Chris's death, although there were plenty of offers. The number of women who approached her for a date in the first few weeks after Chris's funeral still shocked her.

After three years, Laurel began to venture out on an occasional dinner date, but she seldom accepted the offer of a second date. Then four years ago while on a rare weekend trip to the coast, she met Elaine. Laurel had been fishing beneath the dull glow of one of the lights on the Copano Bay Bridge late Friday night. The speckled trout were hitting fast and furious when a young woman stepped from the darkness and asked if she could share Laurel's light. They started talking as they hauled in fish after fish and discovered that besides fishing they shared a love for the outdoors and for traveling. Both women practiced catch-and-release fishing, so when the sun began to paint the eastern sky with warm streaks of pink and blue, all they had to do was clean their gear and pack it away. Exhilarated by the fantastic night of fishing, they agreed to meet for breakfast later that morning. Laurel raced back to her room to shower and catch a quick nap, but found she was too excited to sleep. She hadn't felt that way since before Chris died.

After breakfast, they drove to the Aransas Wildlife Refuge and spent the day exploring several of the short hiking trails. Later, when they went back to Elaine's hotel room on the pretext of resting before going out to dinner, Elaine kissed her and dinner was forgotten.

At the time, Elaine lived in Houston where she worked as an events manager for a major hotel chain. During the next several weeks, Elaine and Laurel traded off making the trip between Houston and San Antonio. If they were short on time, they would meet halfway and occasionally they would return to Rockport for a weekend of fishing. When a vacancy occurred at one of the downtown locations in San Antonio, Elaine submitted her application and was selected for the position of events manager. At the time it seemed logical that she move in with Laurel.

The first two years were wonderful, but then the store began having financial problems. Laurel tried to overcome them by extending the store's hours, which left her working longer days. The drop in business forced her to cut her staff of four full-time and two part-time sales clerks by half. To compensate for the loss of employees she again extended her own hours. She now worked Monday through Saturday from nine in the morning until ten or eleven each night. The store closed at nine, but there was always something left to do afterward. Officially, Sunday was her day off, but it was rare that she didn't make an appearance at the store, and even when she didn't there were so many other things at home to catch up on that she seldom had a free moment.

With a sigh, Laurel pushed away the memories and lightly kissed the photo of Chris before returning it to the desk drawer. She needed to get home. It was already after eleven; Elaine would be upset with her if she arrived home much later. She drained her drink and went to rinse the cup. As she dried it, she thought about stopping by the market to grab a bottle of wine and some flowers for Elaine. She couldn't remember the last time she had taken her flowers. Maybe they could relax and make love later.

"Yeah, right," she muttered as she tossed the dishtowel aside. It had been months since they had made love. There never seemed to be time, or else Laurel was too exhausted from worrying about the store. Besides, she didn't have the money to spend on flowers and wine.

The phone rang as she was gathering her keys and a stack of catalogs she needed to go through. That was probably Elaine calling to check on her.

The caller was Adam Sanchez, who owned a small mystery bookstore. He and Laurel had met at the Alamo Street Book Fair where they had shared adjoining booths. As part of the fair, several writers were scheduled to read. Each time a reading was in session, business would come to a virtual standstill. It was during one of these lulls that she and Adam had started talking. When he discovered she was the owner of the Lavender Page, he told her his brother was gay. She in turn told him her brother was straight. After a brief awkward silence, he started to laugh. By the time the event was over, they were friends. Now they talked several times a month and occasionally had lunch together to console each other over the woes of owning a small business.

"Sorry to call so late," he said. "I expected to get your machine."

"I stayed to catch up on some bookkeeping."

He groaned. "I put it off as long as I can. How was your third quarter?"

She rubbed her jaw. She was the only person who knew exactly how badly the store was doing, even though it was starting to show. Just from her occasional visits, Elaine had commented on the less than fully stocked shelves and the decrease in customers, but Laurel had brushed off her comments. Of course, the women who worked there might have noticed that sales were dropping off, but no one knew Laurel had sunk practically every cent she possessed into trying to save the store. This was not something she would confide to anyone else, not even Elaine.

Her parents, especially her father, had been strict. Their philosophy of life was simple. You worked hard, never gave in or admitted to any weakness and kept your business to yourself. She and her brother had grown up with their father pushing them to excel, because nobody liked a loser. The slightest sign of weakness was an open invitation for the jackals of the world to attack. Maybe she hadn't become the financial success that Daniel had, but she had become an expert in hiding her feelings and fears. She knew that if word got out the store was hurting, even her steady customers would start slipping away.

"Not too bad," she lied.

"That's great. I've seen a small boost in sales during the past month and the holidays are coming. I live for holiday sales."

Recalling the previous year's lackluster holiday sales, Laurel kept quiet.

"Listen," he said. "I'm calling to tell you about an estate sale I went to today. They had several books, some of them feminist or lesbian-related. They were all in excellent condition and the majority of the ones I looked at were first editions. I bought eight boxes of mysteries and they were practically giving them away, so I thought I'd give you a heads-up."

"Thanks. I'll drive by tomorrow and look them over."

Laurel jotted down the address of the estate sale and again thanked him for thinking of her. Before leaving, she considered calling Elaine to let her know she was on her way home but decided against it. Elaine would start nagging her about staying so late, and Laurel didn't have the energy to listen.

CHAPTER TWO

Elaine was sitting on the bed reading a travel magazine when Laurel went into their bedroom. She hadn't crawled beneath the bedcovers yet and Laurel couldn't help but notice the long tan legs that extended from beneath the oversized T-shirt Elaine wore. Elaine was one of the few women she knew who was slightly taller than her own five feet ten inches. Her height had been one of the first things that attracted her.

Elaine glanced up. "You're later than usual," she said as she flipped the page of the magazine.

"I needed to catch up on the bookkeeping." She braced herself for the impending question and was taken aback slightly when Elaine kept reading. When she didn't ask how the store was doing, Laurel experienced a slight ripple of hurt. Confused by her reaction, she went into the bathroom and showered. When she returned to the bedroom, the light was out and Elaine was asleep.

Laurel stood by the bed wearing nothing but a T-shirt. The

publishers' catalogs were in the living room waiting to be reviewed, but the energy required to try and second-guess which books would be the most popular this holiday season left her feeling sick. She didn't want to watch television. Reading might help her fall asleep, but she didn't really feel like reading either. Since Chris's death, she seldom slept more than four or five hours a night anyway. As she slipped into bed, Elaine rolled over and cuddled against her.

"I know the store is in a slump," she mumbled, still half asleep. "I wish you'd let me help."

Laurel stifled a sigh. *A slump.* She wished that was all it amounted to. She waited a few moments for Elaine to fall back asleep before she eased out of bed. Why couldn't Elaine understand that she didn't want to take her money? It was Chris's store. It wasn't right for Elaine to help support it. Besides, it was her responsibility to keep it operational. Chris had entrusted the store to her. Although a part of her appreciated Elaine's offer, she also resented it because it served as a continuous reminder of her inadequate business skills.

Elaine would have a stroke if she ever found out that Laurel had poured all of her personal savings into the store, as well as Chris's life insurance money. During the last two years, she had slashed her salary to the bare minimum needed to pay her share of the household bills and her few personal expenses. After moving in, Elaine started paying half of all the household expenses. There was no longer a mortgage on the house, but she offered to help pay the property taxes and insurance. At first, Laurel refused because the house wasn't Elaine's responsibility, but Elaine argued that she couldn't simply live there without taking on some of the financial burden. Laurel finally saw the rationality of the argument and gave in.

On many nights, Laurel would wake up in a cold sweat wondering what was going to become of her. How long could she go on with no personal savings and next to no income? Her car was twelve years old, and recently a strange pecking sound had begun in the motor. Worse than all of those things was the possibility of having to declare bankruptcy, because then everyone would know she had failed Chris.

Laurel slipped on a thin robe and made her way to the kitchen. The rich oak floor glowed when she flipped on the light. She removed a glass from behind an etched-glass cabinet door and poured herself some milk before turning off the light. The faint glow of streetlights guided her past the dining room and into the family room. Without turning on a lamp, she curled up on the red leather sofa that used to sit in her parents' den until her father died a few years back. Her mother had died the year before Chris.

After their father's death, Laurel and her brother, Daniel, sorted through the decades of accumulated items in their parents' home. After taking what they wanted, they sold or donated the remainder of the things before selling the house. It hurt to sell the place, but they both owned homes and neither wanted to move back there.

Laurel used her share of the proceeds to pay off the remainder of the mortgage on this house—Chris's house, a modest ranch-style painted white with black trim. Chris had purchased the place a few years before they met. The first mortgage had been on the verge of being paid off when Chris decided to refinance her mortgage to renovate the store, which had once been a home. With the new renovations, all the interior walls were torn out and support pillars were installed to replace weight-bearing walls. Sections of the front walls were torn out to make room for display windows and to make the entrance handicapped-accessible. An addition was added to the back for the new office and a larger restroom. A new roof and a more efficient air conditioning unit rounded out the work. Chris died less than a year after the renovations were completed and left almost eleven years of payments remaining on the loan.

Laurel flipped on the television and found some mindless sitcom rerun. As she sipped her milk, she tuned out the droning voices and tried to devise a new advertising twist or an event that would draw customers into the store. She found it hard to concentrate. Her thoughts kept returning to the way Elaine's body felt snuggled against her. She considered going back to the bedroom and kissing Elaine awake, but Elaine might bring up the offer of financial help again, which would more than likely lead to an argument. That possibility kept her on the sofa.

She twisted into a more comfortable position. There must be some way to breathe new life into the store. Chris had made it look so easy. Under her management, the store prospered and continued to grow for fifteen years. After Chris died, red ink had begun bleeding onto the ledger within six years. With the recent appearance of the other bookstore, the nick in the financial artery had ruptured.

Laurel set the glass down and covered her face with her hands. "Oh, Chris, I'm destroying everything you worked so hard for." What could she do to stimulate sales? Surely there was some way to lure the customers back. She dropped her hands from her face and leaned her head against the back of the sofa. As she gazed at the ceiling, a popular jingle for a sandwich commercial began to play on the television.

She sat up slowly as a memory began to surface. She and Chris had been in Dallas for some conference and while they were there, they visited a bookstore that had included a small coffee/sandwich shop. All the way home, Chris kept talking about paying off the loan as quickly as possible so that she could refinance again to build an addition onto the store and open a small coffee bar.

A wave of hope shot through Laurel. "I could do that," she whispered. The local women's organizations were always searching for a place to hold their various luncheons. A small shop that offered a specialized selection of coffee and teas along with a few sandwiches and salads would surely pull in more business. "It's perfect."

She jumped up and began to pace. There were only a couple of openly gay-owned food establishments in San Antonio. They actually catered more to the blue-haired Sunday morning church women than they did to the gay and lesbian community. She could expand the shop and add a few tables and chairs. She would have to hire two or three new people. She stopped suddenly as reality seeped in and shattered her excitement. There was no money to do any of that. She sat down and tried to think. There must be some way she could get the money. She owned the building housing the store. There was plenty of space for an addition, if she used the side parking lot. She could remortgage the building, but if the coffee bar didn't catch on, she wouldn't be able to make the payments. With her reduced salary, she certainly couldn't afford to pay for it personally. The house was also paid for. It could be remortgaged, but that still didn't solve the matter of repaying the loan. There was always Elaine's offer to help. She quickly dismissed the idea. It was one thing to lose her own money, quite another to lose Elaine's.

She could try to find an outside job, but even if she had the time, she only had an associate's degree and, in a few weeks, she would be turning forty. She had worked as a secretary for a law firm for about six years. Maybe she could call them and see if they would hire her. She gave an exhausted sigh. What difference would it make if someone hired her or not? It would take her years to save enough to finance the renovations. The store would fold long before she could accumulate that kind of money. Besides, if she stopped working at the store she would have to hire someone else and she couldn't afford that. She scrubbed her hands over her face. Why was it always a no-win situation with the store? Frustrated, she grabbed the remote control and started flipping through the channels. With over two hundred channels to choose from, there was bound to be at least one program on that could distract her.

CHAPTER THREE

Elaine turned off the alarm and rolled over and reached out an arm for Laurel. All she found was an empty cold bed. She stretched and rubbed the sleep from her eyes. During the past year, she had watched helplessly as Laurel pulled further and further away from her. It was obvious to her that the relationship was falling apart. The pain was worsened by the fact that Laurel didn't seem to care. At times, Elaine found herself wondering why she kept trying. Laurel had never gotten over Chris, and Elaine couldn't compete with a dead woman or a dying store. Sometimes she wondered if Laurel wouldn't be happier alone with her memories.

Elaine tried to imagine how it must be to lose a lover so suddenly. How would she feel if a stranger called her at work today and told her Laurel was dead? *Devastated* seemed too inadequate. Even with the problems they were having, she honestly couldn't imagine her life without Laurel. Sure, Laurel was rarely home, but when she was, there was a comforting sense of rightness in Elaine's world.

She threw off the covers, climbed out of bed and tucked her feet into her much loved but battered old corduroy house slippers. They had once been navy blue, but numerous washings and years of use had faded them to a muted mid-tone of blue. There were two pairs of new slippers in her closet, but they weren't nearly as comfortable and were seldom worn. She pulled her overly large T-shirt into some semblance of order and went in search of Laurel, certain she would find her asleep in front of the television, where she slept more and more often. She stopped in the kitchen long enough to start the coffee and water the sad little ivy that sat in the kitchen window overlooking the backyard.

Myra Reardon, a coworker, had given her the ivy for her birthday. Elaine stood staring at the plant as the water began to seep out of the bottom of the pot and pool into the plastic dish beneath. Myra was in charge of the housekeeping and landscaping staff at the hotel. She was forever bringing Elaine some little gift. She suspected that Myra might have a slight crush on her. At first she tried to ignore it, thinking it would run its course and disappear without incident, but recently she found herself seeking Myra out at work. They started having a cup of coffee together. Then they began going to lunch. That was when they began talking more and Elaine eventually told her about the long hours Laurel was putting in at the bookstore. Myra listened and was very sympathetic but never said or did anything that was inappropriate. Then yesterday, Myra had invited her to a movie on Friday night. The offer wasn't improper, but the small thrill of excitement Elaine experienced from the invitation might be considered so. She had left the invitation open, claiming she needed to see if Laurel required help with anything before making a commitment. In truth, Laurel never wanted her help. She was the most independent woman she had ever known. She was, in fact, irritatingly independent. Elaine moved away from the sink and went to find Laurel. As she made her way past the dining room, she could see the flickering light of the television screen reflecting off the hallway wall. The sound was so low she didn't hear it until she actually came into the room.

15

Laurel was curled up on the end of the sofa with an afghan pulled over her. The dim glow from the screen cast a soft light over her.

Elaine sat on the edge of the massive coffee table and stared down at the woman she loved beyond her wildest imagination. The intensity of her feelings for Laurel had frightened her for a long time. Surely it couldn't be good to love someone so much.

As Elaine sat watching, Laurel moved slightly and moaned. The movement caused a lock of curly, black hair to fall across her face. Elaine swallowed the knot that suddenly crowded her throat. Laurel was dreaming. If she didn't wake her, she would soon start calling for Chris. Unable to bear hearing Laurel call out for someone else again, Elaine shook her awake.

"Baby, wake up."

Laurel opened her eyes with a slight smile on her face.

Elaine watched even though she knew what would happen. Why couldn't she look away and save herself the pain?

As it had so many times before, as soon as reality returned to Laurel, the light in her eyes dimmed and her smile slowly faded. She pushed herself upright and grimaced as she rubbed her neck and shoulder.

"Why did you spend the night in here?" Elaine asked.

Laurel swung her feet to the floor and continued rubbing her neck. "I guess I fell asleep watching the television."

"You were dreaming when I woke you up." Elaine sat down beside her. She had never told Laurel that she called out to Chris in her dreams. There were times when she wanted to, but something held her back. Maybe she was afraid to admit how much Laurel still loved Chris.

Laurel stiffened when Elaine mentioned the dream. "How do you know I was dreaming?"

Elaine hesitated before standing. She couldn't bring herself to speak Chris's name. "You were restless. The coffee should be ready if you'd like a cup."

Laurel followed her into the kitchen.

"Myra asked me to go to a movie with her on Friday night."

Laurel's response seemed to surprise them both. "I'm thinking about adding on to the store," she blurted out.

Myra was forgotten as Elaine looked at her and saw the spark of hope in Laurel's eyes. It had been so long since she'd seen that look. "Can you afford to?" she asked without thinking.

Laurel's shoulders sagged. "No." She took two cups from the cabinet and set them beside the coffeepot.

Even though she knew it was useless, Elaine wanted desperately to put that spark back in her lover's eyes. "You know," she said as she began filling their cups, "I have the money Grandma Devers left me."

"Stop it," Laurel snapped.

Elaine flinched at the harshness of her tone and fought the sting of tears it brought.

"I'm sorry I was abrupt," Laurel said as she reached out a hand.

Elaine pulled away. "Forget it." She set the coffeepot down and quickly left the room. She didn't want to let Laurel see her cry. After rushing back to the bedroom, she stripped off her clothes and stepped into the shower. A few minutes later, she heard Laurel come into the bathroom. She held her breath, praying that Laurel would join her, but she knew she wouldn't. It was too hard for them to be with each other. She watched the blurred image of Laurel's body through the shower doors as she closed the lid on the commode and sat down.

"I'm going to an estate sale today," Laurel called out. "Adam Sanchez called last night and told me about it. He said there were several books that might be perfect for the store."

Elaine shut the shower off. She felt defeated. "That's great." She slid the shower door open and took the towel Laurel handed her.

"Elaine, I'm sorry." She glanced away as Elaine stepped out.

"I know," Elaine replied as she covered herself with the towel. Maybe Laurel simply didn't find her attractive anymore.

"Why don't we go to the coast this weekend?" Laurel asked before quickly standing up.

A spark of hope ignited. It had been so long since they had gone anywhere or done anything together, but how could Laurel afford to get away, with the store doing so badly now? "I could call and make the reservations. It would be my treat."

"I don't need charity!"

Elaine flinched before a stab of anger born from frustration shook her. "That's good. For the record, I wasn't offering any." She forced herself to take a deep breath, but the anger wouldn't let go. "You know what? I don't need this now. I have to get ready for work."

"Elaine, I'm sorry." Laurel reached out and touched her arm.

She pulled free and turned away. "Would you mind closing the door when you leave? It's a little cool in here this morning."

Laurel left, gently closing the door behind her.

Elaine twisted the thumb lock on the door and turned the vanity faucet on before sitting down on the closed commode and crying. It was time to stop kidding herself. Laurel didn't love her. They should simply accept the inevitable and go their separate ways. She dried her tears on the towel and took a deep breath. Maybe Laurel couldn't afford to get away, but she could. She would tell Myra she couldn't go to the movie and instead she would go to Rockport and spend the weekend fishing and relaxing. Besides, the last thing she needed in her life now was another woman.

CHAPTER FOUR

Laurel walked out of the bathroom but stood just outside the door. The running water didn't completely muffle Elaine's crying. She reached for the doorknob but stopped. What could she say or do to help? The store was taking every ounce of her energy. She made a silent promise that as soon as she had the situation with the bookstore under control, she would devote all of her energy into repairing the damage she had done to their relationship. Even as she walked back to the kitchen and used the microwave to warm her coffee, she knew it would be a long time before she could start fulfilling that promise. Things might be a little rough between them now, but Elaine must know how much she loved her. *I just need a little more time—and money.*

As the microwave spun her cup in lazy circles, she thought about Elaine's offer. She knew several couples who kept joint bank accounts and it seemed to work for them, so why was she so opposed to letting Elaine help her out? It wasn't right for Elaine to give her money to bail out the store—Chris's store—but would it have been

19

so terrible to accept the offer of her paying for a hotel room for a couple of nights? A dull ache began to radiate from the base of her skull. She had forgotten to eat dinner again. She took a container of yogurt from the refrigerator and sat at the kitchen table. As she ate, she repeated her vow to patch things up between herself and Elaine. "As soon as I have the store straightened out," she promised herself.

She could hear Elaine moving around in the bedroom. She would come in looking for another cup of coffee soon. She couldn't start her morning without several cups of coffee. *I'll tell her I'll come home early today and we can have dinner together*, she thought. To her astonishment, Elaine didn't come into the kitchen afterward but kept going down the hallway. A few seconds later, Laurel heard the front door open and shut. She raced to the living room window just in time to see Elaine drive away. Elaine had never left the house without kissing her good-bye. Returning to the kitchen, she turned off the coffeepot and rinsed their cups. As she placed them in the dishwasher, she remembered she wanted to drive over to the estate sale. She called the store and left Allie a message letting her know she'd be a little late coming in. After making the bed, she got dressed before finding her street map and locating the address Adam had given her.

By nine, Laurel was sitting in her car with the windows rolled down. The temperatures were unusually warm for the end of October. She was parked across the street from a stately Tudor with a sign in the front yard announcing the estate sale. The dark brick house located in Alamo Heights blended in perfectly with the rest of the sedate older neighborhood. She glanced around at the large oak trees and carefully manicured lawns. It was obvious that no one around here was hurting financially. She studied the tall graceful chimney on the front of the house and found herself hoping the woman's taste in literature was as good as her taste in housing. Adam had mentioned that they were practically giving the mysteries away. Maybe she would be able to get a decent deal on any books she found as well.

Three of her customers were avid collectors of early lesbian fiction. They would be eager to snatch up certain first editions. As she tried to decide on how much she could afford to spend on the books, a black Range Rover swung into the driveway. Laurel watched as a short brunette climbed out and went into the house. Laurel grabbed her checkbook and headed inside. The brunette greeted her as she came in. No one else seemed to be around.

"Let me know if I can help," she called out.

Laurel thanked her and began to look through a box filled with photo frames. She spied the boxes of books sitting in a corner. In an attempt not to appear overly eager, she browsed through several rooms on the lower floor. The upper floor had been closed off with a piece of blue ribbon tied across the banister. She made her way back to the room with the books. There were several titles of general fiction and dozens more of nonfiction. She found four boxes of women's literature and began to inspect the titles. Adam was right. There were first editions, but they were much too new to be of any interest to her three collectors. All she could hope for was a good deal on the lot to help beef up the store's used-books section.

"If you're interested in books, I'll give you a great deal."

She glanced up to find the brunette standing beside her.

The woman waved her hand. "This stuff belonged to my Aunt Maggie. She never had children so I was sort of nominated to handle the sale."

Laurel nodded. "Were you close to her?"

The woman smiled and sat down on a small stool beside Laurel. "No. I hardly knew her. She was something of a recluse and . . ." She hesitated. "I guess you could call her the family's black sheep."

Laurel held up a copy of a lesbian novel. "I'm guessing lavender sheep would be a better description."

The woman smiled and agreed. "I guess you're right." She held out her hand. "I'm Nancy Grady. I don't think I've seen you around before. Actually, I'm sure of it. I would have remembered."

"Laurel Becker." Laurel found her hand being held a moment longer than customary. She pulled away slowly. Obviously Aunt

21

Maggie wasn't the only lavender sheep in the family. She was used to women coming on to her at the store, but Nancy caught her unawares.

"The fact that I only sort of moved here last week might have something to do with it also," Nancy added as she nodded toward the upstairs area. "I've staked out a couple of temporary rooms upstairs."

"Where did you 'sort of' move from?"

Nancy chuckled before replying. "I've been living in Austin. I have a landscaping design firm there. When Aunt Maggie died and left the house to me I decided to move down here, but I'm still spending a lot of time working in Austin. I hope to move my business down here soon."

Laurel nodded. "Welcome to San Antonio. I own the Lavender Page Bookstore. You should come by sometime." She cringed when she realized that her reference to the bookstore would probably drive the price of these books up. "How much are you asking for these four boxes?"

Nancy looked down. "How does a dollar a box sound? I think Aunt Maggie would be happy to know they'd found a good home."

Ecstatic, Laurel reached into her pocket and pulled out a five-dollar bill. "Here, let's make it easy."

Nancy insisted on helping her load the boxes into the car. "Do you have a bulletin board at the store?"

"Yes. Do you want to post something?"

"I'm going to be living here, but the house is so large I thought I would live on the ground floor and rent out the top floor."

Laurel turned to look at the house. "It's a beautiful home and a nice neighborhood. Write something up and bring it by and we'll post it for you."

Nancy thanked her and looked back at the house before saying, "It's such a shame. She spent a lifetime working for all of this and it only takes a few weeks to dispose of it." She smiled sheepishly. "Sorry, I've never had to . . . you know . . . dispose of anyone else's property and I guess it's reminding me of my own mortality."

Before Chris died at the age of forty-four, Laurel would have muttered some platitude about Nancy still being young with a long life before her. Instead, she opened the door to the driver's side and climbed into the car. "Good luck with everything." With a final wave, she drove away.

CHAPTER FIVE

When Laurel arrived at the store, Allie Boyer, the lanky young woman who was one of the full-time employees, was busy dusting the shelves. Dusting was a never-ending chore. Laurel often wondered if the old building didn't somehow generate an unusually high amount of dust.

"How were the books?" Allie called when Laurel walked in with a box. "Did you find any goodies?"

"Not what I was hoping for, but they'll help replenish the used-books section."

"Do you need help bringing them in?"

"No. You finish dusting. I'll bring the books in and get them cleaned up." Laurel carried the boxes back to her office. Whenever she purchased used books, she always flipped through them to remove any old bookmarks or scraps of paper left by the previous owner before wiping off each book. Then a sticker with a special bar code was placed over the original bar code. The new code would allow the cashier to ring the book up at the special used-book rate. She would then update the inventory in the computer and shelve the books.

As she began to remove the books from the first box, she could see they were well cared for. The reader had been so careful with them that in many cases the spine was barely creased. Chris used to say you could always tell a lot about a person by the way they treated books. Laurel wondered what kind of person the owner of these books had been. Had she ever come into the store? Had she purchased these very books here?

"Find anything good?"

Laurel jumped and dropped the book she was flipping through. "Allie, you scared the crap out of me!"

"I'm sorry. I called you, but I guess you didn't hear me."

Laurel picked up the book. "You caught me daydreaming. What did you need?" Allie worked the Wednesday through Sunday day shift, while her counterpart, Gilda Gomez, worked the Friday through Tuesday shift. Cindy Weir, the part-time employee, worked the evening shift, Wednesday through Sunday. Laurel's goal had been to take off weekends to have more time with Elaine, but somehow that hadn't worked out. Before sales had declined so, Allie and Gilda needed Laurel's help to handle the brisk weekend sales. Now, on most days, one person could easily handle the store alone. She knew she should cut her staff again, but she couldn't bring herself to do so.

"Nothing. I just came to see if you wanted some help."

"You can start putting the stickers on those." She nodded toward the books stacked on the corner of her desk.

"What were you daydreaming about?" Allie asked as she picked up a stack of books and moved to the worktable. "As if I didn't already know it was that gorgeous woman you live with."

Laurel ignored the comment. "The woman who sold me these books may be coming by to post an ad on the bulletin board. Her name is Nancy Grady."

"Is she cute?"

Laurel shrugged. "I guess. She's short, brunette."

"Is she interesting?" Allie persisted.

Laurel looked at her and sighed. "Allie, I didn't ask for a personality profile. I spoke with her for maybe ten minutes."

The remark went seemingly unnoticed as Allie continued, "Because I'm so tired of going out with boring women."

"What about that woman you were supposed to have dinner with last night?" A new lawyer had recently opened up a practice on St. Mary's and invited Allie out.

"I should have gotten up and gone home the minute she ordered at the restaurant."

"Big spender?"

Allie snorted. "She ordered meatloaf."

Laurel pulled the last box of books closer and began to remove them. "What's wrong with meatloaf?"

"B-or-ing." Allie dragged the word out into several syllables.

"That's silly. I love meatloaf." When Allie didn't reply, Laurel glanced up. "I won't even remind you who signs your paycheck before I ask you if that silence was an indication that you think I'm boring."

Allie smiled. "Laurel, please. You're not, but it would be all right if you were. You have Elaine, and you're settled."

She shook head. Allie was a great employee and fantastic with the customers, but there were times when her immaturity made Laurel want to wring her neck. "A relationship doesn't necessarily make you boring, just happier," Laurel said.

"Whatever." Allie rolled her eyes.

"Now, back to last night. You can't judge a woman by what she eats."

"Laurel, I've dated enough women to know what I'm talking about. To prove my point, after she ordered meatloaf, she spent the next hour rattling on about tort reform. When I told her the only torte I cared about was the one I could smear all over her body and lick off, she tells me it's unsanitary. Unsanitary!"

Laurel laughed. "I can see where I might agree with her. I wouldn't want someone smearing a pastry all over me."

Allie made a low moaning sound. "Have you ever tried it?"

Laurel blushed.

"Look at yourself, Laurel Becker. You're blushing."

"I am not. It's just a hot flash."

"You're only thirty-nine. You're too young for hot flashes," Allie protested.

"You are never too young for hot flashes," Laurel said. "Now are you going to help with these books or not?" she asked, trying to hide the fact that Allie had indeed flustered her. She hadn't flushed due to embarrassment, but rather the sudden memory of the things she and Elaine had once done with a cone of ice cream.

Allie waved her off. "I'm getting to it."

"Well, get to it faster."

Allie began to resticker the books. "I saw Lou last night."

"Really, how is she doing? She hasn't been by for a week or so."

"She's fine."

Something in Allie's voice made Laurel look up. Was it possible that Allie was blushing? She decided to do a little fishing. "Where did you see Lou?"

"She was at the Rainbow Center. That lesbian military group she belongs to was having a meeting."

"I didn't know you hung out around the center," Laurel pried.

Allie began to fidget with one of the several pastel rubber bands she wore around her wrist. It seemed to Laurel that there was a different color bracelet for every conceivable disease and social condition. "I was just driving by after that loser date. I saw the lights on, so I stopped by to see what was happening."

"I've heard they have a movie night."

"Yeah, sometimes the movies are pretty good, but a lot of them look like they were shot with somebody's camcorder."

Before Laurel could pry further, Allie changed the subject. "When are we going to get a shipment of new books in?"

Laurel's shoulders drooped. New merchandise meant spending money she didn't have. "I'm not sure," she hedged.

"You're worried about the store, aren't you?"

Laurel hesitated. She liked Allie, but she made it a practice

27

never to discuss the store's finances with her employees. She shrugged. "Business is a little slow. I'm sure it'll pick up during the holidays."

Allie seemed to be on the verge of saying more, but Laurel cut her off.

"Would you mind putting the stickers on these also, please? I need to go through that stack of catalogs. I took them home last night and never got around to them."

Allie gave a small chuckle. "Yeah, I bet. If I had someone as hot as Elaine waiting for me at home, I wouldn't even waste my time taking catalogs home."

"You are horrible," Laurel scolded gently. "Get to work."

A buzzer sounded to let them know someone had entered the store.

"Oops, gotta go," Allie said as she hopped up. "There's a customer."

Laurel pushed her back down. "Start putting on the stickers. I'll take care of the customer." She rushed off before Allie could protest.

"There you are," a high shrill voice called out.

Laurel smiled. "Hello, Lou. Where have you been keeping yourself?" Lou Petry was around sixty years old and had more energy than most people a third her age. She was a retired Army major who now spent her time volunteering in at least a half a dozen different organizations that ranged from abused partners to AIDS. She was extremely active in her church and neighborhood, and in her *free* time, she grew an enormous garden that she shared freely with her friends, neighbors and coworkers. She had also been Chris's best friend.

"Oh, here and there," Lou answered as she placed a plastic grocery bag containing several large red tomatoes on the counter before taking her usual place in the chair against the far wall. Not only was the old overstuffed chair the most comfortable in the store, but whoever was sitting in it had a clear view of the door as well as both side windows. The chair was also located near the checkout counter, allowing an unobstructed look at the books each customer purchased.

"How's Dooley?" Laurel asked as she moved behind the counter and sat down on a stool. Dooley was Lou's cantankerous basset hound.

"He's as ornery as ever. All he wants to do is eat, sleep and howl. That's a heck of a life, isn't it?" Before Laurel could comment, Lou rushed on. "Did you hear about Tammy and Ann?"

That was another thing about Lou. She always knew what was going on within the community. A friend of Laurel's had once told her that Lou had known about her impending breakup two weeks before she found out. "No, what happened?" Laurel felt certain she already knew what Lou was referring to. Ann had been to the store a couple of weeks earlier and bought a book on how to forgive a cheating spouse.

"They broke up."

She didn't really want to know the details, but Lou was watching her and waiting for her to ask. "What happened?"

"Tammy found out Ann was seeing someone else."

Confused, Laurel blinked. "Ann was seeing someone else?"

Lou grinned. "Yeah. Little Miss Goodie-Two-Shoes Ann was on the make."

Laurel wondered if Ann had purchased the book for Tammy. "You're right. I'm surprised."

Lou stretched her short legs out in front of her and said, "Of the two I would have pegged Tammy for the butterfly."

"Butterfly?"

"Yeah, you know, flitting from flower to flower."

"Lou, you're horrible."

"Hey, Lou," Allie called as she came out with an armload of books.

"Well, aren't you looking better than a field of daisies to a hungry bee," Lou chirped.

"What's with the floral analogies?" Laurel asked with a frown. "Did I miss a page in the *Lesbian Handbook of Synonyms*?"

"Ignore her," Allie said to Lou in a stage whisper as she set the books on the floor. "Her grumpy meter is running high today."

Laurel's retort was doused when Lou leapt out of the chair. "Did you get some new stuff?" She started digging through the estate-sale books.

Voracious readers of lesbian fiction like Lou were a mixed blessing. On one hand, they bought every available book, but it was impossible to find enough new material to keep them satisfied. On more than one occasion, Lou had left empty-handed because there simply wasn't anything new in stock. When she'd still had the cash flow to place orders, Laurel would spend hours scouring catalogs and numerous Web sites searching for newly released or about to be released lesbian fiction. Even though the number of titles had drastically increased over the years, there still weren't enough to satisfy ravenous readers like Lou.

"I doubt you'll find anything in there that you haven't already read," Laurel said, suppressing a groan. It galled her to have an eager customer with cash in hand and nothing to offer her.

"There's more in the office that I need to put stickers on," Allie said as she glanced at Lou and smiled.

"Maybe I should look through them before I leave, just to make sure," Lou replied with a large smile.

Laurel did a double-take. Was there something going on between those two? She couldn't help but smile as she watched them walk toward her office. The top of Lou's head barely reached Allie's shoulder, and there was almost a forty-year age difference between them. Recalling Lou's flower analogies, Laurel swallowed a giggle as she suddenly saw Lou as a contented little honeybee and Allie as a tall swaying sunflower. "I've got to get out more often," she mumbled as the buzzer sounded and another customer walked in. Laurel smiled and called out a greeting just as the phone rang.

The caller was Cindy Weir. She was the part-time employee who worked the five-to-nine evening shift Wednesday through Sunday. Hiring Cindy was proving to be a dual mistake. First, because there was always something that Laurel needed to stay and tend to, and second, Cindy seemed totally incapable of balancing the register. She knew she should fire her but she felt sorry for her. Cindy was only eighteen and the store was her sole source of contact with the gay community. She still lived at home with her highly devout Catholic parents. Laurel allowed the continued expense of keeping her on because young lesbians like Cindy were one of the reasons Chris opened the store in the first place.

"I can't work Friday night," Cindy said hesitantly. "My aunt is coming in from Chicago and my mom says I have to be home."

Laurel held her tongue. This was the third Friday night in the last six weeks that Cindy hadn't been able to work. "I'll be here, so don't worry about it," she said, trying hard to control her irritation.

"Gee, thanks." Cindy hung up before Laurel could respond.

She stood staring at the phone for several seconds, knowing she should fire Cindy, but also knowing she didn't have the heart to do so.

CHAPTER SIX

Elaine pushed the sliver of cucumber to the edge of her plate. The salad had looked enticing when she bought it but quickly lost its appeal after a couple of bites. She preferred *real* food and thank God had been blessed with a metabolism that could handle something more appealing than salads. *Why did I buy this thing?*

"Sailing to China on that cucumber?"

She glanced up to find Myra standing beside her.

"Mind if I join you, darling, or would you prefer to continue your nautical journey?"

Elaine smiled and put her fork aside. "Stop being silly and sit down." Myra's tendency to call everyone *darling* irritated her.

Myra placed a small green salad and a bottle of water on the table and sat down.

Elaine realized that Myra ate the same thing every day for lunch. "Do you ever eat anything except salads?" she asked.

Myra gave her a grin that for some reason made a wave of heat inch up Elaine's neck. "Sometimes." She speared a small piece of bell pepper. "Darling, are you having a bad day?"

Elaine shrugged. "It's the same as most days. The Hendricks aren't happy with the layout of the Milam Room. We have a group of investment bankers in the Bonham Room and they're complaining that the noise from the historic preservation people in the adjoining room is disturbing them. Food services called this morning to inform me that the one hundred and fifty chicken breasts that were supposed to be served tonight at the Cantus' wedding reception arrived this morning, but upon closer examination, they found that the boxes contained chicken legs. So now, they're scrambling to get the order corrected." She picked up her tea and took a sip. "So to answer your question, no, everything is about par for the course."

Myra chuckled.

"How's your day?" Elaine asked.

"It sounds very similar to yours. A third of housekeeping called in sick. The new maid handling the Presidential Suite walked in to clean this morning and found a rather prominent politician in an extremely compromising position with two young women, neither of whom was his wife. The maid is swearing that there was no sign on the door and that she knocked twice and announced herself. The . . . guest . . . is insisting she simply walked in unannounced."

"Who do you believe?" Elaine asked, completely unfazed. After twelve years in the hotel industry very little surprised her anymore.

"I believe the maid. From the description of the activities going on, the guests were much too busy to hear her knocking."

"Why are men so stupid?" Elaine said, rolling her eyes. "When are they going to learn that if you screw around, you're going to get caught?"

Myra stared at her. "Darling, cheating isn't limited to men, you know."

Flustered, Elaine averted her gaze. "Of course, I know that. It just seems they're more apt to have an affair."

"There's usually a woman involved in each of those affairs," Myra reminded her. She pushed away her barely touched salad and began to pour the bottled water into a glass. "Did you have a chance to ask Laurel if you could go to a movie tomorrow night?"

The insinuation that she needed Laurel's permission irked her. "Are you deliberately trying to piss me off?"

Myra gave a crooked smile before replying. "I do love the way your eyes darken when you get agitated. I can't help but wonder what they would look like when you—" She sipped her water and let the statement hang between them. After a moment she continued, "All I meant was did you manage to get a kitchen pass from Laurel?"

"I don't need a kitchen pass from Laurel or anyone else," she snapped. "I can come and go as I please."

Myra set her glass down in such a way that the back of her hand grazed Elaine's. "Good. Does that mean you'll come tomorrow night?"

Elaine jerked her hand away. She felt off balance. Maybe she was reading more into Myra's comments than necessary. After all, Myra flirted with everyone. To give herself time, Elaine took the napkin from her lap and folded it carefully before placing it on the table. What was the big deal? Why shouldn't she go out to a movie with a friend? It wasn't as if Laurel would be sitting at home waiting for her. When she had mentioned the possibility of going to a movie with Myra, Laurel's only response had been something to do with the store. "Sure, I'll go. It'll be fun." She kept her eyes averted. For some reason, she didn't want to see Myra's response. She was saved from any further conversation when her cell phone rang. After answering the call, she jumped up. "I have to go. The investment bankers and the historical preservation people are having a volume war and now the people in the Bowie Room are complaining about everybody."

"Sounds like the Battle of the Alamo is about to be reenacted," Myra said as she stood. "I should be getting back as well. Shall I pick you up tomorrow night?"

Elaine was already focused on how she was going to solve the problems in the meeting rooms. She turned to Myra, momentarily confused.

"The movie," Myra reminded her. "Shall I pick you up or do you want to meet me there?"

"I'll meet you." Elaine slid her chair back to the table. "Listen, I've got to go. Can we make plans later?"

"Sure. We can make plans over lunch tomorrow."

Elaine nodded before rushing off. As she made her way through the restaurant and across the lobby, she was already regretting her impulsive decision to go to a movie with Myra. Why hadn't she stuck to her decision to go to the coast? By Friday night, she was usually so exhausted that the only thing she wanted to do was go home, climb into a hot bath and listen to some good jazz while enjoying a glass of Chardonnay. *Would Laurel be upset that she was going out with another woman?* She stopped suddenly in the middle of the hallway. She wasn't *going out* with another woman. Why had she thought of the movie date that way? "It's not a date," she said.

"Excuse me?"

She turned to find a young man with a large food rack behind her. She quickly stepped aside. "I'm sorry," she sputtered. "I'm talking to myself."

He smiled brightly. "Sometimes we have to if we want intelligent conversation," he said as he pushed the large cart past her and winked.

She rubbed her head and tried to remember where she had been going. A loud cannon blast echoed from down the hall. The historic preservation people seemed to be making a frontal assault on the investment bankers.

She slipped into the dimly lit room where a film projector shot an ever-widening stream of light onto a screen. A quick glance at the old black-and-white movie brought back memories of her childhood. In grade school, projectors very similar to these had been used in the classrooms.

It took her almost twenty minutes to convince both rooms to call a ceasefire in the war of volume between the historic preservationists' projector and the investment bankers' microphone. In the end, she had to promise to move the investment bankers to another conference room. Both groups were given complimentary desserts to help appease their ruffled feathers.

With peace restored, Elaine headed back toward her office. As she walked, she started trying to think of a way to get out of going to the movie with Myra. Somehow, it didn't feel right. She couldn't quite decide why she was making such a big deal over it but suspected the funny little flutter in her stomach that kicked in every time Myra was near her had something to do with her hesitation. No solution had presented itself by the time she reached her office and her assistant, Tom Miller, handed her a small handful of messages. Tom had been her assistant in Houston. After she transferred to San Antonio and quickly found herself in need of an assistant, she called him with the job offer and he had accepted it immediately.

"It's been a busy day," he said in his soft Lubbock drawl. The overhead light gleamed off his bald head. Rather than try to hide his premature balding as many men did, Tom had chosen to shave away what hair he still possessed. He was a body builder and his shoulders always seemed to be on the verge of bursting through his shirt. To look at him in his fashionable suit and tie, she thought, you wouldn't guess that he worked as a stripper on weekends.

"Let's hope the afternoon is quieter than the morning," she said, thinking about the warring factions in the conference rooms. "Have we received the contract back from Mr. Denny for that birthday party we scheduled for next month?"

He picked up an express-mail envelope and handed it to her. "It came in about an hour ago."

She started into her office and stopped. "Tom, would you mind if Sue went to a movie with some other guy while you were working?" In the three years she and Tom had been working together, a strong friendship had developed. He and his girlfriend, Sue, had moved in together a couple of years ago. Elaine had been upfront with him about her relationship with Laurel from the beginning.

"Yes, I would mind," he replied quickly.

Elaine looked at him, slightly taken aback until she saw him smile.

"She handles my music. I couldn't dance without her," he explained.

"I know that. I meant—" Elaine waved him off. "Never mind. You're no help."

"Is Laurel going out with someone else?" he asked.

"Of course not. She has to work." The statement came out sharper than she had intended.

His eyes lost their teasing look. "It's none of my business, but is everything all right between you two?"

"Yes. Everything is fine." She started into her office.

"Who are you going to the movies with?"

"Myra," she replied without thinking.

"Myra Reardon?" He practically gasped.

She closed her eyes, already regretting bringing up the subject. "Yes." She turned to find him standing with his hands planted firmly on his hips. Something about the posture struck her as being extremely funny and she began to laugh.

"What's so funny," he demanded as her hilarity began to subside.

"Nothing. You just reminded me of that old television commercial with Mr. Clean."

He shook his head. "I have no idea what you're talking about, but you need to steer clear of Myra Reardon."

Tom never spoke harshly about anyone, so his comment about Myra brought her up short. "Why? What have you heard?"

He turned back to his desk and picked up a file. "You're going to love one of those calls," he said and nodded toward the messages he had handed her.

Elaine knew he wasn't going to expound on his comment about Myra. "Which message?"

"The one from Sister Mary O'Reilly," he said.

"Okay, I give up. Who is Sister Mary O'Reilly?"

"She's with the Sisters Against Affluent Bishops."

She saw the smile playing at the corner of his mouth. "Tom, pray tell. What are the Sisters Against Affluent Bishops?"

He was losing the battle to keep from smiling. "They are a

group of ex-nuns who are, and I quote, 'protesting the wealth being accumulated by the male hierarchy of the Catholic Church.'"

She stared at him. "Is this some kind of practical joke?"

He shook his head. "Sister O'Reilly assured me that her organization is legitimate and they would like to host their first annual conference right here in our fair city."

"How big is this organization?" she asked suspiciously.

"According to Sister O'Reilly, they currently have fifteen dues-paying members but are anticipating gathering many more members during their conference."

Elaine rubbed her forehead. "Okay, I'll call her back." She turned to leave.

"Rather than the pink Cadillac that Mary Kay gives to her top sellers, do you think Sister O'Reilly will give away a Saab to the member who recruits the most new members?" he asked.

"A Saab?" she asked, confused.

"You know. Sisters Against Affluent Bishops."

She wrinkled her nose. "That joke is almost as bad as the name. Why didn't you tell her we were booked solid for whatever time-frame she wanted and recommend she call Ramada?"

"Careful," he said, wagging his finger at her. "You know we can't be saying bad things about the guests or competition."

"I didn't say anything bad," Elaine protested.

"Go call her and get it over with."

Elaine went into her office and dropped into her chair. It was days like today that she wished she had gone into a different line of work. She gazed around the office. She loved its soft soothing earth tones. Her district manager had allowed her to redecorate it when she transferred here. There was nothing particularly unusual about the setup. Her desk was a modern oak design with the typical-looking executive chair for her and two green tweed armchairs placed opposite. There was a matching oak credenza behind her chair, as well as a couple of matching file cabinets tucked discreetly in the back corner. A standard green floral sofa flanked by small glass-topped end tables sat along the remaining wall. It was the personal items she had added that made the room feel warm and inviting. Delicate orchids in glossy pots replaced the traditional lamps on the end tables. She had replaced the standard hotel prints with framed posters of places she had been or wanted to go to someday. There were colorful shots of Tuscany, Vera Cruz and Santorini, places she dreamed of visiting. Directly across from her desk was a poster of Big Bend National Park. She and Laurel had spent a week there on their first and only vacation together, and they'd had a wonderful time. On impulse, she pulled her cell phone from her pocket and dialed the store. Her heart gave the same little leap it always did when she heard Laurel's voice.

"What's wrong?" Laurel asked as soon as she heard Elaine's voice.

"Nothing's wrong. Can't I call you occasionally without sending you into a panic?"

"Sure. It's just that you never call me here."

Why was that? Elaine wondered. "Listen, I was wondering if maybe you'd like to go out tomorrow night and do something. We could go to dinner. Maybe even go dancing later." Her heart sank at Laurel's long silence.

"Cindy can't work tomorrow night. I have to fill in for her."

Elaine dropped her head against the back of her chair. "When are you going to fire that woman and hire someone who will do the job?"

"I have customers. I have to go." Laurel hung up before Elaine could say anything further.

Elaine dropped the cell phone back into her pocket and, using the phone on her desk, pressed the preprogrammed button to call Myra. She answered on the second ring.

"Do you have time to talk about tomorrow night?" Elaine asked quickly, before she could change her mind.

"For you, darling, I always have time." Myra practically cooed.

Elaine blinked away tears and wondered if she would ever hear those words from the woman she loved.

CHAPTER SEVEN

Laurel made it a point to leave the store early. She felt bad about hanging up on Elaine earlier. It seemed as though lately they argued more than they talked. Against her better judgment, she had left Cindy alone at the shop in order to go home and spend some time with Elaine. Ignoring her cardinal rule to never use her personal credit card unless she was certain she'd have the money to pay off the balance, Laurel stopped at the grocery store and purchased a bottle of Elaine's favorite Chardonnay and a dozen roses.

When she got back into her car, she had to turn the key three times before the motor finally caught. When it did, the pecking noise that she had been hearing was much worse. She glanced at the wine and flowers and tried not to regret her hasty impulse. The noise lessened as she drove home.

A twinge of nervousness tickled her insides as she thought about the evening before her. She sent up a silent prayer that Elaine wouldn't be overly angry with her for hanging up on her.

She pulled her ailing Ford into the driveway alongside Elaine's new silver Honda Accord, which was only a month old. Elaine had offered her previous four-year-old Honda to Laurel, but pride had forced Laurel to pretend to be too attached to her Ford to part with it. In the dim glow of the streetlights, Laurel sat in her car and studied the Honda. She wondered what kind of car she would have been driving now if she had kept her secretarial job with the law firm. She had enjoyed working there but had decided to quit when Chris needed help at the store. The secretarial job paid well, much better than her current salary, in fact. The hours had occasionally been longer than she had liked, but they always paid her overtime for anything over forty hours. She smiled at the thought of having a job in which she only worked forty hours a week.

She fussed with the roses. Now that she was home, she was hesitant to go in. If Elaine was angry, which she seldom was, then it would be bad. She had only seen her mad a couple of times and she'd rather never see it again. When she was angry, the woman's tongue was sharper than a new razor blade.

To delay going into the house she gathered the wine and flowers and got out of the car. She made a circuit around her Ford, examining it as she might if she were seeing it for the first time. There was a nasty dent over the back fender where someone had hit it at the grocery store. The original hubcaps had been stolen soon after she bought the car. Certain they'd be stolen again if she replaced them, she bought a set of plastic ones from Wal-Mart. Two of those were long since gone and one of the remaining ones sported a jagged hole in the center. A long thin crack ran across the top of the windshield. Luckily, it was high enough that she didn't need to have it replaced. In the dim light, the rest of the body didn't look so bad, but the harsh glare of sunlight would reveal dozens of tiny dings and nicks. The inside wasn't in any better shape. The floor mats were cracked and peeling. The corner of a display stand she had been using at an off-site book sales event punched a hole in the cheap cloth covering of the backseat. The hole had steadily grown larger over the years. The broiling Texas sun had cracked the dashboard and faded it from glossy black to a washed out gray. She patted the hood of the old car and felt a moment of guilt that she and Chris had converted the garage into a family room.

A light came on from across the street. Laurel froze as Mrs. Blackburn, an elderly widow, came out with her equally elderly poodle, Precious. If either of them spied her, it would be an hour before she could get away. She eased down until the car shielded her from their view, before she darted in front of the Honda. The next part would be trickier. She would have to make her way around the hedge that grew along the sidewalk leading to the house. As soon as she turned onto the sidewalk, the streetlights would make her visible. She thought about trying to wait the two out, but sometimes Precious was a little slow in taking care of business. If they moved to the far side of the yard, the Honda would block their view, and she could dash into the house. Rather than stand up and risk being seen, she sat the flowers and wine aside, and then peeked beneath the car to see if she could see either Precious or Mrs. Blackburn's feet.

"What are you doing?"

Startled, Laurel shot up. The back of her head slammed into the Honda's bumper, and for a moment, the proverbial stars of Texas were floating around her head.

Elaine knelt beside her. "Are you all right?"

"Do I look all right?" she snapped, mad and embarrassed at being caught sneaking into her own house. She gingerly touched the back of her head and panicked when she felt a damp spot. "Crap." She moaned. "I think I'm bleeding."

"Come into the house and let me look at it." Elaine tried to help her up.

"Wait," she hissed and pulled Elaine down beside her.

"What is going on?" Elaine demanded. "What's this?" She picked up the wine and roses.

"Those are for you. After this afternoon, I thought I'd come home early and—"

Elaine leaned forward and kissed her softly. "Thank you. That's sweet. Come on in the house and let me look at your head." Again she started to stand and Laurel pulled her back.

"Wait. Mrs. Blackburn is out with Precious."

"Oh, God." Elaine sighed softly. "We could be stuck here all night."

"We'll just have to wait until they get over by those oleander bushes," Laurel said. "She won't be able to see us then and we can make a dash for the house."

"Let me see where she is." Elaine started to stand, but Laurel held her.

"You can't do that. She'll see you." Ignoring the throbbing in her head Laurel lay back down on the sidewalk to peer under the car.

"So, that's what you were doing," Elaine said and giggled.

"Hush," Laurel hissed. "They'll hear you."

"Laurel, Precious hasn't heard anything in at least five years."

Laurel hopped up and grabbed Elaine's hand. "They're by the oleanders. Let's go."

They darted around the hedge and up the sidewalk. Elaine's giggling grew to hysterical laughter by the time they burst into the house.

"Crap, that was close," Laurel said as she leaned her forehead against the locked door.

"I can't believe what we just did to avoid that poor old woman."

"Poor old woman, my ass," Laurel huffed. "The last time she caught me, she talked for forty-five minutes and then shanghaied me into going into the house and moving her living room furniture around." She touched the knot on her head and winced. Her hair felt damp, but there was no sign of blood on her hand.

"Come on into the kitchen and sit down, so I can look at that," Elaine instructed.

Laurel sat in the chair at the end of the table while Elaine gently examined her scalp.

"You have a big knot there already," Elaine said.

"My hair feels wet. Am I bleeding?"

"No. I don't see any blood. I washed the car on the way home. You probably just knocked a pool of water loose or something."

"Are you sure I'm not bleeding?" Laurel whined.

Elaine lightly slapped Laurel's shoulder. "You're such a baby."

"It hurts," Laurel protested.

Elaine leaned over and kissed her head.

"Ouch!"

"Laurel Becker, I didn't even get near the bump."

Laurel looked at her skeptically. "It felt like you did," she muttered.

"Well, that's what you get. A grown woman out there hiding like a baby."

"Excuse me, but I seem to remember you were running up the back of my heels trying to get into the house."

Elaine giggled. "I wasn't running. You were dragging me."

"Bull, you were running." Laurel looked up at her. "And very fast, I might add."

Elaine waved her off. "I picked up a pizza on my way home. I was about to eat before I found you doing your James Bond impersonation. Are you hungry?"

"Starved," Laurel admitted as she started to get up to help.

Elaine pushed her back down. "Sit still. I'll get it after I get these in water." She picked up the roses and went to the sink, then turned back and smiled in a way that nearly sent Laurel's heart into a new biorhythm.

Laurel watched as Elaine reached into the top shelf of a cabinet, searching for a vase.

"I guess I moved the vases to the utility room closet when I cleaned out the cabinets," Elaine said as she closed the door. "I'll only be a minute." The phone rang as she turned to leave. They both stared at it. "Let it ring."

"I left Cindy alone at the store. She's probably having problems."

"If it's really serious, she'll call back. Please, don't answer it," Elaine pleaded.

Laurel nodded slightly and gave a small smile.

"Thank you," Elaine replied as the phone stopped ringing. "I know how hard that was for you." She started out of the room.

"I'm going to change into my pajamas while you're doing that," Laurel called.

"Okay. The pizza will be ready in about five minutes."

As soon as Laurel was out of Elaine's sight, she practically ran to the bedroom. She snatched up the phone to call and check the message, but the message wasn't from Cindy. A wave of nausea washed over her as she listened. Unable to believe what she had heard the first time, she replayed the message.

"Elaine, darling. It's me. I do hope you'll be able to get away tomorrow night. I can't wait. Are you sure Laurel will be working late? We wouldn't want her coming home early and you having to explain where you were. Until tomorrow, darling, I say good night and pleasant dreams."

Laurel pushed the erase button, but the words still echoed through her head. Had she misunderstood? Was Elaine seeing someone else? As she mentally replayed the message, she heard Elaine moving around in the kitchen. She hung up the phone and tried to make herself think clearly. She needed to change clothes, get back to the kitchen and pretend nothing unusual had occurred. There was still time to save their relationship. If she didn't lose her head and make a big scene, everything would be all right. She would stop working weekends and come home earlier at night. If Cindy couldn't handle the job, she'd replace her. Laurel tried to make herself stand, but her legs no longer seemed to function properly. She didn't know how long she'd been sitting there on the side of the bed when Elaine walked in.

"I thought you were going to change. The pizza is ready." Light suddenly flooded the room.

Laurel closed her eyes against the sudden glare. Elaine was

seeing another woman. How long had it been going on? Who was she?

"Laurel, are you all right?" Elaine knelt in front of her and took her hand.

Laurel opened her eyes and found Elaine looking around the room as though she were searching for something.

"Did something happen?" Elaine asked. "You look as though you've seen a ghost."

"I don't feel well," Laurel said in a voice that was barely more than a whisper.

"Sweetheart, what's wrong?"

"I just don't feel well."

Elaine placed a hand over Laurel's forehead. "You don't have a fever. You were fine a few minutes ago. I can't imagine what happened. Oh, my God. Do you think you have a concussion? Maybe you hit your head harder than I thought. There is a rather large knot." She moved to sit beside Laurel on the bed and wrapped an arm around her. "Let me help you up. I'll take you to the emergency room."

Laurel studied the woman she had spent the past four years with. Tears sparkled on Elaine's cheek. She reached out to touch one. "You're crying."

Elaine's voice shook when she spoke. "Laurel, you're scaring me. I'm going to call nine-one-one." She reached for the phone, but Laurel stopped her.

"It's not the fall. I think it was the tuna I had for lunch," she lied.

"Tuna? Where'd you get tuna? We never buy it. I thought you didn't like it."

It took all of Laurel's willpower not to jump up and start screaming that she didn't like the idea of Elaine seeing other women either, but that didn't seem to stop her. Instead, she forced herself to smile. "Allie made some sort of tuna concoction and I ate some of it not long before I left the shop. I don't think I should have."

Elaine eyed her skeptically. "Are you sure? I seem to remember reading somewhere that a concussion can make you feel nauseous."

So can finding out that your girlfriend is cheating on you, her brain screamed. "I think I'll just lie down for a while."

"No. I know they never let people with head injuries sleep."

"Then I'll just close my eyes and rest." She stretched out on the bed and welcomed the pain it caused her injured head.

Elaine crawled up beside her and took her hand. "I'm going to sit right here and make certain you don't fall asleep."

Laurel wasn't sure she'd ever sleep again. Each time she closed her eyes all she could see was Elaine kissing a stranger. The other woman was in a dark shadow and no matter how hard she tried, Laurel couldn't see who it was.

"Thank you, for the flowers," Elaine said as her hand closed over Laurel's arm. "They're beautiful."

CHAPTER EIGHT

The night that followed was one of the longest of Laurel's life. Long after Elaine fell asleep beside her, she lay staring at the shadows the streetlights cast upon the ceiling. A light breeze kicked up, making the shadows from the oak tree in the front yard dance upon the ceiling in a wild frenzy. Elaine had wanted to go out tomorrow night to dinner and maybe dancing. Would they have danced with the same wild freedom as the shadows were? Was it after she hung up on Elaine that Elaine had decided to go out with the strange woman who called? Was this the first time they had gone out?

"Laurel," Elaine whispered as she sat up and shook her gently.

She considered not answering, but if she didn't Elaine would probably assume she was in a coma and try to rush her to the hospital.

"Laurel." This time there was a touch of concern in her voice.

"Yes."

"How do you feel?"

Like someone blew a big hole in my chest, she wanted to scream. Was this how Chris felt when her heart exploded? No, the doctor had assured her that it had happened so fast that Chris wouldn't have felt anything.

"Laurel." Elaine shook her again.

Laurel made herself move. "I feel fine, just sleepy," she mumbled.

"Are you sure?" Elaine persisted.

"I'm fine. Go back to sleep."

Laurel pretended to sleep, but it was a long time before Elaine finally dozed off. When she heard Elaine's breathing slow into a steady rhythm, Laurel mentally reviewed each sentence of the woman's message. She took each word and carefully analyzed it to decide if there was some way she could have misunderstood the message. It was the word *darling* that she kept coming back to and stumbling over. After going over the message several times and not being able to find any other explanation, she felt the sting of tears start to build behind her eyes. She squeezed her eyes closed and willed the tears away, determined not to cry. She was stronger than anyone realized. Burying a lover had taught her how to harden her heart against pain. Anger began to burn. Why couldn't Elaine understand how much the store meant to her? She was exhausted and there was no end in sight. If the store was going to survive she would have to work twice as hard. Maybe even find a part-time job. And, rather than support her effort, Elaine was having an affair. Her body began to tremble with anger. Why should she chase after Elaine if she wanted to be with someone else? She wasn't going to allow herself to fall into that mindless trap that so many women did and give up everything to try and save a failing relationship. If Elaine wanted her freedom, fine, she could have it. Laurel might be turning forty, but she knew there were plenty of women who still found her attractive. Rather than sit around and mope about what Elaine was doing, maybe it was time she went out and had some fun. The heck with women. If she were single she wouldn't have to find time for anyone else. She could focus all of her attention on the store. Once it began showing a consistent profit, she could work on getting her personal life back on track.

At some point Laurel dozed because the next thing she knew the alarm was ringing. Elaine turned off the alarm and leaned over her. "How are you feeling?"

"I'm fine. Would you mind if I shower first?" The house had two full baths, but the shower in the guest room had a leak and Laurel had turned the water to it off. Since Elaine had to be at work earlier, she normally showered first.

"No, go ahead. I could use a few more minutes of sleep," Elaine said with a yawn.

I'll bet. Wouldn't want you to be too tired for tonight, Laurel thought as she crawled out of bed. She took a long shower, not caring if she used up all the hot water. Elaine was making the bed when she came out.

"I may be home a little late tonight," Elaine started.

"Fine. I have a lot of things to do," Laurel replied as she yanked clean underwear out of the drawer. She could feel Elaine watching her.

"Are you mad at me?"

Something evil pushed at Laurel to confront Elaine. Instead she looked her in the eye. "Have you done anything that I should be mad about?"

"No," she replied in a voice that didn't sound too certain.

"Then why would I be mad? You're going to be late if you don't hurry."

As soon as Elaine was in the shower, Laurel quickly dressed and left. There was no way she could watch Elaine pick out clothes that might be removed by some other woman in a matter of hours.

The store was a twenty-minute drive from the house. Laurel was almost there when her cell phone rang. When she saw her home number appear on the cell, she turned the phone off and dropped it into her bag. Suddenly, she wasn't in much of a rush to get to the store. Instead, she stopped at a McDonald's for a cup of coffee and drove aimlessly. There was a time before Chris's death when Laurel felt like she'd had several close friends. After losing Chris, she slowly but determinedly pushed them away. She knew she had chosen to disengage rather than endure the pain of possibly losing them, but the effort had been futile because she ended up losing them anyway.

She lost track of time. When a familiar building caught her attention she realized she was back on the streets of her childhood. She hadn't been here since shortly before her father had his debilitating stroke almost seven years ago. Due to his excessive medical needs she and Daniel had been forced to place him in a nursing home where he had remained until he died five years ago.

The late 1950s ranch-style house she grew up in was still standing. Her parents had worked for civil service at Fort Sam Houston and diligently saved their money until her mom found out she was pregnant with Laurel. Only then did they start looking for a house to purchase to raise their family in. The house they fell in love with was near both a grade school and a high school. There was a Lutheran church for them to attend less than four miles away. Two miles beyond that was a shopping mall with a grocery store. The area had everything they needed. Two years later when Daniel was born, they converted the garage into an extra bedroom and eventually added a second bathroom. Every five years her father painted the exterior.

Laurel stared at the house. Despite her strict upbringing, her childhood had been happy. There had never been a time when she questioned her parents' love. Growing up, she had found them to be unbelievably boring. Now, she longed for those simpler times. She drove to a nearby park where her father had taught her and Daniel to play baseball, basketball and, to their total embarrassment, horseshoes. The memories made her smile and suddenly she missed them both. She and Daniel weren't as close as they had once been. He was a botanist and worked at a research and development company near Dallas. She had been to his elaborate home once several years before, after his only son, Zane, was born. She tried to remember how old Zane would be and was amazed when she realized he must be ten or eleven. Daniel and his wife, Judi, an oncologist, divorced soon after Zane's ninth birthday. She was ashamed to admit that she hadn't seen Daniel since their father's funeral. They occasionally talked on the phone, usually at Christmas and sometimes on their birthdays. Somehow everyone had slipped away from her.

Laurel grabbed her lukewarm coffee and made her way across the park to a picnic table. It was gray with age and names had been scratched into every conceivable area. She read a few of them, but didn't recognize any of the young lovers.

Thoughts of Chris and Elaine tried to sneak in, but she slammed the door on them. Suddenly too hyper to sit still, she went back to the car and drove to the site of her first apartment. The building was gone. In its place were a Diamond Shamrock and a Krispy Kreme Doughnut shop. From there she drove across town to the house she and Pam, her first lover, had lived in. She wondered where Pam was. That relationship had simply ended. It was almost as if they had both woke up one morning, looked at each other and said, "This isn't working." Of course, there was probably a lot more to it than that. If so, she no longer remembered what it was. She hadn't heard from Pam in years. The last time had been a Christmas card from Seattle.

After splitting up with Pam, Laurel had moved to another apartment, but there was no need for her to drive there to see it, because she knew it was gone. The sixteen-unit complex had burned a couple of years after she moved in with Chris.

Her grumbling stomach made her glance at the clock on her radio. She was shocked to see it was after ten. Allie would be wondering where she was. She didn't feel like digging the cell phone from her bag and instead turned the car around and drove toward the store. As she drew close, she found she still wasn't ready. She needed to be alone, completely disconnected from the store for a little while longer. Her stomach grumbled again and she used it as an excuse to stop at a pancake house and order waffles and a side order of bacon. Her mouth practically watered in anticipation of the food's arrival, and then a tall woman with auburn hair walked in. The resemblance to Elaine was too much. The smell of the cooking food suddenly made her stomach churn. Laurel dropped a ten-dollar bill on the table and left.

CHAPTER NINE

As soon as the district manager ended the meeting, Elaine practically ran to her office. She had been worried ever since she got out of the shower and found Laurel gone. She tried calling Laurel's cell several times, but there was no answer. Before coming in to work, she drove over to the bookstore, but Laurel wasn't there. Since then she'd lost track of the number of calls she had placed to the house, Laurel's cell and the store. She had almost cried with relief when Allie answered at the store, but the relief quickly evaporated when she learned that Laurel hadn't shown up for work yet.

"Has she called?" she asked, racing into her office.

Tom shook his head. "Are you sure she didn't mention having a meeting with someone or something? What about that group of bookstore people?"

Elaine shook her head. "Allie checked her calendar. She didn't have anything scheduled." She collapsed in the chair beside Tom's desk. "I can't imagine where she is. I wouldn't be so worried if it weren't for that bump on her head. I didn't think it was serious, but maybe it was worse than it looked." She pounded the chair arm. "Why did I make fun of her and just blow it off as being nothing? I should have made her go to the hospital and have it checked."

Tom grabbed her hand. "Elaine, don't let your imagination run away with you. From what you've said the bump on the head was exactly that and nothing to be overly concerned with. She strikes me as a very capable woman. There are a dozen different simple explanations as to where she is."

"Why did she just take off and not say anything to me? She never does that. She certainly wouldn't fail to show up at the store without letting Allie know where she was."

"Maybe she had car trouble and isn't where she can call you."

"She has a cell phone!"

"And you said yourself that she's notoriously bad about recharging it."

Elaine sat up suddenly. "That's it. She's been having problems with that clunker she drives. I'll bet it broke down on her way to work." Her shoulders drooped. "No. It didn't. I went to the store. I would have noticed her car."

"Not if she managed to pull it into some parking lot. If the car started acting up she may have been able to drive it to a repair shop. Does she use any particular shop? We could call and see if she's there."

"No, she uses whoever is the cheapest."

"Elaine, it's almost noon. You're not going to get anything done here today. Why don't you go home? I can reschedule your afternoon meetings. There's nothing pressing."

She took a deep breath and slowly exhaled. "Maybe you're right, but if she calls you tell her to call me right then, but don't let her off that phone until you know exactly where she is."

He nodded.

"Then you call me and tell me where she is."

He stood. "I know what to do. Get your stuff and get out of here."

The phone rang as she started to walk away. She turned to grab it, but he stopped her.

"It may not be her and I don't want you to get stuck on the phone." He answered the call.

Elaine didn't realize she'd been holding her breath until it exploded from her chest in a cry as Tom smiled and nodded toward her office. She didn't bother closing the door as she snatched the phone up. "Laurel, is that you? Where are you? Are you all right?"

"Yes, it's me. I'm at the store and I'm fine."

Elaine was stunned by the curtness of Laurel's answers. "We've been looking for you. No one knew where you were and you left the house this morning without saying good-bye. Are you sure you're—"

Laurel cut her off. "I told you I'm fine. I had some things to take care of."

"Why didn't you let Allie know where you were?" Elaine's concern was rapidly evaporating. She had been worried sick and Laurel's snotty attitude was pissing her off.

"Maybe I didn't think I needed to check in with an employee."

"What about me?" Elaine snapped. "Did it ever occur to you that I might have been worried about you? Would it have been such an imposition for you to let me know that you didn't plan on going to work this morning?"

"I suppose you tell me everywhere you go and everything you do?"

Something in the tone of Laurel's voice made Elaine hesitate. She was trying to decide what Laurel was hinting at when Laurel gave a harsh laugh.

"That's what I thought. Well, since I seem to be the only one who needs to check in, I'll let you know now that I'll be home late tonight." Before Elaine could respond Laurel hung up.

Elaine stood staring at the dead phone in her hand. *What was that all about?* she wondered as she replaced the handset. What was going on with Laurel? She sat down and massaged her temple.

The nagging headache that had been plaguing her all day was getting worse. There was a discreet knock. She looked up to find her door was closed. "Yes," she called.

Tom opened the door and stepped inside. "Are you okay?"

Embarrassed by all the drama she had caused, Elaine fiddled with a pen on her desk. "Laurel is at the store now. Apparently, she had some errands she needed to run."

Tom seemed on the verge of saying more but stopped. "I'm glad she's okay. I'll be at my desk if you need anything." He started to leave but again hesitated. "Should I reschedule your afternoon meetings?"

"No. I'm staying, but could you find me a couple of aspirins or something for a headache?"

When he returned with a bottle of Tylenol and a glass of water, she took two and asked him to close her door on his way out. She sat staring at the Big Bend poster for several minutes before reaching for her cell phone. Laurel owed her an explanation and she intended to get it or . . . or . . . Allie answered the phone before she could complete the thought.

"Laurel's not here," Allie informed her.

"Do you know where she went?" Elaine tried to control the anger that was steadily building in her.

There was an awkward pause before Allie said, "She called Gilda and asked if she could change her hours to work tonight and then come in later tomorrow."

"Cindy can't work tonight. She has some kind of family obligation," Elaine said, grateful that she at least knew some things.

"Laurel fired Cindy this morning and then she put a sign in the window."

Elaine flinched. Had Laurel fired Cindy because of her thoughtless lashing out? "What kind of sign?"

"She's changing the store hours. We're only going to be opened from ten until six thirty." Allie hesitated. "Elaine, she's acting really weird. When I asked her what was wrong, she got super pissed and told me to mind my own business. What's going on? I know she has been worried about the store, but this is different. She's so angry."

Elaine heard her sniffle. "Did she say anything else?"

"She said . . . she said if I didn't mind my own business, I could join Cindy in the unemployment line." Allie was sobbing.

"Allie, I don't know what's going on, but I'm sure Laurel would never fire you. She thinks the world of you. She knows how lucky she is to have you working there." Elaine gave her a moment before asking, "Do you have any idea where she went?"

"No. She just left. If I had known she was going to fire Cindy, I wouldn't have told her about the register being out of balance."

"You're not the reason she fired Cindy. That was my fault. I said something stupid and apparently she was listening for a change." She spun the pen on her desk. "Listen, when she comes back will you please call me, but don't let her know you're calling, all right?"

Allie took a second to respond. "Look, I like both of you guys. I don't want to get in the middle of anything."

Elaine swallowed her irritation. Allie made it sound like they were breaking up. Why couldn't she see it was the damn store that was causing all the problems? She wished it would hurry up and close, so Laurel could get on with her life. Anyone with a half of brain could see what it was doing to her. She stopped her mental ranting, took a deep breath and exhaled slowly. "You're right, Allie. Forget I asked. It's not your problem. I'm sorry." She made a lame excuse about being late for a meeting and said good-bye. She continued spinning the pen as she struggled to take in all that had happened. Where would Laurel go? She carefully reviewed a mental list of their friends and family, but no one in particular jumped out at her. Laurel was a very private person. It wasn't her nature to share her pain and worries with others. A light tap on the door interrupted her thoughts. "Yes, Tom."

The door eased open and Myra poked her head in. "I'm not Tom, but can I come in anyway?"

Elaine hesitated. She wanted to be alone, but maybe Myra could help her sort this mess out. She waved her in. "Come in. I warn you in advance that you may be sorry you did."

"What's going on? Is there another war between the conference rooms?" Myra sat in one of the chairs in front of the desk.

Elaine considered the advisability of discussing her personal problems with Myra. After all, they were coworkers. She tried not to notice when Myra crossed her shapely legs. In a moment of flitting curiosity, she wondered what she would be like in bed. Horrified by the thought, she sat forward in her chair and began to play with the pen on her desk again. "No, everything is actually rather quiet here today. I'm a little concerned about Laurel."

"Did something happen?" Myra leaned forward, a worried look on her face.

Elaine was touched that she cared. "I don't know. It's . . ." She wavered. Laurel would have a cow if she ever found out that she was telling anyone about the store's problems, but Elaine needed to talk to someone. She was tired of not being able to confide her worries. "You know that Laurel owns the Lavender Page and it's having financial difficulties."

"It's those horrible chain stores," Myra said and waved her hand.

"Precisely. Small businesses like Laurel's can't compete, but she is so stubborn. She'll never give up."

"What can I do to help, darling? I'm ashamed to say I don't read much, but I could go over and buy gift certificates for all my friends."

Elaine felt a sudden rush of warmth for this woman's generous heart. "Thank you. That's so sweet of you. It's a wonderful thought but a temporary fix. Nothing short of a miracle would save the store. I've offered to help her financially, but she calls it charity and refuses my attempts." She stopped and rubbed her forehead. "Something happened last night. She came home early and brought me flowers and a bottle of wine. We were having a great time, and then somehow everything went bad." She shook her head. "I don't know what happened." Myra's hand was covering hers. She hadn't noticed Myra pulling the chair closer to the desk.

"Tell me exactly what happened and maybe I'll see something you missed," Myra said as her thumb caressed the back of Elaine's hand.

Elaine started to pull her hand away but stopped. Myra was only trying to comfort her and it felt good to be touched. She started her story with her finding Laurel crouched in front of the car. Myra didn't interrupt until she mentioned the phone ringing.

"Who was calling?"

Elaine shook her head. "I guess it was Cindy, the woman who works nights at the store. She seems to have trouble balancing the register. That's why Laurel stays so late each night."

"It sounds like Laurel needs to find someone else," Myra offered.

Elaine's headache was returning.

"So she answered the call," Myra prompted.

"No. Either it went to voice mail or whoever it was hung up. I don't really know. I was so ecstatic that for once Laurel put us before the store." She stopped, suddenly embarrassed by her admission.

Myra patted her hand and urged her on. "What happened after the phone rang?"

"I went to the utility room to get a vase for the roses."

"Where was Laurel?"

"She went to the bedroom to change, but she never came back. I found the vase and took care of the flowers. When she didn't come back, I called out to her, but she didn't answer. I went to check on her and found her sitting on the side of the bed. She seemed sort of . . ." She struggled for the right word to describe Laurel's behavior. "Stunned."

Myra's thumb stopped its soothing massage of Elaine's hand. "Did you ask her what was wrong?"

"Yes. She told me she didn't feel well. I became concerned that maybe she had hit her head harder than I thought."

"What about the phone call? Did you ask her about that?"

A twinge of irritation stabbed her. Why was Myra so concerned about the phone call? "We didn't answer—" She stopped. "Maybe that was the trouble. Maybe Cindy left a message. That's why Laurel went to change clothes. She wanted to check the damn voice mail. She knew Cindy would leave a message." She jumped up and began to pace alongside her desk. "I guess that explains why she couldn't wait to go tearing out of the house this morning. The precious register was out of balance." The last of her concern faded away. *Just wait until she saw Laurel again.* She was going to tell her exactly what she thought about . . . everything!

"Darling, please calm down," Myra said as she placed an arm around Elaine's shoulders to stop her pacing. "Perhaps we should cancel tonight so you can go home and be with Laurel."

At this moment, Laurel Becker was the last person on earth she wanted to be with. "No," Elaine insisted. "I'm going to that movie. In fact, let's go to dinner and then catch a late movie." *Let Laurel come home to an empty house for a change. Maybe she'd see it wasn't so much fun.*

CHAPTER TEN

Going to the Lavender Page that morning quickly proved to be a colossal mistake. As soon as Laurel walked in Allie started ranting. She demanded to know where Laurel had been and why she hadn't called in to let her know she was going to be so late. People were calling for her, the cash drawer was three dollars and sixty-seven cents short, and Cindy hadn't bothered to leave a note. Allie grumbled that this would have caused her end-of-day drawer to be out of balance if she hadn't taken time to double-check it. In addition to the cash drawer, Cindy had failed to batch the credit card sales. The counter was a mess, and the table displays were in disarray. Laurel tried to escape by taking the phone messages and retreating to her office.

All of the messages were from Elaine. Laurel tossed them in the trash. She didn't want to talk to her. In fact, she didn't want to talk to anyone. As she sat staring into space, she began to feel guilty. There was work that needed to be done, and she should call Elaine to let her know she was all right. She picked up the phone and dialed Elaine's number. Everything might have gone smoothly if Elaine hadn't tried to sound so concerned about her. How could she care for her when she was making plans to be with another woman tonight? When Elaine started bombarding her with questions, Laurel could barely keep from shouting at her that she knew the truth.

Hanging up on her proved to be less satisfying than Laurel thought it would be. In fact, the childish act left her feeling so bad, she actually reached for the phone to call her back to apologize, but then the woman's voice came back to her.

"I do hope you'll be able to get away tomorrow night. I can't wait."

The words seemed to pound in her head.

"Don't forget that payroll checks are due tomorrow," Allie said as she came into the office.

"Have I ever failed to give you your check on time?"

Allie flopped down on the old couch and sighed. "When are you going to order some new books? I don't know how you expect sales to improve without new stuff. I'm tired of listening to customers complain about—"

Laurel's anger was building dangerously high. She took a deep breath and tried to rein it in. "In case you haven't noticed, sales are in the sewer. Maybe you would enlighten me on how you think I can order new books when we aren't selling the ones we already have."

"Can't you order them on credit and pay for them later?"

Laurel turned to her computer and tried to focus on the detailed listing of the previous night's sales. To describe them as meager would have been generous.

"When are you going to do something about Cindy? I'm tired of cleaning up behind her."

Laurel whirled to face her. "And I'm sick and tired of your constant whining." The thin thread of control unraveled. "You're right." She grabbed the phone and hit the speed dial to call Cindy. Months of helpless frustration boiled over as soon as Cindy answered. "Please, tell me what is so damn hard about adding the nightly sales and then subtracting the one-hundred-dollar beginning balance. Why is that so hard? I know everything was balanced at five when Allie left."

"Ah, ah—" Cindy began to stutter, but Laurel cut her off.

"Even if you can't count, is it too much to ask of you to straighten up the displays? I mean, honestly, how many people were even here after I left. Judging from last night's sales, I'd venture to guess six or eight sales." She didn't slow down enough for Cindy to answer. "And how many times have I reminded you about batching the credit card sales? Why can't you remember that?" She stopped short and tried to control her thudding heart. "I'm waiting." She jumped up, but stopped when Allie leapt off the couch, her eyes wide with fear.

"Oh," Cindy mumbled. "I thought you were just taking a breath so you could yell at me some more."

The meekness in Cindy's tone that normally would have shamed Laurel simply made her madder. "You know what? Never mind. Don't even bother coming back in tonight. You're fired. I'll leave a check for what I owe you with Allie, and you can pick it up whenever you want." She hung up before Cindy could respond.

Before her anger burned out, she dialed Gilda's number and basically told her if she wanted to keep her job she would change her hours and work that night. Moving at manic speed, she grabbed a cardboard divider from the stack they used for shipping orders and with a black marker made a sign announcing the new store hours.

She thrust the sign into Allie's hands. "Here, post that in the front window. If no one else cares about this store, why in the hell should I?" She grabbed her keys from the corner of the desk and started to leave.

"What about—"

Whirling, she cut Allie's question short. "If you don't want to join Cindy in the unemployment line, start minding your own damn business."

After storming out of the store, she drove home. The minute she entered the house memories began to assault her. She tried to watch television, but there was the afghan, the one her grandmother Nelda had given her the year before she died, lying across the back of her parents' old couch. Retreating to the kitchen she spied the dimple in the dining room wall where Chris had accidentally punched a hole in the sheetrock while painting the ceiling. She had been acting silly and hit the wall with the end of the extension rod used on the roller. Chris had patched the damaged area, but a small indentation remained. Laurel ran her hand over the old wound and smiled. Things would have been so different if Chris had lived. She would have known how to bring the customers back to the bookstore.

Laurel made her way into the kitchen to get a soda. When she opened the refrigerator door, she found the pizza and the bottle of wine she and Elaine had been planning to have for dinner the night before. She grabbed a can of soda and slammed the door. The roses she had bought Elaine were sitting on the counter. Again, there were too many memories. She started into the bedroom but stopped at the doorway. Even worse memories lurked here. If she hadn't checked the voice mail, her life would still have some semblance of order, some meaning. Why had the woman left a message? Hadn't it occurred to her that she rather than Elaine might be the one who heard it?

Every nerve ending in Laurel's body went numb. The unopened soda can slipped from her hands and bounced silently on the carpeted bedroom floor. Could that be why she left the message? Had the woman wanted Laurel to know about her? Maybe Elaine was being hesitant about breaking it off and this woman was trying to speed things along.

Laurel glanced at the clock on the bedside table, amazed to see it was already five thirty. Elaine normally left work around six. Would she come home first or would she go straight to this woman? As she stood in the doorway, a plan began to form. She was going to find out who the woman was, and then she was going to confront them both. She pulled her car keys from her pocket and headed for the door.

It normally took her thirty minutes to drive downtown. Today she pushed her battered car and made it in less than twenty. It took her a while to find a parking spot where her old clunker was out of sight but she could still see the exit to the parking garage. As the minutes ticked off, she began to worry that she had missed her already. Just as she was ready to give up, Elaine's shiny new Honda pulled out. A disgustingly beautiful sports car followed it out of the garage.

Laurel held her breath as she turned the key. The engine kicked over on the second try. She kept two cars between her and Elaine. It quickly became obvious Elaine wasn't going home. After a few blocks, Laurel realized that the sports car was still behind Elaine. At the next light the car between her and the sports car turned. Taking a chance, Laurel closed the distance, but the car's windows were too darkly tinted for her to see the driver. She was staring at the sports car so intently that she almost missed Elaine's car turning in to a parking lot. The signal light on the sports car came on and Laurel began to feel sick. They were going to the Arbor. Elaine had taken her there to celebrate their first anniversary. The restaurant was located on a corner. Laurel turned onto the side street and parked at a meter. The Arbor was one those odd places often found in San Antonio. The menu carried a hodgepodge of dishes ranging from hamburgers to rosemary chicken, which was Elaine's favorite. They baked their own bread and stocked over two hundred different brands of beer, as well as an excellent selection of wines. One side of the building featured a large patio with an arbor that was covered with massive grapevines, hence the name. The patio would be filled to capacity most nights regardless of the weather. If it was cold or rainy the large bamboo screens were lowered and locked into place. When the summer heat became too intense, the misters kicked on to offer welcome relief. Even at this early hour, there were already several cars in the lot. She jumped out and darted between the cars before stopping behind a white SUV. It took her a minute to spot Elaine in the maze of vehicles, but there she was, with a woman who looked vaguely familiar. As they drew closer, it only took a moment for Laurel to remember her name—Myra Reardon. Elaine had introduced them last year at the Christmas party the hotel threw for its employees and their families. As they walked past her hiding spot, the sound of Elaine's laughter reached her. She didn't know how long she stood behind the SUV, but the voice of a security guard finally snapped her back.

"Can I help you?" he asked, eyeing her suspiciously.

She looked up and shook her head.

The guard appeared to be in his late twenties and had a tattoo of some kind of bird on his arm. "Ma'am, are you okay?"

"Yes." She ducked her head and hurried away toward her car. The last thing she needed was to be arrested. The car thieves were so prevalent and daring in San Antonio that they could practically strip your car with you sitting in it. As soon as she was safely inside her car, all she could do was sit and stare out the window. Elaine really was having an affair. All day a part of her had been holding out hope that she had misunderstood the message, that it had been some sort of horrible mistake.

After several minutes, she noticed the security guard standing by the edge of the parking lot watching her. She needed to leave, but where could she go? She couldn't go back to the house and just sit there until Elaine came home. The store wasn't an option. Gilda would be there and Laurel was too embarrassed by the way she had treated her on the phone. Gilda deserved an apology from her, but she wasn't ready to face up to that yet. She finally cranked the car and drove to Pinky's, the only women's bar she knew of.

Once inside the bar she gave a small sigh of relief. At this early hour, there were only a handful of women and she didn't know any of them. She bought a beer and found a seat near the back by the dance floor. It would be hours before the place began to fill up and by then she hoped she would have some idea of how to straighten out this mess.

She was on her third beer and feeling a little lightheaded when a short, stocky woman asked if she could join her. Laurel motioned to the empty chair across from her.

The woman introduced herself as Casey and Laurel mumbled her name in return.

"I'm from Indiana. I'm here for a conference."

"Where are you from in Indiana?" Laurel asked, not really caring.

The woman gave a grimace. "When I tell you, promise me you won't sing that stupid song."

Laurel watched her as her memory searched for a song about Indiana. She smiled and the woman groaned.

"Could it possibly be that you're from . . . Gary, Indiana?" She tried to decide whether to sing or not.

The woman pretended to cover her ears. "Please, don't sing it."

Laurel held out her hand. "I'll make you a deal. I won't sing if you promise you won't ask me where I work."

Casey grabbed her hand. "You have a deal. We'll talk about everything except that."

After that, Laurel lost track of time. She and Casey talked and laughed. Fresh beer kept appearing on the table, and Casey's jokes kept getting funnier. Laurel had no idea what time it was when a hand landed on her shoulder and a familiar face loomed near hers.

"Laurel, what's going on?" Lou asked.

"I'm having a beer with my friend Casey," Laurel said and swallowed a hiccup. She tried to look up at Lou, but Lou kept swaying from side to side. It was making her dizzy.

"Looks like you've had more than one." Lou motioned to the bottles covering the table.

It wasn't until she moved that Laurel noticed Allie standing behind Lou. "What do you want? Need somebody to count your cash drawer?"

Lou tapped Laurel's shoulder. "Knock it off. She's with me."

"With you?" Laurel struggled unsuccessfully to keep her words from slurring. "Why is she with you?"

"Because I want to be with her," Allie replied with a touch of defiance. "Who are you with?" She eyed Casey with ill-hidden suspicion.

Casey glanced back and forth nervously. "Look. I don't want any trouble. We were just having a few beers."

"There's no problem," Lou assured her. "Our friend here has had too much to drink, and we're going to take her home before there is a problem." She looked directly at Casey. "Okay?"

Casey nodded vigorously. "Sure." She turned to Laurel and smiled. "Hey, thanks for not singing."

Laurel grinned back. "Thanks for not asking."

Casey nodded and disappeared into the crowd.

"You didn't have to run her off," Laurel grumbled. "We weren't doing anything."

"Never said you were," Lou answered. "Come on. We'll drive you home."

Laurel sat staring at the bottle of beer in front of her. It seemed to be moving across the table on its own accord. She reached for it so that it wouldn't fall off the table, and suddenly all the bottles on the table were falling. She tried to catch them, but it was useless. It wasn't until people at the tables near her began to turn and stare that she realized the bar was full. When had all of these women come in?

She watched indifferently as Lou and Allie helped the waitress pick up the bottles and place them into a large plastic tub. Then Lou's hand was under Laurel's arm and lifting her up off the chair.

Laurel's legs began to buckle. Allie grabbed her other arm and steadied her. Laurel wanted to protest that she wasn't ready to leave, but she was having trouble keeping her feet beneath her. She stumbled every time she turned to Lou to talk. She finally gave up trying to talk and concentrated on placing one foot in front of the other. After a less than graceful exit from the bar and equally awkward path across the parking lot, she was draped unceremoniously over the side of the bed of Allie's truck. She tried to stand upright but simply didn't have the energy.

She heard Allie say something about no room, and they seemed to have a long discussion. The next thing she remembered was being dumped into the bed of the pickup.

"Come on, Laurel. Help us." Allie grunted.

"Help me sit her up against the cab," Lou said as she again grabbed Laurel beneath the arm and dragged her. At last, Laurel was propped up against the cab. The night air held a slight nip, but the metal of the truck bed still held a hint of the warmth from the day's sun.

"Are you sure you'll be okay back here?" Allie asked.

Laurel was about to answer when Lou said, "I'll be fine. Remember, if I start pounding on the cab you pull over as soon as you safely can."

"Lou, I don't like this. Can't we just find her car and drive her home?"

Laurel suddenly shot up to her feet. "I'm not going home," she shouted. To her surprise, her feet flew from beneath her and she was again on her butt in the truck bed. Lou was in her face.

"Laurel, it's been forty years since I decked anyone, but so help me if you try that one more time, I'm going to deck you." She grabbed Laurel's chin and forced her head up. "Listen to me. I'm not taking you home. We're going to my house. You can stay there. Are you okay with that?"

"Yes," she answered weakly.

Lou let go of her chin and wrapped an arm around Laurel's shoulder. "Good. Allie, let's go."

The cool wind whipping around the sides of the truck felt good. She tried to close her eyes and lean back against the cab, but the minute she did everything began to spin wildly. She opened her eyes and leaned forward slightly. Lou's arm tightened around her.

"I'm not going to jump," she mumbled. The wind carried the words away before they left her lips. As the truck continued across town, they drove to within a few blocks of the Arbor. She wondered if Elaine was still there with Myra. Or had they gone somewhere else, like to Myra's place? She knew without a doubt that Elaine would never insult her to the point of taking Myra to their house. The image of them together was too much for her to bear. To drive away the threatening tears she began to sing the silly song about Gary, Indiana. The stronger her pain grew the louder she sang. By the time they pulled into Lou's garage, she was howling at the top of her lungs.

CHAPTER ELEVEN

Soon after the waiter arrived with their orders, Elaine knew for certain that Myra was interested in more than friendship. All during dinner, Myra continued making small innuendos. At first, they were rather benign, but they gradually became less subtle. Then Myra started running her stocking-clad foot along the inside of Elaine's calf. The first time she simply twisted away and showed her disapproval with a raised eyebrow. The second time she decided that coy wasn't going to cut it with Myra. "Stop doing that."

Myra shrugged. "You're so beautiful, I can't help myself." Then with a wink, she added, "I'm a bad girl. You should spank me."

"I don't want to spank you," she whispered, unable to determine if she was angry or flustered by Myra's comment.

Elaine turned her attention to her rosemary chicken. Myra's throaty laugh flustered her more. Elaine mentally cursed Laurel; this was all her fault. She was the reason she was in this pickle. She wouldn't be here if Laurel came home at a decent hour and didn't spend her every waking moment thinking about saving that blasted bookstore. *Stop it*, she told herself. *Laurel has enough on her mind without me whining and making it worse.* The bookstore was important and she should be helping Laurel, not making things harder for her. When Elaine first came out, it was a women's bookstore she had turned to for information on where to go and meet other lesbians. Since then, that store, like so many others, had been forced to close its doors. Where did young women who needed help go to today? She certainly had never seen a bulletin board at any of the big chain stores advertising any lesbian events. Maybe Laurel was beating a dead horse, but despite all the problems it caused, a part of Elaine was proud of her for her persistence. *This is silly*, she realized. She didn't want to be here with Myra. She wanted to be with Laurel. An idea struck her. She waved the waiter over.

"I'd like to place a to-go order," she told him and proceeded to order the flame-broiled chicken breast that Laurel liked so much. If Laurel was too busy to go to dinner with her, she would start taking the dinner to Laurel. As soon as the waiter left, she turned to Myra. "I'm really sorry, but I think I may have misled you."

Myra looked surprised. "What do you mean?"

"I love Laurel. I get upset with her sometimes and there are plenty of times when she makes me so mad that I want to scream, but I love her." She looked Myra in the eye. "I'm not in the market for anything else."

Myra nodded and signaled the waiter back for the check.

They remained silent until after they left the restaurant and were standing by Elaine's car. "Let me know if you ever change your mind," Myra said. Before Elaine could respond, Myra kissed her long and hard. Her actions surprised Elaine so, she almost dropped the carryout bag. "I hate losing," Myra replied calmly before walking away.

All the way home, Elaine berated herself for not slapping Myra or telling her off. How could she have simply stood there and allowed Myra to kiss her like that? To say nothing of the look of smug satisfaction Myra had given her just before she left, leaving Elaine standing with her mouth hanging open. How was she going to face her at work Monday morning? The most troubling aspect was that she couldn't deny that she had enjoyed the kiss and the spark of desire it had stirred within her. To her discomfort, she felt herself getting aroused just thinking about the kiss. As she squirmed in her seat, she suddenly pummeled the steering wheel. "Damn you, Laurel Becker, you've got to stop working so late."

She turned on the radio to distract her traitorous thoughts, but every song seemed to be about cheating, lying or, worse, making love on some sandy beach. Finally, in desperation, she switched the radio to an AM talk-radio station that hated everything she liked. Even that couldn't completely chase away the memory of Myra's kiss.

Thirty minutes later, she was sitting in bumper-to-bumper traffic on Loop 410, waiting for a major three-car accident to clear. The wonderful scent of the chicken she had ordered for Laurel filled the car and made her regret her hasty decision to leave her own practically untouched dinner behind.

By the time she reached the bookstore it was almost eight. As she approached the entrance she noticed a handwritten sign announcing new store hours. She released a frustrated sigh when she realized Laurel was probably at home waiting on her. She pulled the cell phone out and called the house to let Laurel know she was on her way home. When there was no answer she tried her cell and hung up when the voice mail kicked in.

It was only a little after eight when Elaine got home. She wasn't overly surprised to see that Laurel's car wasn't in the driveway. She was probably still pissed about the confrontation from that morning and out with Lou somewhere, or maybe the new store hours didn't apply to her.

Elaine changed into a pair of comfortable old sweats before warming up the chicken she had brought for Laurel. She probably wouldn't be home until ten or later and hopefully they would both be too tired to fight by then. If so, maybe they could talk.

After eating and cleaning away her mess, she turned on the computer to check her e-mail. It was the easiest and cheapest way for her to keep up with her parents and her two sisters, who all still lived in Houston.

Laurel still wasn't home when she finished her e-mail, so she began playing Solitaire. She told herself she should be doing something constructive, but she was too tired. She lost track of time as she played round after round. It was only when she went to the kitchen to grab a bottle of water that she noticed the clock on the stove read twelve-fifty-two. She stared at it in disbelief. How could the time have gotten away from her so? Laurel was never this late. She called the store and Laurel's cell again, but there was no answer. She started to dial Lou's number but stopped. Lou wasn't a night owl. She was one of those early-to-bed, early-to-rise women. Besides, if Laurel, with her strong sense of privacy, found out she had been calling around looking for her, it would only make matters between them worse. Elaine tried to convince herself that if anything bad had happened, someone would have called her. Laurel would be home any minute now, so all she could do was sit back and wait.

By one thirty, she could no longer sit still. She tried to call the store again. When there was no answer, she grabbed her keys and drove over there. The parking lot was empty. She killed the engine and forced herself to calm down and think. Where could Laurel possibly be at this time of night? She glanced around the well-lit but secluded lot and refused to let her mind focus on all the horrible things that could have happened to Laurel.

"Think," she hissed. Where would Laurel go at this time of the morning? Other than Lou, Laurel really didn't have any close friends she hung out with. There were no family members around whom she would go to. As far as going out by herself, San Antonio wasn't exactly New York. At this time of the morning, the number of places still open was pretty much limited to bars, and Laurel wasn't much of a drinker. Even if she went to one, she would never go to a straight bar, so her choices were severely limited. Elaine tried to remember where the gay bars were. Suddenly she remembered the women's bar off of San Pedro. They had gone there once a couple of years ago with Lou. She glanced at her watch. The bars would be closing in less than thirty minutes. She dialed Laurel's cell and the home number one last time before pulling out of the parking lot.

The bar wasn't where she remembered it being. She had almost given up when she spotted the rainbow flag flying from the rooftop. By the time she finally pulled into the parking lot it was almost three. She practically shouted with relief when she spotted Laurel's car parked near the end of the lot. As she pulled into a spot closer to what she thought was the entrance, she alternated between being relieved and seriously pissed. At least she knew where Laurel was, but why hadn't she bothered to call her and let her know she was going to be so late in getting home? At the very least she could answer her cell phone. It took her a moment to find the entrance at the side of the bar.

There was a woman standing just outside the door. She held up a hand to stop her. "Whoa, honey. We're closed."

"I'm here to pick up someone," Elaine explained.

The woman gave her a wide, lazy grin. "Lucky me. I'm the only one left, except for the owner and she's spoken for."

Elaine rubbed her head and tried not to snap at the woman. "Look. A friend of mine called and said she'd had too much to drink. She asked me to come and get her."

The woman became serious. "Sorry. I was just teasing you. I'm positive there aren't any customers left, but if it'll make you feel better we can check. I'm Dana, by the way."

Elaine nodded. "I'm Elaine." She forced herself to relax and smile. "Thanks for checking for me."

The woman opened the door and waved her inside. Elaine stepped into the now brightly lit bar. She didn't see Laurel anywhere. An older woman with long salt-and-pepper hair was standing behind the bar. She looked up as they approached.

"Jan, you checked the restrooms for sleepers, right?" Dana asked.

"Yeah, everyone's gone," the woman said, eyeing Elaine. "Why?"

"A friend called needing a ride," Elaine explained.

Jan began slowly wiping down the already clean counter in front of her. "Who's your friend?"

"Laurel Becker," Elaine said. "A tall woman with black hair and—"

"The woman who owns the bookstore," Jan interrupted.

"Yes. Have you seen her?" There was something in Jan's guarded expression that was beginning to concern Elaine.

Jan nodded. "She was in here earlier. She left sometime between eleven thirty and twelve. I didn't see her leave. She was here when I took a break and she wasn't when I came back."

"But her car is still outside," Elaine protested. A sick feeling was forming in the pit of her stomach. Dana and Jan exchanged glances and looked away from her.

When she realized that they were probably thinking she was being played a fool, Elaine tried not to look away, but it was hard and she could feel tears burning the backs of her eyes. "Was she with someone?"

Jan nodded.

"Who?" Elaine felt certain it was one of their friends. Laurel had probably stopped by for a drink and run into someone she knew.

Jan stopped swiping at the counter and looked at Elaine. "I don't know who she was. I've never seen her in here before. She was a short, heavyset woman with a Midwestern drawl. They were both pretty loaded when I went on break, and like I said, when I came back they were both gone."

Elaine hated the pity she saw in both women's eyes. She quickly thanked them and left. Before going to her car she ran across the lot to Laurel's old clunker and prayed she was sleeping it off in the backseat. The car was empty. She went back to her car and slowly drove home.

The first thing she did was to check the voice mail to see if

Laurel had called. There were no messages. With nothing left to do but wait, she made a pot of coffee. She sat in the kitchen drinking it and watching the minutes slowly give way to hours. As the sun began to climb above the horizon, Elaine finally allowed herself to admit the truth. Laurel wasn't coming home. She had met some woman at the bar and gone home with her. Only then did she let the tears come.

At eight, she gave up hoping Laurel would call. A quick shower did nothing to ease her tear-swollen eyes or the headache they had brought on. Regardless of how hard she tried to hold them back, the tears returned when she pulled her suitcase out and packed her clothes. She brushed the tears away harshly as she loaded the luggage into the car. One of the great things about working for a large hotel chain was that she could almost always get a room without worrying about reservations and at steeply discounted rates.

When she checked in, she left her sunglasses on and told the desk clerk that she had been having some renovation work done on the house and mold had been discovered. She elaborated that the contractors weren't sure how long it would take to get the mold cleaned up, but it could take several days. If the man behind the desk doubted her explanation, at least he didn't dispute it. By ten thirty, she was hanging her clothes in the closet of a luxury suite normally reserved for visiting VIPs. She hadn't bothered to leave Laurel a message telling her where she was, because Laurel obviously didn't care.

CHAPTER TWELVE

Laurel turned over and grabbed her throbbing head. Her initial thought was that she must be coming down with the flu. She reached out to touch Elaine and encountered empty space. She opened her eyes to complete darkness. Sick and confused, she reached in the opposite direction and ran her palm along what felt like the back of a sofa that was covered by some type of slightly fuzzy material. She sat up, causing the room to whirl madly around her. She clung to the sofa and took several deep breaths until she could orient herself enough to swing her feet off the sofa. Her bare feet touched a cool tile floor. This definitely wasn't home. As she tried to clear her head enough to remember where she was and why Elaine wasn't with her, something warm and wet slithered across her toes. She screamed and yanked her feet back onto the couch. A dog began barking somewhere very close to her. Confused and frightened, she scrambled as far back on the sofa as she could. Without warning a door flew open and flooded the room with blinding, skull-splitting light. Just before she squeezed her eyes shut and clapped her hands over them, she was almost certain she saw Allie and Lou. She squeezed her eyes tighter and reached for Elaine. Obviously, she was having a nightmare.

"What's going on?"

"Are you all right?"

Laurel snuck a peek through slitted eyes, because these apparitions even sounded like Allie and Lou. The sight before her temporarily made her forget about her aching head. Allie was dressed in a granny gown that was much too short for her. She had rollers in her hair. Lou was in a similar gown, but her hair was simply poking out in all directions. The three women continued to stare at one another until finally an overweight basset hound plopped itself down on its rump beside Lou's foot and began to howl.

Laurel grimaced in pain and covered her ears.

"Dooley," Lou scolded. "Be quiet."

The dog gave a large sigh and flopped to the floor with his head resting on his paws. As he lay there, it seemed to Laurel that he was looking at her with a deep-seated resentment.

"Why is he so mad?" she croaked.

"You're in his bed," Lou said and nodded to the sofa.

Laurel tried not to look guilty. She wasn't really a dog-lover and apparently Dooley had figured her out. "Where am I exactly?" she asked as she glanced around at a small room filled with odds and ends of furniture. There were nearly a dozen boxes stacked against the far wall.

"My house," Lou answered.

"Where's Elaine?"

Lou and Allie glanced at each other. "I'm going to get dressed and make some coffee," Allie said as she left the room.

"Why is she making coffee in the middle of the night?" Laurel asked.

"It's actually morning. This room used to be a darkroom."

Embarrassed and still confused on what was going on, she grabbed onto the information as though it were a lifeline. "Lou, I didn't know you were a photographer."

"I'm not. I had the room converted for an ex-girlfriend. After she left, I never changed it."

Laurel nodded carefully as she slowly unfolded herself from the corner of the sofa. She noticed that she had slept in her clothes.

"Do you remember anything from last night?" Lou asked as she sat on the other end of the sofa.

Laurel grew still as flashes from the previous day came back— the bar, Casey, and finally, Elaine with Myra. Along with the memories came a violent wave of nausea. Her hand flew to her mouth and Lou quickly guided her across the hall to a bathroom. As she hugged the commode, she remembered why she never liked to drink. Several minutes later, as she stood leaning against the vanity trying to control her shaking body, she heard Lou's voice through the door telling her she could find whatever she needed in the corner cabinet.

It was almost an hour later when, freshly showered and slightly less hung-over, she wandered out of the bathroom. She found her shoes in the room where she had slept and put them on before following the sound of voices down a hallway into a large cheerful kitchen bathed in the glow of the morning sun. It seemed almost obscene that the sun could shine so beautifully when her world was shattering again. A quick glance at the clock on the stove announced it was nearly ten thirty.

Allie got up and took two small juice glasses from the refrigerator. Both were about two-thirds full. "Here, drink this. It's guaranteed to cure any hangover." She handed her a glass of something that looked like weak tomato juice.

"What's in it?" Laurel asked suspiciously.

"There's nothing in there that will hurt you, unless you're allergic to tomatoes."

Laurel took the glass and eyed it skeptically.

"You have to drink it all at once. Don't sip," Allie instructed.

The small smirk on Lou's face should have warned her, and maybe she would have paid more attention if she hadn't been so miserable. Laurel gulped the strange mixture down in two rapid swallows. She was about to admit it wasn't that bad when her sinuses began to burn. A thin film of sweat broke out over her body. When she tried to inhale, her throat erupted into a fiery misery. While she was gasping, Allie pushed the other glass into her hand.

"Drink it quick. It'll stop the Tabasco burn."

Laurel gulped the second glass and the burning stopped almost instantaneously. "What in God's name was that?" she rasped.

"That's Allie's secret cure for a hangover." Lou chuckled as Allie picked up the glasses and rinsed them before sitting back down at the table.

Laurel sat down across from her.

"Don't you think you should call Elaine?" Allie asked.

Laurel shook her head.

Lou reached into her pocket and handed Allie some money. "Would you mind going over to the little place on the corner by the library? I'm hungry for some *barbacoa*. You know the kind I like."

Laurel's stomach threatened to rebel again at the mention of food. She struggled to get it under control as Allie nodded and left.

Laurel heard the sound of a car engine crank. As it drove away, Lou turned to her and took a deep breath. Laurel braced herself for the lecture she knew was headed her way.

"Laurel, I've known you for a long time, and your personal business is exactly that. However, I figure I owe it to Chris to sort of look after you and help you when I can."

Laurel started to stand up, but Lou gently took her hand and stopped her.

"No. You're going to listen to me. I don't know what's wrong between you and Elaine, but that little stunt you pulled last night sure won't help things. If it's the store—"

"Elaine is seeing someone else." The words were out before Laurel could take them back.

Lou looked at her dumbfounded. "She wouldn't do that. She's crazy about you." When Laurel didn't respond, Lou sat back and scrubbed a hand over her head. "Are you sure?"

Laurel nodded. "The woman called the house and left a message. I heard it. Then—" She stopped and swallowed. "I saw them together last night. It's someone she works with."

They sat in silence for a long moment.

"What are you going to do?" Lou asked.

Laurel shrugged. "What is there to do? Elaine is a grown woman. She makes her own choices."

"Maybe so, but I'm betting you would still have a lot of influence over those choices."

"What do you mean?"

"I mean, maybe you should spend more time at home and less at the store."

Laurel leaned back in her chair and tried to hold her temper. Of all people, Lou should understand how important the store had been to Chris. Why couldn't anyone understand how important it was to her that the store continued to thrive as it had with Chris? She looked into Lou's eyes and saw only concern. Maybe it was the hangover, or perhaps she was just tired of carrying the burden alone for so long. For whatever reason, she gave in. What did it matter anyway?

"The store is going under," she said. "I don't see how I can keep it open much longer."

"So close it."

Laurel looked up, shocked. "How can you say that? You were Chris's best friend. You know how she loved that store."

Lou nodded. "Yes, I do. I also know how much she loved you. Laurel, she wouldn't want to see you struggling and hurting the way you are. She would have burned the place down rather than have it hurt you the way it has."

Laurel shook her head. "You don't understand. She loved the store. It was her whole life. She opened it to help women."

Lou rolled her eyes. "Stop being a nitwit. You were her life. It was you who brought her joy. The store was a means of income that allowed Chris to be her own boss. Sure, it helped a lot of women and Chris was good with people, but she was also an independent soul who couldn't face the bullshit of a nine-to-five job. She opened the store as a way to avoid that. She never had some starry-eyed dream of creating a lesbian Nirvana. Heck fire, the truth is Chris didn't even like to read. I was the one who read the books and told her what they were about."

"That's not true," Laurel protested. "Chris talked about books all the time. She loved to read."

Lou shook her head. "Did you ever see her reading a book?"

"Of course she read."

"Name one single book you *saw* her reading."

"She read lots of books. She read . . ." Laurel struggled to remember a book. Suddenly, vague memories began to surface. Laurel had always loved to read in bed, but Chris said it gave her a headache. There were cold, rainy Sundays when she would snuggle up under a blanket with a book, and Chris would be off working on some project she had started. She gripped the table as she realized that Lou was right. She couldn't recall ever seeing Chris reading. "She read at the store when no one was around."

Lou slid her chair closer and took a firmer hold on Laurel's arm. "Chris was a wonderful person. She was a good friend who would do anything for you and she'd gladly give you the shirt off her back if you needed it. But, Laurel, she was only human, not the icon you've turned her into."

"What are you saying?"

"I'm saying that if Elaine is cheating on you, it might be because she got tired of trying to compete with a dead woman."

Laurel yanked her arm away and jumped up from her chair. "I can't believe you would say that. You're supposed to be Chris's best friend." She turned and ran out of the house. She heard Lou yelling at her, but she kept running until she was several blocks away. She finally found a bus stop and climbed on the first bus that came by. She didn't care where it was going. There was nowhere she wanted to go anyway.

CHAPTER THIRTEEN

It was almost dark when Laurel finally made her way back to her car at the bar. Exhausted, she drove home. She wasn't sure things between her and Elaine were salvageable, but Lou might have a point. Maybe it was time to lay all their cards on the table and see if there was anything left to save.

The driveway was empty. When she went inside, the same silence and emptiness that had filled the house after Chris's death was back. She wasn't overly surprised to find Elaine's side of the closet empty. Without bothering to get undressed or even pull back the comforter, Laurel fell across the bed and slept.

It was mid-morning before she woke. She stripped off her clothes and showered. When she came out she noticed the message light on the phone blinking and knew it would be Lou. She turned the machine off without checking the message, got dressed and packed two large suitcases. She called and systematically arranged for all the utilities to the house to be temporarily turned off, effective the following day. The final bills were to be charged to her credit card. She called and stopped her cell phone service. Then, she went online to put a hold on her mail and to arrange for Elaine's to be sent to her work address. Afterward, she dumped everything from the refrigerator into the trashcans and set them out in the alley for pickup. As soon as she was certain everything at the house was in order, she went back inside to call Elaine's cell. Even as she dialed the first three numbers she knew she wouldn't be able to talk to her. She opted for the coward's way out and sat down at the kitchen table with a pen and pad. She forced herself to remain detached as she wrote.

Elaine. I apologize for leaving you a note. I would have preferred to discuss this in person, but I didn't know where else to contact you.

I think we both know that things between us have not been as they should be for quite some time. I'll accept the bulk of the responsibility for that and I'm sorry. Please believe me when I say I never meant to hurt you. At this point, I think it's best if we go our separate ways. I'm moving away from San Antonio and selling the store. Since you have a place to stay, I'm closing up the house as well. At this time, I don't know whether I will be placing it on the market or not, but in case I do, I would appreciate it if you would remove your things as soon as possible. Laurel

She tore the page from the pad and stared at it. Now that it was finished she couldn't make up her mind whether she should mail it to Elaine's work address or simply leave it here on the table and assume she would find it when she came for the rest of her stuff. After a lot of deliberation, she finally decided to leave it on the table. With nothing else to do, she locked up the house and drove to the cemetery. It was time to say good-bye.

When she reached the section of the cemetery where Chris was buried, she parked her car and walked slowly across the grounds to the gravesite. After Chris died, Laurel had spent a lot of time here, but over the years her visits had tapered off to once a month. She brushed a few stray leaves off the unique headstone that was shaped like an open book. An engraved sketch of the Lavender Page filled the left-hand side. On the right was Chris's name, along with the dates of her birth and death.

Laurel sat down beside the stone. "Chris, I've failed your trust in me. I tried my best, but it just wasn't good enough." She wiped away the tears that were beginning to slip down her cheeks. "I've messed everything up and don't know how to fix it." She ran a hand over the stone. "I miss you so much. You always made things better. It seems as though no matter how hard I try or how hard I work, I can't seem to do anything right with the store." She took a deep breath. "People were depending on me and I let them down—you, your customers, Allie, Gilda and Cindy." She closed her eyes. "God, Chris, I was so ugly to Cindy. I fired her. I made a mistake in hiring her, one that you would never have made. She wasn't suited for the job. I don't know why I kept her on. Maybe it was because she's so young. Letting her go was the right thing to do, but I'm so ashamed of the way I did it. The poor kid was crying." She tried to push away the memory. "I know you would have found a way to help her. You would have handled it so much better than I did." She stopped and wiped her eyes again. "Lou is mad at me. I got drunk last night and made a complete fool out of myself. Lou was only trying to help, but I wouldn't listen. I didn't want to hear what she had to say." She smiled slightly. "Why didn't I notice that you never read? I've always pictured you as a voracious reader. How could you have owned a bookstore and not liked to read?" She shook her head. "Only you could have pulled that one off." She sat in silence for a long stretch before continuing. "I came by to tell you that I'm going to be gone for a while. I don't know how long yet, but I've got to get away." She took a deep trembling breath. "I've decided to sell the store. I'm sorry, because I know how much it meant to you, but I just can't keep doing this. Please, forgive me, baby." Tears blinded her as she kissed the stone lightly before jumping up.

She ran back to the car and headed toward the bookstore. This had to be done quickly, before she lost her nerve.

Allie and Gilda both avoided her when she came in, but that was all right with her. She was too ashamed of what she was about to do to talk to either of them. She went directly to her office and closed the door. She turned on her computer and typed out two letters of recommendation. She printed them off and folded each one carefully before removing the ledger from her desk and writing out payroll checks for Allie and Gilda. She added a week's salary to each of the checks. It wasn't much, but it was all she could afford. She placed the checks and letters in envelopes. With that done, she wrote each woman's name on the appropriate envelope. Then she quickly wrote a note to Cindy and apologized for the way she had fired her. Cindy had been a bad employee, but she hadn't deserved the tongue-lashing. She addressed the envelope and placed a stamp on it before tucking it into her back pocket.

With nothing left to do, she reached into the bottom drawer and removed the nearly empty bottle of amaretto, along with Chris's photo. She set the photo on the desk, raised the bottle in salute and drained it in two swallows. The alcohol burned her throat, but she ignored it as she picked up the phone to place the hardest call she'd ever had to make.

After making an appointment with a realtor, she went to the front of the store and flipped over the closed sign. With a heavy heart, she locked the door.

"What's going on?" Allie asked.

Laurel ignored the question as she motioned for them to follow her back into the office. She saw the nervous glances they threw each other. As soon as they were in the office she handed them the envelopes.

"Here are your checks. I'm sorry I couldn't do more and that I didn't give you more notice." She took a shaky breath before continuing. "I've included a letter of recommendation." She nodded toward the envelopes they were holding. "I know it's not much, but maybe it'll help you find another job." She couldn't look at them when she spoke so she concentrated on the envelopes they held.

"What's going on?" Allie asked, her voice tinged with doubt.

Laurel took a deep breath. "I've decided to close the store."

"When?" they both asked as once.

She ran a hand over the back of her neck and stared at the floor. "Today. Now," she added. Silence filled the room. She could feel them staring at her. As always, it was Allie who found her voice first.

"You can't do that. How can you just close it without even talking to us about it?"

A spark of anger tried to flare, but Laurel pushed it down. "It's my decision to make," she replied as calmly as she could. "I've held on as long as I could."

"Why didn't you ask for help?" Allie asked. "This store means too much to too many people for you to make that decision alone."

Laurel wanted to shout and demand to know where those people had been during all those long, lonely nights she'd spent trying to come up with ways to keep the store. If it meant so much, why had most of the customers fled to the chain store? Instead she curbed her anger and said, "I'm going to place it on the market."

She had already made up her mind that if the store didn't sell by the end of December, she would simply close the doors. Either way, she was not going to start another year with the store hanging around her neck.

Allie started to say something, but Laurel held up her hand and stopped her. "Please, don't make this any harder than it already is."

"But I like working here," Allie argued. "I don't want you to sell the store." Tears flowed freely down her cheeks.

"Damn it, Allie, grow up," Laurel snapped. "Life doesn't always hand you what you want. The store is closed and that's that." She tried to rein in her anger. "You two should go. I still have a couple of things to do before the appointment."

Gilda stepped forward as if to hug her, but Laurel seemed incapable of moving. Gilda finally gave an awkward wave and rushed out.

Allie wasn't so easily dismissed. "So, like, this is it?" Allie asked. "You just walk in and say the Lavender Page is closed and we have no say-so in the decision."

Laurel looked into the tearstained face looking up at her and realized for the first time how much Allie meant to her. She would miss the daily interchange with the energetic and sometimes irritating young woman. Was there ever a time in her life when she had been so young?

"Allie, I've already told you. It was my decision to make, and it wasn't an easy one. This has been a long time in coming." She reached out to wipe a tear from Allie's cheek and Allie grabbed her in a tight embrace.

"When am I going to see you again? Lou is worried sick about you."

"Tell Lou I'm fine. I just need some time to get my life back on track. That's why I'm going away for a while." She had debated not telling anyone but knew Lou would worry.

Allie stepped away. "Where are you going? Is Elaine going with you?"

Laurel focused her attention on the back window where a flock of sparrows were frolicking in the ash tree. "Elaine moved out. When I got home yesterday her clothes were gone. I don't even know where she went."

"Don't you think you should find out?"

After years of keeping her feelings to herself, they were suddenly trying to pour out. She cleared her throat to give herself time to get her emotions under control. "I don't know if Lou told you, but Elaine is seeing someone else." On an impulse, she leaned forward and kissed Allie's forehead. "Go on now. I have lots to do."

"I can stay and help you," Allie said, her eyes brimming with tears.

"No. I need to do this alone. Go on and take care of yourself." She turned and began to clean out her desk. She waited until she heard the door close and the sound of the lock turning before she dropped into the chair and cried.

When she had cried herself out, she got up, washed her face and went to the register to close it out for the last time. As she ran the credit card batch, she tried not to think about how many times she and Chris had done the same thing together. Afterward, she went about the store and carefully put everything in order, silently saying good-bye as she went. Finally, with nothing left to do, she picked up Chris's photo and left, being careful not to look back.

Laurel's heart started to pound as a new fear began to germinate. What if no one stepped forward to pick up the reins for the Lavender Page and it didn't sell? She didn't have a job. How was she going to pay her bills? Beads of sweat popped out along her hairline. This was a mistake. She couldn't afford to close the bookstore. Despite the lack of newly released material, the store's inventory was still significant. It would take hours to sort through the remaining stock, pack it and then ship it back to the various distributors. How much of the stock would she be able to return? What would she do with the remainder? After she paid the shipping costs and restocking fees, the refunds wouldn't come close to paying off the debts she had incurred. It was the memory of the stack of bills in her desk drawer that brought her up short. She had no choice but to close the store. Whether it sold or not wasn't the issue. The important thing now was how she recovered and moved on with her life. She had to find some way to get things back on track.

From the bookstore, she drove to the appointment with the realtor and signed the paperwork necessary to place the store on the market. The realtor didn't offer much hope of selling the business intact, but she was optimistic that if not, the building and fixtures would sell quickly.

It was almost four by the time Laurel left the realtor's office. With nothing else left to do, she turned her car south toward Corpus Christi.

After over an hour on the road, her stomach began to complain, reminding her she needed to eat. When she finally spotted a drive-through burger joint, she pulled in and ordered a cheeseburger and a soft drink. As she waited for the food, she found herself wondering what Elaine was doing. She pushed the thoughts away. It was too soon to probe those wounds.

As she drew nearer to the Gulf coast, she rolled her window

down and took a deep breath of the tangy salt air. As the slightly chilled breeze washed over her, she again found herself thinking about Elaine. Was it only a few hours ago that the two of them had briefly discussed coming to the coast for the weekend? If she had agreed, Elaine wouldn't have been free to go to dinner with Myra.

Laurel thought of the long hours she had spent at the store. Was that the reason Elaine turned to someone else? Along with these thoughts came a trickle of doubt. Had she acted too hastily in running away? If she had stayed and confronted Elaine maybe they could have worked through their problems. Or had she jumped at the first opportunity to leave Elaine? She pushed aside the disturbing thought. Now wasn't the time to explore it. She was too tired and the pain still too raw. That was why she had headed for Corpus—to give herself time to heal and think.

Chris didn't particularly like the coast so there were no burning memories of her here. Elaine loved going to Rockport, but they had never gone to Corpus together, so there was no history with her there either. Corpus would be hers alone.

A blinking sign of a dancing palm tree caught her attention. Kitchenettes could be rented by the week at the Seafarer's Paradise Motel. To experience this paradise she must take the next exit. She pulled in to check it out.

The short, chubby woman behind the counter could have been anywhere between forty and seventy. Her short gray-streaked hair framed a face with skin the consistency of leather. She was wearing a sleeveless shirt that had faded to a dull red and a pair of baggy, blue-checkered, knee-length shorts. Her feet were clad in the inevitable flip-flops.

"I only have two empty units," she said as she pulled keys from a cigar box she took from beneath the counter. She led Laurel down a covered walkway and unlocked the door. "It's nothing fancy," she said, "but I run a clean, quiet place." She peered at Laurel. "What you do here is your own business as long as I don't get any complaints from my other tenants." She pushed the door open and flipped on a light before stepping back to let Laurel pass.

The room was one large space with a cheap leather couch

flanked by plastic end tables. Across from it was a television on a swivel base that could be turned and watched from the bed in the far corner. Across from the bed was a small kitchenette with a refrigerator and stove. A coffeepot and microwave sat on the counter. Worn mottled green linoleum covered the entire area. Everything was old and cheap, but it was clean.

"What are your weekly rates?"

"One hundred and fifty if you only want it for a week, but if you take it for a month or longer, it's one hundred and forty a week."

Laurel thought about the four hundred dollars in her pocket. It would have to carry her until she found work. "I'll start with a week."

After taking care of the paperwork, Laurel took her luggage from the car. It only took her a few minutes to put away her clothes. Afterward she walked back to the office. The woman was sitting behind the counter reading a *Reader's Digest*.

"I'm sorry to disturb you, but is there a grocery store nearby?" Laurel asked.

The woman stood up and smiled. "I'm Ella Mae, by the way, and you're not disturbing me. I like talking to people." She gave Laurel directions to a store that was only a few blocks away.

Laurel thanked her and turned to leave.

"If you don't mind my saying so, you don't look like you're here on vacation," Ella Mae said.

Laurel stopped. "I didn't know people looked different when they were on vacation."

"Sure they do. They smile a lot, are always in a hurry and wear loud, flashy clothes they wouldn't be caught dead in at home. Are you looking for work or hiding?"

Her bluntness caught Laurel off-guard. "You're not shy, are you?"

"I can't afford to be, not in this business. I take it as my personal responsibility to make sure I protect my tenants as much as I can."

Laurel traced a grout line on the floor with the toe of her shoe. "I'm looking for work. I'm not in any kind of trouble, and the only thing I'm hiding from is life."

Ella Mae nodded. "My husband, Earl, works the office during

the day, but I'm always around here until at least ten each night, if you ever want to come over and watch television or just talk about the weather."

"Thanks. I might take you up on it some night." She started to leave, but Ella Mae stopped her again.

"If you're not opposed to getting a little dirty, Jim Rawlins over at the Oyster Hut on Water's Edge is looking for a shucker."

"A what?" Laurel asked, frowning.

"An oyster shucker. He's over by the bridge if you're interested. Tell him I sent you."

"Thanks. I'll go see him tomorrow morning."

Ella Mae pulled a pack of cigarettes from her shirt pocket and lit one. "The place doesn't open until around eleven, but go on over there earlier. Jim will be around somewhere."

"Okay, I can do that." Laurel went back to her car and drove to the grocery store. She bought coffee, milk, eggs, a package each of bologna and cheese and a loaf of bread. As she stood in the check-out line, her gaze drifted to the rack of books by the counter. She almost laughed when she realized she still owned a bookstore, but she hadn't brought a single book to read. She decided she would get a library card if she decided to stay. *Of course, I'm staying*, she told herself. Wasn't that the point in coming here in the first place? Wasn't her goal to find a job and a small cheap apartment? On the way back to the motel she decided she would drive over to the Oyster Hut the following morning and apply for the job. She had never shucked an oyster in her life, but there was a first time for everything.

After putting away her meager groceries, she turned the small television toward the bed and crawled beneath the crisp white sheets. She fell asleep watching *The Golden Girls* finagle their way out of yet another crisis. Life would be so simple if all her problems could be solved in thirty minutes or less.

CHAPTER FOURTEEN

A strange chirping sound pulled Elaine from a troubled sleep. She reached for Laurel as her brain struggled to identify the sound. When her hand made contact with the cold empty spot beside her, she remembered where she was. She turned off the alarm on the hotel clock and struggled to wake up. Despite the fact that she had slept most of the previous day away, she still felt exhausted. Mondays were usually hectic. She prayed today would be an exception.

After a large yawn, she forced herself up and sat on the side of the bed. She stared at the phone, worried that Laurel might have forgotten to turn on the alarm clock before she went to bed. "What a pathetic wuss I am," she said as she headed toward the bathroom. Sleep probably wasn't playing a big role in Laurel's life right now. She remembered how at the beginning of their relationship they had made love and talked away the night. Tears threatened to start, but she pushed them away. She had to be at work in a couple of hours, and if she started crying again, she wasn't sure she'd be able to stop.

As she stood beneath the stinging spray, she tried to decide what the best approach was to handle Myra. Their first encounter was bound to be awkward after that kiss. For a moment, her mouth felt the pressure of Myra's kiss. If she weren't with Laurel . . .

You're not with Laurel, a small voice prodded.

Elaine grabbed the safety bar to steady herself. What was wrong with her? One minute she was bawling her eyes out because Laurel had left and the next minute she was thinking about kissing Myra. When all she should be thinking about was how to find Laurel to try and salvage their relationship before it was too late. Or was it already too late? She grasped the bar tighter. Was her relationship with Laurel over? When she left, had she done so with the intention of never returning? No, she told herself. She simply wanted Laurel to see how it felt to be ignored and taken for granted. She rinsed the soap from her body and turned off the water. As she toweled herself dry, she admitted there was more to her leaving. She couldn't handle Laurel's indiscretion. *If there was one*, she reminded herself. Part of her didn't believe Laurel would ever pick up a stranger at a bar, but it was pretty hard to deny the facts. As surprising as it was, Laurel had gone to the bar. The question was, if Laurel did go home with someone she'd picked up there, could Elaine ever forgive her infidelity? This time the answer was a resounding no.

With the towel wrapped around her, she stepped over to the vanity and began to comb her hair. She needed to work through this infatuation for Myra, if indeed that's all it was. She slowly allowed herself to remember Myra's kiss. As the event replayed in her mind, she was fairly certain that there had been at least a brief moment when her body responded and she had kissed Myra back. Did that mean she had committed her own small infidelity? If the situations had been reversed, how would she feel about Laurel going to dinner with another woman? *A dinner that ended with a somewhat mutual kiss*, the voice prodded again. "I wouldn't like it," she told her mirrored image. She threw the comb on the vanity.

This wasn't getting her anywhere. They needed to sit down and talk like rational adults. It was time for them both to make some decisions. If Laurel wanted to keep the store, then it was time to hire someone who could help turn the business around. Otherwise, Laurel should either sell the damn thing or close it. *It's time I told Myra Reardon to stop sniffing around, and I need to stop encouraging her.* Regardless of all these other things, she and Laurel had to remember they loved each other and needed to work together rather than ripping each other apart all the time.

She didn't want to take a chance of Laurel hanging up on her again, so she made plans to go to the house later that night. She would give Laurel plenty of time to close the shop and get home before she arrived. It didn't seem right to be there waiting for her when she got home.

Elaine was already in her office working when Tom arrived and stepped into her office.

"You're an early bird this morning." He stopped sharply when he saw her. "What's wrong?"

She pretended to search for something in her desk drawer. "Nothing. I came in early because I wanted to follow up on a couple of things before it gets crazy. We have that nursing conference starting today and the seminar with the real estate people. The nursing group should be almost three hundred people, so we need to stay on top of that." She grabbed a pad of sticky notes before turning to her computer and opening her contact list. "When you get a chance, call the rental company and confirm that they'll be here by six tonight with those extra chairs we ordered for that banking seminar in the Bowie room, and make sure housekeeping has the placards for the lobby."

He nodded. "How was your weekend?"

His question caught her off-guard. "It was . . . um . . . fine." She stood. "Have you eaten? I got here so early I didn't take time to eat. I thought I'd run over and grab a bagel or something."

"I ate at home, but if you like I can go over for you. I need to drop by Anderson's office anyway to see if they have the new promotional brochures ready."

She nodded. "Thanks, I'll make a fresh pot of coffee while you're gone." She continued to piddle at her desk until he left. She was grateful she could delay leaving her office. She wasn't in any hurry to run into Myra, and there was always the possibility that Laurel might call.

From that point forward everything about Elaine's day went wrong. At nine she received a call from an angry spokeswoman for the nursing conference complaining that the continental breakfast they had scheduled for eight thirty had not yet arrived and that the delay was playing havoc with her schedule.

Elaine called the kitchen and cringed when she learned that the truck that normally delivered the hotel's pastries had been involved in an accident. She hung up. It was days like today that she wished she had listened to her mother and become a teacher. She pasted on her best smile and decided she would take the easy way out by offering to comp the breakfast. The gesture rarely failed to soothe even the most ruffled feathers, and this time was no exception.

With the situation temporarily under control, Elaine went to see the head chef to beg for his help.

"I need food for my guests," she informed him. She found him whipping up a large bowl of what appeared to be pancake mix.

"Fine," he replied, "I can do a buffet of scrambled eggs, meat and toast."

Elaine cringed at the extra expense the hotel would have to absorb, but it couldn't be helped. The participants had to be fed. "How long before it's ready?"

He shrugged. "Twenty or thirty minutes."

She nodded. "Thanks. That'll have to do."

He grabbed a pad of paper from his pocket. "How many people do you want to feed?"

"Better make it for three hundred."

He slowly raised his head. "Did you say three hundred?"

"Yes." She took a step back as his face began to flame red and a tiny vein on his forehead expanded dangerously. When his face escalated to deep purple and he started to roar that he couldn't feed an additional three hundred people, Elaine assured him she would make other arrangements and ran.

As soon as she was back in her office, she and Tom got on the phone and started calling every bakery in the downtown area. It took seven different orders, but by nine forty-five the food was beginning to arrive.

As the hungry horde of participants ingested the mounds of pastries, Elaine leaned over to Tom and whispered. "I thought nurses were health-conscious."

"I have to leave," he replied. "They're starting to scare me."

Elaine stood at the back of the room until she was certain everything was under control. She was on her way back to the office when her cell rang, and a frantic maintenance man informed her that the audio system in the large training room where the insurance folks were had shorted out, and the room was filling with smoke.

"Should I activate the fire alarm?" he asked.

"Have you seen any fire?" Elaine started walking as fast as possible without drawing unwanted attention.

"No, but there's a lot of smoke in here."

"Get everyone out of the room, but don't do anything else until I get there. I'll be there in a minute." The elevators were packed, and she didn't have time to run to the other end of the building to the maintenance elevator. Instead, she ran up the three flights of stairs from the first floor to the training room. As she went she called Tom and had him standing by in case an evacuation order was needed. "Start searching for a backup system," she panted as she raced up the final flight of stairs.

To her relief, she found only a minimal amount of smoke. Most of it was coming from the irate trainer who was ranting about needing to get the lecture started because she had to catch a six thirty flight back to Chicago that night. "My company won't pay for an additional night at a hotel," she insisted. "I'll have to pay the additional expenses out of my own pocket. I absolutely have to wrap up this training by three in order for the participants to take a test on the—"

At that point Elaine politely interrupted her. "Let me just get things started on correcting the problem." She stepped away and called Tom. "I have to have an audio system and I need it now. Steal it if you have to, but get it up here now!"

"I've called Randy's Audio and they're on their way, but it will take them at least forty-five minutes to get here and set up."

Elaine took a deep breath and told herself to calm down. "Okay, but see if you can get him here faster," she said. She returned the phone to her pocket as she turned and put on her best smile once more. "Have you folks had breakfast?" she asked the trainer.

"Breakfast," she practically bellowed. "It's almost time for lunch."

Elaine spied a large stack of manuals on a nearby table. She took the woman's arm and began to move her gently away from the podium. "I'm going to call the chef and have him prepare you and your class a complimentary lunch. In the meantime, perhaps the participants could start reading the materials you brought. If the training is completed on time, I'll send around the hotel's limo to take you to the airport. If not, I'll see to it that you're put in one of the hotel's luxury suites at no charge and I'll personally take care of updating your travel arrangements."

By the time Elaine left, the trainer was laughing and telling the class to settle down and start reading the first booklet. Elaine headed back toward the kitchen and prayed the early-morning chef's shift had already ended.

By the time Elaine left her office that night at seven thirty, she was so exhausted she could barely make it back to her room, but all of her guests had left happy and well fed and she had the expense sheets to prove it. Her manager would blow a fuse when she handed in all those comp tickets, to say nothing of the invoice for the pastries she had purchased that morning.

She dropped across the bed intending to catch a quick nap. There was still plenty of time. Laurel wouldn't be home for a couple of hours yet.

The sound of the industrial garbage trucks woke her. She squinted at the clock. It was ten minutes after six. It was time to start her day, but first she needed to talk to Laurel. She put on a pot of coffee. As it started brewing, she dialed the home number. The phone rang once before an automated voice clicked on to tell her that number was temporarily out of service. Thinking she had dialed the wrong number, she hung up and redialed, only to get the same message. Without waiting for the coffee to finish brewing, she turned it off and quickly changed out of her rumpled suit into a pair of jeans and a shirt. Minutes later, she was driving home. She made excellent time on the nearly empty freeways. Her heart sank as she pulled onto their street and saw the empty driveway. She circled the block and drove to the store, where she found a large For Sale sign. Confused and scared, she drove back to the house and this time went in. Even though it was beginning to get light outside, the house was still dark inside. She flipped on the living room light, but nothing happened. She tried the switch to the porch light, again nothing. Pulling open the drapes to allow the weak illumination of dawn helped, but she still couldn't see much. She made her way to the kitchen, trying various lights as she went. In a cabinet drawer she found a flashlight and began searching the house for clues. On heavy feet, she made her way to the bedroom. The bed was neatly made. When she checked the closet, she discovered that several items of Laurel's clothes were missing, as were Laurel's suitcases. Her hopes faded when she opened the refrigerator and found it completely empty. When she finally accepted that Laurel was really gone she slowly made her way back through the house that she had never liked living in. This was Chris's house. She had agreed to live here because Laurel loved it so. When she decided to move in, she knew Laurel was still deeply in love with Chris but had thought that with time Chris's looming presence in Laurel's life would fade to warm, precious memories. For a while, it seemed like that was happening, but then things started going bad at the store. That was when their relationship started to decline.

As she stepped back into the kitchen the beam of the flashlight flashed across the table. As soon as she saw the sheet of paper, she knew what it would say, but she forced herself to read it anyway. Despite everything that had happened, the pain caused from reading Laurel's note took her by surprise. Laurel had left without giving them another chance. Their relationship didn't mean enough to her to try and salvage.

Elaine moved toward the front door. The house felt odd to her. It felt foreign. The sense was more than being alone in the house. She was always the first one home each evening, so she had spent many hours here alone and had never noticed this feeling before. It hit her as she reached the door. The house felt empty. Laurel was gone and she didn't have a clue as to where to start looking for her.

CHAPTER FIFTEEN

Laurel sat on the hood of her car on a section of the public beach and watched as the sun slowly appeared on the horizon. As it rose, the gulf waters seemed to catch fire. Today was the proverbial first day of her new life. In a few hours she would start looking for work. She would take whatever job she could find that would provide her with some income. Her plan was to try the Oyster Hut that Ella Mae had recommended. If that didn't pan out, she would start applying at various temp agencies. Thanks to the years of working as a secretary for the law firm her typing wasn't bad and she knew how to use Word, Excel, Access and a handful of lesser programs. She possessed years of sales experience, although she really didn't want to go back into any type of a retail business unless absolutely necessary. For now, all she wanted was a nine-to-five job where the biggest decision she would have to make was where to go to lunch. Eventually, she might need something more challenging, but not now. Memories of Elaine kept trying to sneak in, but she deliberately held them at bay.

It was almost nine before she drove back to the motel and changed the shorts and tank top she was wearing for the only pair of dress slacks and blouse she had packed. It occurred to her that she probably should have packed more clothes, but she brushed away the worry. She could always drive back on a weekend and pick up anything she needed. Before she left on her job search, she found the card the real estate agent had given her and called their toll-free number. The young woman who answered the phone informed her that her agent was out, but she'd be happy to page her and have her return Laurel's call.

Laurel declined the callback. She gave the woman the motel's phone number to be used as her new contact number if anyone showed a serious interest in buying the store. With the card tucked safely back into her wallet, she went to look for work.

She found the Oyster Hut with no problem. When she entered the outside patio, a short Hispanic woman dressed in a white T-shirt and denim cutoffs was wiping down tables and opening umbrellas.

She glanced up and saw Laurel. "We don't open until eleven."

"I'm not here to eat. I'm looking for Jim Rawlins."

The woman nodded toward the bay. "He's fishing on the pier."

Laurel turned and saw several people standing on the pier. "I don't actually know him. What does he look like?"

The woman laughed. "You can't miss him. He'll be wearing a lime green shirt."

"Thanks." She started to walk away.

"You looking for work?" the woman asked.

"Yes. Someone said he was looking for an oyster shucker."

The woman grimaced. "Trust me. You don't want that job. Jim is looking to hire another waitress. It's a better job. The pay is better and the tips aren't bad." She opened another umbrella. "Jim will try to scare you at first by being gruff and such. It's all bluff. He's okay."

"Thanks, I appreciate the tip."

She reached across and extended her hand. "I'm Nina."

"Laurel," she replied. As they shook hands, Laurel's gaydar clanged loudly.

"Good luck."

She made her way across the street and down the pier. She was approaching the midway point when she spied the lime green shirt. As she grew nearer a wave of nervousness ran through her. It had been a long time since she'd applied for a job. She was trying to remember the dos and don'ts of an interview when she suddenly smiled. This wasn't going to be a typical interview. After all, she was standing on a fishing pier about to ask for a job from a man wearing a baseball cap and T-shirt so brightly colored it could be used to signal planes in with.

Jim Rawlins was a barrel-chested man with huge, gnarled hands that were a living testament to a life of hard work. An anchor with the word *Navy* beneath it was tattooed on his left arm.

"Mr. Rawlins."

He turned and squinted up at her. As he did so she could see the words Oyster Hut in bold red letters emblazoned across the front of his shirt. "Who's asking?" he asked.

"I'm Laurel Becker. Ella Mae at the Seafarer's Paradise said you might have a job opening."

He looked again. "You always been so damn tall?"

"No, I was much shorter as a child."

He chuckled. "Ella Mae would send me a wiseass."

Laurel kept quiet.

"What job did Ella Mae say I had?"

"She said you needed an oyster shucker."

He reached out and took her hand. Turning it palm up, he shook his head and grunted. "You ever shucked oysters before?" he asked, releasing her hand.

She considered lying but knew it would eventually catch up with her. "No, but I'm willing to learn."

"You'd probably cut your fool hand off before you learned anything." He reeled his line in and cast it back out.

"I heard you might be looking for a waitress as well."

"Yeah, that's one of the problems with hiring college kids. Too many of them only want to work long enough to get a few dollars in their pockets and then quit." He paused. "You ever worked in a restaurant before?"

A stab of guilt prodded her conscience. She wasn't planning on staying around long either. She would be leaving as soon as she could secure a better paying job. "No, but I've been in retail for the last—"

"I'm not running a department store."

She bit her tongue.

"You married?" he asked, looking her over.

She folded her arms across her chest. Enough was enough. "No. I'm a lesbian. Does that bother you?"

He sighed and stood up. "Hell, yeah, it bothers me. I'm an ugly old man. Any additional competition bothers me."

Confused, Laurel stared at him.

"Do you fish?"

"Every chance I get."

He studied her again. "There's an extra pole." He nodded to a reel leaning against the rail of the pier. "There are live shrimp in that bucket."

"I don't have a fishing license," she admitted.

"I thought you fished," he barked.

"I said I did when I had a chance. I've been living in San Antonio—"

He snorted. "Don't know how anyone can live in that madhouse. There ain't no rhyme nor reason to the street layout. You can't get from one place to another without taking five detours. There are people everywhere you look. Go ahead and grab that rod. If JT, the game warden, comes out, I'll tell him you're with me and it'll be fine."

She took the fishing pole he indicated and checked the rigging before she dipped her hand into the bucket and snatched up a plump shrimp. He was watching her as she baited the hook and cast her line. It made her nervous, but her cast was smooth and long. She began to jig the bait back in.

"You're not going to catch anything doing that," he practically growled. "Cast it back out there and let the shrimp do all the work."

"I don't like to fish that way." She kept jigging the line. "I prefer to—" The hit was one of those solid ones that anglers dream about getting. Laurel set the hook, and the line screamed as the fish made its first run. She planted her feet and the game was on. Every time she would gain a few inches of line, the fish would make another run and take it back. It took her almost twenty-five minutes to bring in the big flounder.

Jim netted it and hauled it onto the pier where he quickly measured it. "Whew! Would you look at that? Eighteen inches," he yelled. "Now, there's a fish that'll melt in your mouth." He must have sensed Laurel's hesitation, because he turned to look at her. "What?"

"I practice catch-and-release."

He stared at her as if she had suddenly grown two heads. "It's a flounder," he said, astounded.

"I wouldn't even know how to cook it, to say nothing of cleaning it."

"You let me worry about that. Let me take this fish and I'll fix you some of the best food you've ever tasted."

Laurel shrugged. "Well, it was your bait and fishing rod, so I suppose you have some vested interest in it." She laughed when he began to do a little jig.

"Hot damn," he sang. "We're having fresh flounder." He put the flounder into an ice chest and began to pack up his gear.

"Mr. Rawlins—"

"Call me Jim."

"What about the job?"

He stopped packing and looked up at her. "You don't have any experience in food services?"

She stared across the bay. He wasn't going to give her the job. "No, I don't."

"Do you plan on staying around a while or are you going to be looking for a better job?" He was watching her closely.

She considered lying but remembered all the employees she had hired, only to have them quit two or three months later when something better came along. "I'll probably be moving on, but I promise you, I won't leave without giving you at least two weeks' notice."

He took a deep breath and pushed the brim of his cap up higher on his head. "Well, I need a waitress. It's a split shift. You'll work Monday through Friday. The lunch shift is from ten until two and then dinner is five until nine. The pay is two-seventy-five an hour plus tips, and there are two free meals, if you want them. You eat after your shift ends, but don't let me catch you snatching a nibble off a customer's plate." He practically glared at her. "And I don't care how mad somebody makes you, if I ever see you doing anything stupid like spitting in the food I'll fire you on the spot. I know it happens a lot in some of those big-city places, but I run a clean kitchen."

She nodded and wondered if she would ever again enjoy eating in a restaurant after working in one.

"We get a good mixture of customers, tourist and locals," he rushed on. "When can you start?"

"Now," she replied, unable to believe her luck.

He handed her the two fishing rods before leaning over to pick up the ice chest. "Well, let's go. It's almost time to open the door."

As they walked back down the pier, Jim stopped several times to talk with other anglers. Each time he would set the ice chest down and show off the flounder Laurel had caught. Then he would tell how Laurel and the fish had squared off for an epic battle. Each time he told the story, the struggle to land the fish magnified in intensity.

When he started telling the story for the third or fourth time, Laurel tuned him out and mentally calculated her weekly salary.

She swallowed a groan when she realized that her salary wouldn't even cover her weekly rent at the motel. The free meals would help. Hopefully, the tips would be decent and make up for the low hourly rate. She banished the thoughts. If the job didn't pan out, she could always go back to San Antonio. She was tired of worrying about money. For a little while, at least, she was going to relax and enjoy listening to Jim entertain everyone with tales of her fishing skills.

When she turned her attention back to the pier, Jim had his audience's full attention. She watched their amused eyes as he flailed his arms in an exaggerated reenactment of her fighting the fish. It was easy to see that these people cared for and respected Jim Rawlins. This little group of people was not so different from the one that passed through the door of the Lavender Page. She took a deep breath of the salt air and slowly released it along with a few slivers of the pain and fear she'd been carrying around for so long.

CHAPTER SIXTEEN

By the time Laurel and Jim arrived at the restaurant, it was already starting to fill up with customers. Laurel was impressed. She hadn't expected the tiny place to have such a brisk business.

"Kate," Jim bellowed as he led the way to the kitchen.

"What do you want, you old coot? I'm right here, so stop your hollering."

Laurel turned to find a short, heavyset woman with an enormous beehive hairdo and makeup thick enough to have been applied with a palette knife.

Jim waved her off. "This here is . . ." He turned to Laurel. "What did you say your name was?"

"Laurel Becker." She extended her hand to the woman.

"I hired her to replace Tiffany."

"Tonya," Kate corrected.

"Whatever." He waved her off again. "Just get her settled and show her what to do." He rushed off with the ice chest.

Kate looked her over from head to toe as she shook her hand.

"I'm Kate Reid. I'm a part-time cook, waitress and hostess. There have even been occasions when I've been known to bus tables and wash dishes. You ever worked as a waitress?"

"No."

Kate rolled her eyes. "Come on. Let's get you fixed up before we hit the floor. I swear that old fart doesn't know shit from Shinola about hiring people. It's a wonder he's still in business."

"How long has the restaurant been open?" Laurel asked as she struggled to keep up.

"It's going on twenty years."

"Wow! That's a long time. He must be doing something right."

Kate shrugged. "What can I say? He's a helluva cook, when you can pry that fishing pole out of his hand." She led them into a small storage room where she removed an apron from a large stack on a shelf, an order book and a couple of pens. "Everyday when you come in, you'll come back here and get the things you need. You may need to change aprons during a shift. If something gets spilled on you, get a clean apron. You'd never know it to look at him, but Jim's a fanatic about neatness. At the end of the shift, throw the apron in that bin over there." She pointed to a tall plastic container by the doorway before leading Laurel to the other side of the room where a cabinet stood. Each of its several drawers had individual locks. Some had keys dangling from them. "Pick whichever one of these with keys that you want. You can store your purse and stuff in them."

"I don't carry a purse."

Kate glanced back at her and shrugged. "Well, they're here if you want to use one." She headed out of the room. "Since it's already so busy, we'll worry about getting the paperwork filled out later. For now, come on and I'll show you the ropes. You'll have tables nine through fifteen. You won't see any numbers on the tables so you need to remember the layout. Table nine is to the left of the entrance door. Your area starts there and flows around to the kitchen door. Odd numbered tables are against the wall; even numbered ones are in the center."

Laurel wasn't sure why the tables needed numbers. Why didn't Kate just tell her to work the tables on the left? She decided not to ask. If it was a big deal the answer would be obvious soon enough.

"That's Nina," Kate said as she nodded toward the woman Laurel had talked to on the patio.

"We sort of met earlier."

"Good. We're sort of like a family here. We all have our individual duties, but if things get crazy we pitch in where we're needed." Kate took the first couple orders before turning it over to Laurel. "That's all there is to it," Kate told her as she led Laurel over to a table with two elderly women. "You take this one."

Laurel pasted on her brightest smile as she approached the table. This was really not much different than the bookstore. Rather than discovering which book her customer was searching for, she was simply finding out what food they wanted. "Good afternoon, ladies. What can I get for you today?"

"What kind of fish are you serving today?" a woman with almost orange hair asked.

"The specials are—" Before she could continue, the woman sitting next to Orange Hair interrupted her.

"I want a shrimp salad and don't bother bringing out any those puny little things he tried to pawn off on me last week. I want good plump shrimp. Don't fill up the bottom of the bowl with lettuce. If I wanted lettuce I'd order a dinner salad. And to drink I want—"

"You never did tell me what the specials are," Orange Hair interrupted.

"Ida Faye," the second woman interrupted again. "I was just about to tell her what I want to drink. Now if you can just hold your horses long enough to let me finish." She looked up at Laurel. "I want a Bloody Mary with—"

"Junie, you know you can't have any alcohol. Dr. Ramos told you so," Ida Faye said.

"Oh, hell's bells, what does he know? If that man had been around when Jesus turned the water into wine, he would have made him switch it to iced tea, unsweetened at that." Junie flipped a dismissive hand. "But again, what can you expect from a Yankee?"

"He's not a Yankee. He grew up right here in Corpus. As did his parents. You know he told you that his grandfather was from Mexico."

"Yes, and I'm sure it was northern Mexico."

Laurel glanced at Kate for help, but Kate simply shook her head and smiled.

"Ma'am," Laurel began, "the specials—"

"Do I look like a ma'am to you?" Ida Faye asked loudly.

The back of Laurel's neck grew warm as she realized customers from the surrounding tables were turning to stare. Ida Faye and Junie were glaring at her, waiting for an answer. Laurel had no idea what she was supposed to say. Finally, she simply started scribbling on the order pad. "The specials today are fried cod with fries and coleslaw"—Ida Faye tried to interrupt, but Laurel pushed on— "and grilled tuna steaks with broccoli or green beans and a dinner salad."

The two women had apparently finished harassing her because they settled down and placed their order without further argument.

Despite the rough beginning, Laurel soon discovered that the hardest part about the job for her was weaving through the crowded room with the heavy trays. After arriving at the wrong table with an order a couple of times, she realized that the numbering system for the tables was intended to help her get the correct orders to the intended table. The best part of the job was that she was too busy to think about Chris, Elaine or the bookstore.

It was almost one thirty when the last two diners left her station. Laurel's feet and back ached and she was looking forward to sitting down. Her anticipation was dashed when Kate pushed a sweeper into her hands.

"We've gotta clean up and set up for dinner. If anyone comes in, I'll put them in Nina's section. It's not likely we'll get another rush before dinner."

Laurel forced a smile as she began running the sweeper over the floor. Kate began covering the laminated tables with bright red tablecloths and laying out silverware. When the last of Nina's customers left, she started setting up her tables. Since Kate had set up Laurel's tables, she continued on with the sweeper and finished the floor. When she finished, Kate told her to put the sweeper away and to meet them on the patio. Laurel's feet ached as she discarded her apron and washed up before making her way to the patio where Kate and Nina were sitting. As she went over to join them, she pulled the warm salt-laden air deep into her lungs.

"Nina, this is Laurel Becker," Kate said. "Laurel, Nina Delgado."

Nina extended her hand. "We actually talked a little when you came by earlier today."

Laurel nodded and shook her hand again.

"Welcome aboard," Nina said.

Nina appeared to be in her mid to late forties. Fine lines were etched into the corners of her eyes. There was a liberal sprinkling of gray mixed in her short black hair. Laurel suspected Nina was an avid swimmer, judging from the slim, well-toned lines of her body. She was about to ask when Jim interrupted them.

"Come and get it," he shouted as he walked out of the kitchen with a large platter.

"Finally," Kate grumbled.

"Whenever the weather allows we eat out here on the patio," Nina informed Laurel as they gathered around a table.

A delicious aroma tickled Laurel's nostrils as Jim placed the food in front of her. She visually devoured the mouth-watering dish of baked fish filets topped with tomato and cucumber slices and resting on a bed of wild rice. She inhaled deeply and detected a slight aroma of garlic. "Gosh, that smells wonderful. What it is?"

"This is my specialty, baked flounder," Jim replied. He carefully spooned rice onto a plate before adding a generous filet. He placed it in front of Laurel and watched her with anticipation.

She picked up a fork and broke off a small portion of the flaky fish. "It looks delicious." She could feel all of their gazes on her as she tasted the fish. In addition to the minced garlic, she detected a subtle hint of butter, green pepper and onion. She closed her eyes in appreciation as she chewed. There was a subtle suggestion of wine and something slightly tangy. *Lemon*, she decided. She swallowed and smiled with delight. "It's wonderful, but there's something I can't quite place." She quickly named the items she tasted.

"Dang it," Kate grumbled.

Laurel opened her eyes and saw the disappointed looks in the women's eyes and the smug smile on Jim's face. "What's wrong?"

Nina passed plates over for Jim to fill. "We've been trying to figure out what he puts in the dish for ages and he won't tell us."

"There's a reason I call it a secret recipe," Jim replied as he continued to serve. "If I told everybody who asks what's in it, then it wouldn't be a secret."

"He has customers who come all the way from San Antonio and Houston just for this dish," Kate said as she cut into her food.

Conversation slowed as they enjoyed their meal. Laurel couldn't help but think about how much Elaine would have enjoyed the dish. She continued to eat, but for some reason it no longer tasted quite as good as it had before.

After they finished eating, they all pitched in to clear away the table. Then Kate snagged her to fill out the necessary employment papers.

"The way you choose to handle reporting your tip earnings is up to you," Kate said.

"What do you mean?"

"You will be the only person who knows how much you make in tips. What you choose to tell Uncle Sam is between you and him."

Laurel shook her head. "My memory is too bad to lie."

"Just remember that taxes aren't being withheld on the tips and come April that will come back to bite you in the butt. Just make sure you're prepared."

Laurel thought about the tax-related headache that closing the store was bound to cause. Somehow a few dollars in tips didn't seem to be a big deal.

It was almost four when Laurel climbed into her car. It was overly warm from sitting in the sun. She rolled the windows down. She was physically tired, but it felt good. The second shift would begin in an hour. The drive to the motel was less than twenty minutes, but at the moment it seemed overwhelming. She leaned her head back and closed her eyes. The coarse laughter of the laughing gulls filled the air. In the distance she could hear the low roar of a speedboat. The gentle breeze teased her hair as the sounds of the gulls and lapping water soothed her. The music of nature was sweeter than any manmade music she'd ever heard.

"Hey."

Laurel opened her eyes and blinked.

"Are you all right?" Nina asked.

Embarrassed, Laurel sat up. "Yeah, I guess I must have dozed for a moment."

Nina chuckled. "I think it was probably more than a moment."

Laurel noticed that Nina was no longer wearing the T-shirt she'd had on earlier. She groaned when she saw the sun low on the horizon. "Don't tell me I've been sleeping all this time."

Nina smiled. "I think so. It's time to start the dinner shift."

Laurel glanced down at her wrinkled shirt. "I guess I was more tired than I thought."

"You'll get used to it in a couple of days." She patted the door. "Come on or we'll be late."

Laurel rolled up the car window and got out.

"Do you swim?" Nina asked.

"Yes. I used to swim a lot."

"I work as a part-time night clerk over at the Ramada on

Surfside and one of the perks is I can use the pool whenever I like and I can bring a guest. I usually go over every morning around seven and swim for a couple of hours. It's early enough that not many guests are out at the pool yet." They had to wait for an RV pulling a boat to pass before they could cross the road. "You're welcome to join me if you'd like."

Laurel started to decline the offer, but she really did like to swim, and the motel where she was staying didn't have a pool. There was always the public beach, but as much as she loved the coast she didn't like swimming in the gulf waters. Accepting Nina's offer would get her out of her tiny room and provide her with some much needed exercise.

"I might just take you up on that," she said as they made their way across the street.

CHAPTER SEVENTEEN

Elaine was at her desk putting the final touches on a contract for a wedding reception when Tom came in.

"There's a woman here to see you." He made a slight adjustment to the position of one of the chairs in front of her desk.

Elaine's heart leapt. Laurel was back.

Tom must have seen the look on her face, because a deep look of sadness crossed his as he rushed on. "Her name is Lou Petry."

"Lou?" Elaine felt as though she had been punched in the gut. She flinched when she noticed a look that she construed as pity in Tom's eyes. Of course it wasn't Laurel. He knew Laurel and wouldn't have announced her. Elaine took a deep breath. "Send her in."

Tom started to say something but stopped when he saw her warning look. He nodded instead and rushed out of her office.

Elaine wondered what Lou was doing here. She had never been by to visit before. In fact they had never even had lunch together.

It wasn't that she felt disliked by Lou—in fact, the opposite was true. But there was no getting around the fact that Lou had been Chris's best friend and that her true loyalty lay with Laurel. Lou would know where Laurel was. Elaine tossed the contract aside and stood when Lou came in. There was an awkward moment when Elaine couldn't decide if she should greet Lou with their customary hug or not. Once more she was saved by Tom's intervention.

"Would you care for something to drink, Ms. Petry?" he asked.

"No, thanks." Lou pushed her hands deep into the back pockets of her jeans and glanced around at the posters on the wall.

He gave a slight nod and left, discreetly closing the door behind him. The awkwardness returned as soon as Tom disappeared.

Elaine struggled to regain control of herself. "Hi, Lou." She made her way from behind the desk and motioned Lou toward the couch.

"Sorry to bother you at work, but I wasn't sure how to get in touch with you after work," Lou said as she sat on the edge of the couch.

"Do you know where Laurel is?" Elaine blurted, unable to remain still any longer.

Lou glanced up. "You mean you don't?" Her shoulders slumped when Elaine shook her head.

"No. I haven't seen her since Friday morning." She took a seat beside Lou. When Lou didn't respond, Elaine went on. "She left the house on Friday morning without saying good-bye. She didn't answer her cell, and she wasn't at the store when I tried to call her. When she finally did call me, she was angry. She had fired Cindy and changed the hours at the store. I waited up for her. She never came home. When I went looking for her, I found—" She had to stop and swallow the knot in her throat before she could continue. "I found her car in the parking lot at Pinky's. The bartender said she had left with some woman."

"So that's when you put two and two together and came up with five, huh?" Lou said with a huge sigh.

119

Irritated, Elaine looked at her. "When she didn't call or come home, it didn't take a genius to see what was happening."

"And what exactly do you think was happening?" Lou asked.

Elaine tried to control her frustration and reminded herself that Lou was Laurel's friend. "Don't you think it's obvious? She's having an affair."

Lou snorted and rolled her eyes. "Now, ain't that amazing. According to Laurel, it's you who's having the affair. She seems to think that while she was getting plastered at Pinky's, you were carousing with some other woman." Lou quickly filled her in on what she knew about the events that had occurred at Pinky's.

Elaine shook her head in confusion. "That's ludicrous. I'm not having an affair."

"According to Laurel she saw you with some woman on Friday night."

Elaine's breath caught sharply. "Oh, my God. She saw me with Myra."

Lou looked at her with disappointment clearly reflected in her eyes. "Well, I see I can still be surprised," she said with a touch of sadness.

It took Elaine a moment to recover. Lou was about to stand when Elaine reached over and took her by the arm. "Please, don't go. Let me explain."

"What is there to explain? I'm not your mama or your girl-friend."

"You don't understand. Laurel was mistaken in what she saw." She stopped. "I mean, I was with a woman."

Lou's eyebrows drew together in a deep frown of disapproval as she glared at her.

Elaine stood and took Lou's hand. "I swear to you, I'm not having an affair. I went to dinner with a coworker Friday night. I only went because I was tired of being alone." She released Lou's hand and sat down. Everything was so screwed up. "If I hadn't jumped to conclusions and taken off, maybe this could have all been avoided."

Lou blew out another sigh and sat back. "When was the last time you two had a good talk?"

Elaine shrugged. "There doesn't seem to be time to talk anymore. We seem to be rushing full tilt in opposite directions." She picked at imaginary lint on her slacks. "Even if there was, we don't seem to remember how to talk to each other."

"Bull." Lou shook her head in disgust. "What's there to remember? You say something. She says something."

"What's the point? We'd only end up arguing."

"So, argue. There's nothing wrong with a healthy argument sometimes."

Elaine looked at her skeptically. "I'm not sure I agree with you on that."

"Well, I don't give a rat's patootie if you agree with me or not. All I know is that in your infinite wisdom of silence, Laurel thinks you're having an affair and you think she's having one."

Elaine couldn't believe that she had lost the best thing that had ever happened to her. She had to do something. There must be some way to make things right between them again. "Where is she?"

Lou shook her head. "I don't know. That's why I came to see you. I was hoping you knew. She got mad at me and stormed out of the house Saturday morning. I haven't heard from her since. I've called or driven by the house half a dozen times, but I can't find her. I guess you know she placed the store on the market."

"Yes. I drove by there this morning looking for her and saw the sign. Lou, I tried to help her financially, but she wouldn't let me."

Lou patted her hand. "A lot of people tried to help her. Laurel is too stubborn for her own good. I wish Chris had never left her that store."

Elaine had experienced the same feeling many times but resisted vocalizing it.

"Somewhere along the way," Lou continued, "Laurel got this crazy idea in her head that by hanging on to the store, she was holding on to a piece of Chris."

"She never got over losing her."

Lou gazed at her for a moment. "Trying to measure up to Chris couldn't have been much fun for you." She squeezed Elaine's hand.

"I never wanted to measure up to Chris. I wanted Laurel to love me for myself. From the very beginning I knew I could never compete with Chris. I thought Laurel was over her enough to move on." She leaned back into the couch. "I was wrong."

"No, you weren't. It has been hard for her, but she has slowly been letting go." She shook her head slightly. "Her letting go of the store was the last anchor holding her back. Things will change. You'll see."

"That doesn't do me much good." Elaine rubbed her temple where the headache was threatening to return. "She has already moved on."

"No, she hasn't. She still loves you. She just needs to be reminded of how it once was. You two have lost touch with each other. You need to rediscover that special spark that brought you together in the first place."

"How are we going to do that, if I can't find her?"

Lou stood up. "We'll find her. Humans are creatures of habit. Think about it. Where would she run if she were hurting?"

"To you."

"Maybe before, but she's upset with me. Where would her second choice be?"

Elaine thought about it for a moment and smiled. She knew exactly where Laurel was. "She's at the coast. She loves it down there."

Lou smiled. "See? Now all you have to do is go find her."

Elaine's mind began to formulate a schedule. She had plenty of vacation time coming to her, but with the holidays rapidly approaching, it would be almost impossible for her to get away. There was no way she could leave before the weekend. "I'll drive down to Rockport on Saturday morning." Her excitement wilted. "What if she doesn't want to see me?"

"Do you still love her?"

"Yes."

"Do you think she still loves you?"

Elaine's shoulders drooped as she pondered the question. "I don't know. Maybe not. If she still cared, why did she run away?"

Lou brushed aside the question like she would an annoying gnat. "You two are wearing me out. I don't have the energy for all this dyke drama."

Elaine flinched.

Lou rolled her eyes and Elaine was certain she was doing a slow count to control her frustration.

"For what it's worth, I know she still loves you," Lou said. "All you two need is some serious talk time."

"What if you're wrong and she doesn't love me anymore?"

They stared at each other for a long moment before Lou spoke. "Then you'll have to move on with your life without her."

"I don't know if I can."

Lou patted Elaine's arm. "I don't think it'll come to that, but if you have to you can. It won't be easy, but you'll make it."

Elaine sat at her desk staring into space for several minutes after Lou left. She wasn't so sure Lou was right in her last prediction. She honestly couldn't imagine life without Laurel.

It was later that afternoon when Elaine finally ran into Myra. Elaine was on her way back to her office after a staff meeting and Myra caught her in the hallway.

"There you are," Myra said.

"Oh, hi."

"I was beginning to think you were avoiding me."

Elaine considered pointing out the fact that Myra obviously hadn't been searching for her too hard but decided against bringing it up. It was time to put an end to this silly flirting. "Look, Myra. I know I'm partially responsible—"

Myra held up a hand to stop her. "Darling, if this is where you tell me you only want to be friends, let me save us both a lot of heartburn. If I wanted cuddly friends I'd buy a dog. If you're not interested in sex with me, say so and I'll move on."

Elaine tried to hide her shock but knew she wasn't doing a very good job. She finally gathered her wits about her enough that she could respond. "All right then. If that's how you feel about it, I guess there's nothing else for us to discuss." She turned to leave.

"Just like that you walk away?"

Elaine stopped. "I thought that's what you wanted."

"Of course that's not what I want." Her gaze traveled down Elaine's body. "Don't you understand how much fun we could have? And no one needs to get hurt."

A thought suddenly occurred to Elaine. "Did you call my house last Thursday night?"

The brief flash of guilt in Myra's eyes gave her away. "I might have called to remind you about our dinner date."

"That was a crappy thing to do." Elaine tried to control the anger that was building. "In case you care, someone has already been hurt with our childish flirting and I pray to God she gives me a chance to make it up to her." Without waiting for a response, Elaine walked away.

CHAPTER EIGHTEEN

It was a few minutes before eight when Laurel arrived at the pool the following morning. Nina was slicing through the water with seemingly little effort. She stood and watched as Nina reached the end of the pool and did a lithe flip before heading back toward her.

"Hey, you came," Nina said as she surfaced and clung to the edge of the pool.

Laurel shrugged. "Are you sure it's okay?"

Nina smiled and said, "Sure it is. Come on in. The water is perfect."

As she slipped out of her shirt and shorts she recalled the day Elaine had purchased the bathing suit for her. The suit was much bolder than anything she would have ever chosen, but Elaine had insisted it looked great on her. It was a one-piece suit, with the legs cut high. The front V-shaped opening plunged provocatively between her breasts to her abdomen. Just below her breasts the opening was held together by a small gold buckle that served only to draw more attention. Laurel suddenly thought of Elaine. A slight stab of guilt hit her, but she pushed it away. The brief gleam of appreciation in Nina's eyes did little to make her feel better. *Elaine left me*, she reminded herself. *There's no reason I should feel guilty about being here, even if I were up to something, which I'm not.* She eased into the pool and stifled a sigh of contentment as the warm water engulfed her. With slow deliberation she began to swim laps without bothering to count them. She swam until her arms began to tire. When she reached the end of the pool and draped her arms over it to rest, a family with three young boys was splashing around the shallow end. Each time water hit the youngest, he would shriek. It was hard to tell if it was a howl of pleasure or fright. Laurel pulled herself out of the water and grabbed her towel. As she dried off, she realized it was Halloween. She glanced at the three kids again and wondered if they would be going trick-or-treating tonight. A quick memory of her and Daniel going trick-or-treating made her smile.

She looked around. Nina was nowhere to be seen. She wondered if she should leave, but exhaustion prevailed. She wasn't used to such vigorous exercise. She grabbed her stuff and stretched out on a lounge chair as far away from the uproar as possible and was on the verge of dozing when Nina spoke.

"Do you suppose winter will ever get here?"

Laurel forced her eyes open and found Nina sitting on the chair next to her with two fruity-looking drinks in her hands.

"Sure it will, and both days will be in February," Laurel replied as she sat up.

Nina handed her one of the drinks. "This is my own special secret concoction. It's a great energy booster."

Laurel sipped the drink and immediately detected the flavor of pineapple, coconut and vanilla. "It's good."

"And it's good for you," Nina said as she popped the chair into an upright position and stretched her nicely toned legs out in front of her.

Laurel couldn't help but to compare Nina's legs to Elaine's long sexy legs. She squirmed as the memory sparked a flame of desire.

"Are you okay?"

Laurel shelved her thoughts of Elaine and made herself focus on the moment. "I'm fine."

Nina glanced toward the rowdy family. "Sorry about all the noise. There's usually no one but me around at this time of the morning. If you want we can move over there." She nodded to a large potted palm at the other end of the pool.

Laurel nodded and they gathered their things. After settling in at the new location, an awkward silence hovered between them.

"Does your family live in Corpus?" Laurel asked to fill the silence.

"Yeah, we all live within ten miles of each other."

"That must be nice." Laurel thought about how seldom she saw her brother, Daniel. "Is your family close?"

Nina chuckled. "God, yes." She held up a hand. "Don't get me wrong. I love my parents and siblings. I have an older sister and brother and one younger brother. There are times when I just want to hide under my bed for a week. Sometimes there's too much family time. You know what I mean?"

Laurel shook her head. "No. I only have one brother. He lives in Dallas, but I seldom see him. When we do get together, we get along okay. I mean, I love him, but we're just not a real close-knit family."

"What about your parents?"

"They're both dead."

Nina touched the small silver cross at the base of her throat. "I grumble a lot, but honestly, I don't know what I'd do without my family. They're one of the reasons I'll never move from here." She glanced toward Laurel and seemed to come to a decision. "My partner, Rachel, is in the Navy. She's a nurse and was stationed here at the naval base until six months ago when they transferred her to Iraq."

"Oh, my gosh. How much longer will she have to stay?"

Nina sipped her drink before answering. "She'll be there at least six more months. Maybe longer if they extend her tour. She wants to retire in eighteen months." Nina shrugged.

Laurel thought of Elaine. What would the upcoming months be like for them? She quickly smothered the pain the question caused and turned her attention back to Nina. "How long have you two been together?"

"It'll be twenty-one years in January."

Laurel blinked in genuine surprise. "Wow. That's a long time."

"When I was nineteen I was still living at home with my parents and youngest brother. My two older siblings had already moved out. I was working in my Uncle Berto's restaurant and hated it. I decided I wanted to see the world. I love the water, so joining the navy seemed to be the logical way to go." She set her glass down. "Rachel was a recruiter then. She started telling me about all the benefits of the navy and before I knew it, one thing led to another." Nina looked up and smiled. "I never did get around to enlisting. Six months later, I moved in with Rachel and followed her from here to California. Then we went to Hawaii, Connecticut and Maryland. This is actually her second trip to Iraq. She was there on a hospital ship in nineteen ninety-one. After that she was stationed in Virginia and several other places. Whenever I can I move with her."

"So you got to see some of the world after all."

Nina nodded and turned away, but not before Laurel saw the glimmer of tears.

"You miss her a lot, don't you?"

Nina brushed her eyes quickly. "I try and tell myself she'll be okay, but I can't stop worrying about her." She wiped her eyes again. "We bought a house that we both love about eight months before she got her orders. It needs a lot of work, but it's a great place. I spend most of my free time doing what I can to fix it up. It helps to keep me from worrying so much."

"It's good that you're so close to your family. They must give you a lot of support."

Nina nodded. "They've all been wonderful." She smiled. "My mom sends Rachel a big tin of cookies every month."

As they both drifted off to their own thoughts, Laurel wanted to ask how they had managed to stay together for so many years but decided it was stupid question. From looking at Nina's face whenever she spoke about Rachel, it was obvious why they were still together. This time she couldn't stop thoughts of Elaine from flooding in. "I can only imagine how much you must miss her."

Nina leaned forward slightly. "I get the feeling that you're missing someone yourself. Do you want to talk about it?"

Laurel glanced at her. Were her feelings so transparent? For an instant she considered telling Nina everything, but years of suppressing her feelings came forward and kept her mute. Instead she jumped up. "I didn't realize it was so late. I need to go home and get ready for work." She said a hasty good-bye and dashed off before Nina could say anything further.

CHAPTER NINETEEN

By eight thirty Friday night, Elaine was approaching the out-skirts of Rockport. Due to the unexpected arrival of a regional vice president, her week had proven to be more hectic than she had thought it would be. His appearance also forced her to move out of the luxury suite. Since the hotel wasn't at full capacity she was allowed to move into a regular guest room. Overall, the relocation wasn't a major inconvenience, since she had very little to move. The upside to the move was that in all the confusion over the change, she had been authorized an extra week in her current room, so she still had some time before she had to start looking for an apartment.

She had planned to wait and drive down tomorrow morning, but as soon as she got off work she knew she wouldn't be able to wait. After throwing a few clothes in a suitcase, she started out. Now, as she drove into the city limits, a sudden case of nerves hit her. Despite what Lou had told her, a tiny sliver of fear remained that Laurel wasn't here alone. Even if she was, there was a good chance Laurel wouldn't want to see her. She dismissed the possibility and told herself that things between them could be worked out. Everything could be rectified if she could just find Laurel and they could talk out their problems. Once the store was sold, Laurel could move on with her life. A twinge of guilt struck her. She knew she shouldn't be feeling so relieved that the store was closing, but in her heart she felt certain that all of their problems were directly linked to it.

Elaine rolled her window down and let her fears drift away on the warm gulf breeze. As soon as she turned onto the main drag, she immediately began to see changes. It seemed as though everywhere she looked there was a sign for a new art gallery. A newly built hotel, which still had Halloween decorations dangling from its balconies, stuck out like a large mole on the end of a nose. Its parking lot was filled with luxury cars. The sleepy little fishing town that she had fallen in love with was starting to take on a new look that she wasn't sure she cared for. She drove on down to the Fulton marina and was relieved to see that some things hadn't changed. The Fulton Pier still had its share of older pickups in the parking lot and the bright lights dotting the long wooden structure continued to illuminate the determined night fishermen.

She had only a vague plan on how to search for Laurel. She would start at the Gulf Side Motel, where Laurel had been staying when they first met and where they stayed on the rare occasions when they came down afterward. They had gotten very close to the Harwells, the older couple who had owned the motel for the past thirty-odd years. If by some slight chance Laurel wasn't there, Elaine would simply check every motel in the Rockport/Fulton area. The two towns were so close that for the most part they had become a single municipality. She was so sure she'd find Laurel at the Gulf Side that her plan hadn't developed much beyond that point.

When she pulled into the parking lot of the Gulf Side Motel her nervousness increased. She slowly made her way to the tiny office that was actually the front room of a small four-room, stand-alone unit that also served as home to the Harwells. The actual motel rooms were strung out in a large horseshoe arrangement around this unit.

She could see Vera sitting at a small table. As soon as she opened the door a faint scent of lavender and vanilla teased Elaine's nostrils. Vera Harwell with her crown of silvery hair and still-vibrant blue eyes glanced up from the silk floral arrangement she was creating.

As soon as she recognized Elaine, the smiled deepened. "I thought you'd dropped off the face of the earth," she called out as she came over to hug Elaine.

"No. Just busy."

"You girls need to move out of the city and away from all that stress."

"I'd love to," Elaine declared. "Unfortunately, there's a little thing called money that keeps getting in the way."

Vera laughed. "Now, you know Edgar's theory on money."

"The more you have the more you need," Elaine repeated.

"Hey, who's that talking?" Edgar called out as he shuffled from their living quarters behind the office.

Elaine was shocked by how stooped he had become. He appeared to have aged drastically in the last couple of years. She quickly gathered her composure. "Hello, Edgar. How's life treating you?"

"Well, I'll tell you, since you asked. The government is going to hell in a handbasket and this town is going right along with it. Now everything has to be artsy-fartsy and smell pretty. Used to be a fellow could fish all night and stop off for breakfast on his way home. Now, you walk into one of these fancy-shmancy restaurants in your fishing breeches and they get all bent out of shape and put you way back there by the kitchen door where you can just forget about being waited on. And even if they do wait on you, all you get is that stinking old flavored coffee and some fancy-sounding food that'll cost a working man a half of day's pay."

"Edgar," Vera cautioned softly. "You know you're going to get your blood pressure up."

"I need my blood pressure up," he scolded. "That's what's wrong with the world today. Nobody cares enough to get worked up over anything."

Vera patted his arm. "I'm sure you get worked up enough for everyone."

"Where's my girlfriend?" he demanded as he peered over his glasses and out the door behind Elaine. Over the years he and Laurel had become great friends and occasional fishing partners. As a result, he had dubbed her his girlfriend. The reference had bothered Elaine at first, until she realized that Edgar's roving eye started and stopped with his wife of forty-plus years.

Elaine swallowed her disappointment. She had thought Laurel would be here. "She wasn't able to get away, but she sends her best and promises to get down as soon as possible." She looked up to find Vera studying her closely.

Edgar sighed softly before starting toward the back room. "That's too bad. I was looking forward to seeing her again before I go."

Stunned by his words, Elaine turned to Vera, whose gaze was locked on Edgar's slow departure from the room. When she turned to Elaine her eyes were brimming with tears.

"Before he goes? What's going on?" Elaine asked as she took Vera by the arm and led her over to the table where she had been working on the floral arrangement. "What's wrong with Edgar?"

Vera pulled a tissue from her dress pocket and wiped her nose. "Nothing, except the old fool has decided he's going to die."

"Has he seen a doctor?"

"Yes. They've run all kinds of tests on him and can't find anything. It all started when Aaron Deering died."

The name didn't mean anything to Elaine.

Vera went on to explain. "Aaron and Edgar were in the Air Force Academy together. As you know Edgar retired after he put in twenty years, and we moved out here."

Elaine nodded. She vaguely remembered that the Harwells were from Cincinnati.

"They kept in touch over the years. Then Aaron and his wife, Kathy, moved here after Aaron retired." Vera put a finger to her chin. "I guess it was about seven or eight years ago." She fell silent for a moment.

"You mentioned he died," Elaine prompted.

Vera looked up. "Oh, yes. He died about six months ago. That was when Edgar got it in his head that he was about to die, too."

"Can't his doctor convince him otherwise?"

Vera made a rude sputtering noise and her voice rose in frustration. "Edgar is too hard-headed to listen."

"I'm not deaf," Edgar called from the back room.

"That's right," Vera called back. "You're just a bullheaded, stubborn old fart."

He began to mumble, but Vera ignored him and turned her attention back to Elaine. "You're not here to listen to us fuss. Did you want a room?"

Elaine nodded. She tried to think of a way to bring up Laurel's name without making it obvious that they were having problems, but nothing came to her.

After checking in and unpacking, she decided it would be best to wait until morning to start her search. After a quick shower she settled between the crisp, white sheets and flipped the television on. She spent the next several hours tossing and turning as she half-watched one mindless show after another, never allowing herself to admit that she wouldn't find Laurel in Rockport.

The following morning she was up early to start her search. The temperature had dropped considerably overnight and storm clouds were building on the horizon. She stopped by the motel office with the intention of grabbing the continental breakfast and saying a quick good morning to the Harwells. Unfortunately, Vera insisted she join them for a more substantial meal of her famous pecan waffles and bacon. An hour and a half flew by before she could slip away. When at last she left the office a fine mist of rain had begun to fall.

It only took her a couple of hours to drive to every motel, bed and breakfast and hotel in the area to see if Laurel was registered there. After leaving the last one without finding Laurel, she sat in her car and brooded. It was obvious the trip was for nothing. Laurel wasn't in Rockport.

The rain stopped, but heavy clouds hinted at more to come. Not wanting to return to her room, yet needing to be alone, she drove through Aransas Pass, planning to ride the ferry across to Port Aransas. She normally loved riding the ferry. From its deck there were always great views of dolphins frolicking in the bay and brown pelicans perched on the enormous pilings along the water's edge, while gulls glided overhead, always on the prowl for any offered tidbits of food. Today she barely noticed any of these things.

As soon as she was on the ferry she started to regret her decision to take it across. She should have gone back to the room, packed her things and driven back to San Antonio. Determined not to give in to her mood, she drove down to the beach and was pleasantly surprised to find it nearly deserted. The slapping waves soon enticed her out of the car and toward the water's edge. As she strolled along the wet sand some of the jumbled pieces of her life slipped into place. Once she took time to fully examine it in detail, Lou's explanation of what happened to Laurel made sense. In her heart, she couldn't believe Laurel would betray her trust. What was in doubt was whether Laurel was still interested in trying to salvage the relationship. That couldn't be answered until they talked.

When that avenue of thought hit a stalemate, she began to probe her own actions and feelings. It didn't take a genius to know why she had flirted with Myra. She was lonely, and on some level she wanted to show Laurel, and maybe even herself, that there were women who found her desirable.

It was hard to maintain the proper distance needed to analyze her feelings, but she was determined to do so. She wanted to work things out with Laurel, but some things would have to change. With a little soul-searching she realized that the long hours Laurel devoted to the store weren't so much the issue as Laurel shutting her out. They were a couple and as such she felt they should share both the good and the bad. She could sort of understand Laurel's reluctance to not take the proffered financial help, but not Laurel's refusal to let her in emotionally. Again, these were items they needed to sit down and discuss. A tide of anger washed through her. Where in the heck was Laurel?

A cool, brisk wind began coming in off the water. She regretted not bringing a heavier jacket. At this time of year the South Texas weather could be more fickle than usual. She started to jog back toward her car. The brisk pace helped to warm her. As she ran she realized that regardless of all the other issues, the bottom line was she loved Laurel and wanted to be a part of her life. She had to find her so they could work through this.

It was too cold to get out of her car as she crossed back to the mainland on the ferry. She used the time to check her voice mail and to call Lou to let her know Laurel didn't appear to be in Rockport. Lou didn't answer, but Elaine left a voice message. As she drove back toward Rockport, she decided she would return to San Antonio tonight. She'd tell Vera and Edgar something had come up at work and she needed to get back. It was time she started looking for an apartment. The hotel room wouldn't be available to her indefinitely.

Her plans changed as soon as she walked into her room and saw the flashing message indicator light on the phone. Certain it was a message from Laurel, she quickly called the front desk. Vera answered.

"I had a message?" Elaine asked.

"That was me. Edgar and I thought you might like to join us for an early dinner. I put on a pot roast this morning, so there will be plenty."

Elaine struggled to hide her disappointment.

"Tell her I'll be on my best behavior," Edgar called out.

"Did you hear that?" Vera asked.

Elaine smiled. They were sweet. She didn't have the heart to tell them she intended to drive back tonight. She could just as easily leave in the morning. "Yes. I heard. I'd love to join you guys. May I bring something?"

"No. Everything's covered. Come on over. It's ready."

Elaine freshened up some before going to join the Harwells for dinner. As she walked across the parking lot, she almost stopped in her tracks when a new thought occurred to her. What if Laurel was here with someone else and the room was registered in that person's name? She tried to shake off the thought, but it kept nagging at her. "She's not with anyone else," she whispered to herself over and over until she reached the motel's office.

There were times during dinner when Edgar seemed to be his normal spry self, then without warning his shoulders would droop and he would start talking as though his time on earth was narrowed down to a matter of hours or perhaps even minutes. After the meal was finished he told them good night and trudged back to his room.

"I hate to see him this way," Elaine said. "It must be really hard for you."

Vera traced the large hibiscus imprinted on the tablecloth. "The old coot is driving me crazy," she said. "I'm scared to death that he's so bullheaded that he'll lay down and die just to show me I was wrong."

Elaine couldn't help but smile. "I doubt if he'll take it that far."

"I hope you're right, but you saw how he is. There are days when I can barely get him out of the office. He hasn't been fishing in weeks. He used to like to sit outside and watch the hummingbirds. Now I can't even get him to prepare the nectar for their feeders."

Elaine frowned. She didn't know what to do to help them. "I wish Laurel was here. Maybe she could get through to him."

Vera looked up hopefully. "Do you think she would come to visit him?"

Elaine gave herself a swift mental kick. She hadn't intended to verbalize her wish. Something in her expression must have shown itself.

"Oh, my," Vera sighed as she reached across the table and took Elaine's hand. "You have troubles of your own, don't you, dear?"

"It's nothing." Elaine turned away, blinking rapidly to control the tears that sprang to her eyes.

"Is something wrong with Laurel, or are you two having problems?"

Elaine started to deny any problems, but the denial stuck in her throat. "Things between us have been a little rocky," she admitted.

"Is that why she isn't with you?"

"Actually, I'm down here looking for her. She left a few days ago. I assumed she would come to Rockport."

Vera shook her head. "We've not seen her since that last time you were both here."

Vera's comment on not seeing Laurel made Elaine admit the truth. There wasn't any need to bother checking the piers for Laurel. Regardless of who she was or wasn't with, if she was in town, she would have been by to see Vera and Edgar.

CHAPTER TWENTY

On Friday morning Laurel delayed meeting Nina at the pool. She needed to return a call from Angela Ramirez, the realtor. Angela had left the message at the motel yesterday and asked her to call her between eight and nine Friday morning. As she headed to the pay phone on the corner, Laurel said a silent prayer that Angela had found a buyer for the Lavender Page. She had been at the Seafarer's Paradise Motel for almost three weeks and it was already starting to wear on her nerves. In truth, she was rarely in the room. She swam with Nina each weekday morning before work and rather than returning to the room during the break between her shifts, she spent the time walking along the shore or sitting on the pier talking with the locals. Now, the weekend had rolled around again and she was trying to think of a way to fill the hours until Monday morning. She was tired of sightseeing. She considered trying to fish some but still hadn't purchased a fishing license, and she needed to hang on to every spare dollar. The two free meals Jim let her eat at the restaurant each day helped tremendously. What little money she had accumulated would be eaten away when her credit card statement arrived.

Laurel dialed the number and was relieved when Angela answered on the second ring.

"Your timing was perfect," Angela said after a quick exchange of greetings.

"I wasn't sure the message was correct. I was concerned it was too early to call."

"I like to get here before things get too crazy. It gives me a chance to get caught up."

In the background Laurel could hear a muted symphony of ringing phones, the low hum of office machines and voices.

"It sounds like everyone's already working," Laurel said.

Angela chuckled. "The real estate market in San Antonio is growing so rapidly we can't keep up."

Laurel wondered why her business hadn't sold if the market was booming.

Angela quickly got to the point. "Laurel, I'm not much of one for beating around the bush, and I take my responsibilities to my client seriously."

There was a brief pause and Laurel thought she heard her sipping coffee.

"When you first came in, you kept stressing how much you wanted to sell the business to someone who would keep it open." Angela rushed on, "I didn't have a lot of hope in selling the bookstore intact, but I felt I owed it to you to try."

Despite being on the phone, Laurel nodded in agreement.

"As you already know," Angela said, "there have only been two lukewarm inquiries on the store. Quite honestly I don't think either prospect will call back."

"What do you think the problem is?"

Angela hesitated a brief moment before answering. "Honestly, there's not much of an interest in a lesbian bookstore in San Antonio. I think it's remarkable that you managed to keep it open as long as you did."

This wasn't news to Laurel, but she had been holding onto a thin thread of hope that someone would step forward and pick up the reins. "I understand. So are you saying I should remove it from the market?"

"On the contrary. What I'm suggesting is that if you want to get rid of the responsibility completely then clear out the merchandise and fixtures and sell the building. I can get you a good price for it and I'm positive someone will snap it up immediately. The real estate is in a prime location. I know that large bookstore down the street hurt you, but the mall and the surrounding business construction has practically doubled land prices in that area over the last year."

"I'm glad to see it was worthwhile for something," Laurel said.

"Is there another store you could sell the merchandise to or maybe even donate part of it? I know it hurts to give your inventory away, but it might prove to be beneficial on your taxes."

"I could return some of the books for credit and donate the rest. I left so quickly I honestly didn't give it much thought."

"Think about it." Angela hesitated a moment. "Have you ever thought about leasing the space? I'm certain I could lease for you without any trouble and that would provide you with some regular monthly income."

"I hadn't thought about that. What could you lease it for?"

"Well, as I said, you're in a prime location. It's a wonderful building with a lot of charm, new outside paint and great parking. I think I could easily lease it for an annual rate of around sixteen dollars per square foot. There's a little over twenty-two hundred square feet, so you're looking at"—the clacking chatter of a calculator sounded in the background—"definitely thirty-plus thousand a year."

Laurel grabbed onto the phone for support.

Before Laurel could find her voice, Angela continued. "Of course, you might have to put a little cash in upfront. The carpet should probably be replaced. If I remember correctly some of the bookshelves were attached to the walls and those would need to come out. But, overall, I think it would be well worthwhile."

"What about ongoing costs?" Laurel asked when she could finally speak.

"You'll still be responsible for property taxes, and certain maintenance issues, but those can be stipulated in the contract, and you'll certainly want to continue your insurance on the building. Even with those expenses you'll still have a nice chunk of change left over."

Laurel didn't tell her that for the past two years she had been living on less than twenty thousand dollars annually.

"Laurel, I have another call, but think about what I've told you. If you still want to sell the building I'd urge you to think about clearing everything out and focusing on the building itself. I'll be around the office until about six, and of course you can always reach me on my cell."

After agreeing to think about her options, Laurel walked back to her room and put on a pot of coffee. She decided she wouldn't meet Nina at the pool at all today. She needed to think about Angela's advice.

As she drove to work, she made up her mind to make a trip into San Antonio over the weekend. She needed to pick up her mail, and she wanted to see Lou and patch up their little spat. By the time she pulled into the parking lot at the Oyster Hut she was whistling softly and anticipating her trip. She told herself that the sudden uplift in spirits had nothing to do with the possibility of running into Elaine.

Despite a restless night, Laurel was on the road to San Antonio before eight. The Saturday morning traffic was light, allowing her to make good time. About an hour outside of Corpus she stopped at a convenience store and bought a cup of coffee. As she stood by her car sipping the hot brew, a small car, crowded with two young couples stuffed in among piles of bags, pulled in next to her. Laurel smiled at the ice chest tied to the top of their car. When the two men and women piled out of the car, they were chattering excitedly about their upcoming weekend in Corpus.

Laurel wondered at the irony of it. Here she was excited to be going home for the weekend, while they were anticipating getting away. The crisp mid-November wind cut her musings short. She got back into the car and headed out. As she drove she found herself growing more and more excited about getting back. Since Lou's house was closer than her own, she went there first. The first twinges of nervousness hit her as she pulled into Lou's driveway.

What if Lou was still mad at her? They had never really had an argument of any consequence before. She slowly made her way up the sidewalk, wondering what she would say when Lou opened the door. Laurel decided she would apologize for the way she had ran out of the house the last time she was here, and she would apologize for not letting anyone know where she'd been for the last three weeks. As she reached out to ring the bell, the door flew open and Lou grabbed her in a tight bear hug. She was trying to recover from that shocker when a bigger one hit her as Allie came flying out the door. Laurel found herself in the center of a massive group hug. Lou and Allie were talking and laughing so hard that Laurel could barely understand them.

She hugged them back as much as her pinned arms would allow. When they finally loosened their grip enough so that she could pry herself from their clutches, she quickly wiped the tears from her eyes and berated herself. How could she have ever thought Lou would be so angry at her that she wouldn't want to see her? She gave a relieved carefree chuckle and instantly regretted it when Lou planted her fists on her hips.

"Where in the hell have you been?" she demanded. "We've been worried sick about you."

"I went to the coast. I needed time to think."

"The coast! Where were you at the coast? Elaine went down to Rockport looking for you and could find neither hide nor hair of you." She leaned her short frame closer.

"I'm living in Corpus. I found a job there."

"A job! Why would you want to get a job in Corpus?"

Laurel glanced at Allie for support and found her glaring at her with her arms crossed tightly across her chest. "I told you I needed to get away." She reminded herself to keep her anger under control. "I need to make a living."

"Why couldn't you do that right here?" Lou persisted.

"I left because I didn't want to have to worry about running into Elaine with another woman." As soon as the words were out of her mouth, Laurel wished she could snatch them back, but she realized they were true. She hadn't moved to the coast simply because she loved it down there.

An awkward silence fell between them until Lou finally spoke. "Well, now we're getting somewhere." She motioned for her and Allie to follow her. "I think it's time we all went inside and had a long talk."

CHAPTER TWENTY-ONE

Dooley, Lou's cantankerous basset hound, released a low pathetic howl when the three of them entered the house.

"Stop that," Lou ordered.

He flopped to the floor. With an exaggerated sigh he dropped his head onto his front paws.

"Poor Dooley," Allie said as she sat beside him and began to scratch above his ears.

"You're going to spoil him," Lou said.

"Yeah, like he's not already," Allie replied.

Laurel took a seat on the comfortable couch. It, like so much of Lou's furniture, was old but had been built with quality materials that seemed to improve with age. Laurel noticed several items of furniture and various knickknacks that indicated Allie was now living here. A worm of guilt wiggled through her. Maybe Allie's layoff had forced the arrangement. She glanced at the two women and wondered when their relationship had started. They made a rather odd couple, in that Lou was somewhat reserved while Allie was like a pressure cooker with all her youthful energy and optimism building until it was on the verge of exploding. There was at least a forty-year age difference between them. Perhaps that was why it did work for them. Each perfectly balanced the other.

Allie looked up and met Laurel's gaze. "Should I leave? I mean, if you two would be more comfortable talking alone."

Laurel shook her head. "No. That's fine." Her curiosity got the best of her. "So, how long have you two . . ." She waved a hand at each of them.

Allie smiled brightly. "We've been seeing each other for a couple of months."

Lou sat in a recliner across from Laurel. Her short legs barely allowed her toes to touch the floor. "I know what you're thinking, with me being so much older—"

Laurel held up a hand to stop her. "Actually, I was just thinking you both are exactly what the other needed. Besides, who am I to judge what's best for you?"

Allie gave Lou a small smile. The intimacy it conveyed caused Lou to blush and duck her head, but not before Laurel saw the pleased look in her eye.

Feeling like a voyeur, Laurel quickly changed the subject. "So, what have you two been up to?" The implications of the question made her cringe.

Ironically, it was Allie who came to her rescue. "I found a job."

"That's great. Where?"

She laughed. "At a temp agency. You'll never believe what else. I applied at UTSA. I'm going to get my Bachelor's of Science in architecture."

"I'm impressed," Laurel said. "That is really wonderful. I'm proud of you. That took a lot of courage to move into something so different from anything you've tried before."

"Lou helped me a lot. I wouldn't have had the guts without her encouragement."

Lou waved away Allie's compliment. "You'll be the one who's

doing all the work." In what appeared to be an effort to divert the attention away from herself, Lou turned to Laurel. "We need to get this mess between you and Elaine straightened out."

"What is there to straighten out? Elaine met someone else and moved out."

Lou shook her head in frustration. "No. No. No. That's why you two need to talk. She's not having an affair."

"I saw her."

"You saw what you wanted to see," Lou insisted.

Laurel's eyes widened. "Excuse me. Exactly why would I want to see my girlfriend with another woman?"

"Well, I'm no psychologist," Lou said. "Maybe you were looking for an excuse to push everyone away so you could wallow in your own little pool of self-pity."

"Lou," Allie said softly.

But Lou was on a roll. She scooted to the edge of the recliner and planted her left elbow against her knee. The right arm became a pointing, slashing sword of indignation. "Laurel Becker, you know I love you like you were my own flesh and blood, but the truth is they should have buried you in that same coffin they used for Chris, because you died the same day she did."

Stunned, Laurel started to stand.

"You sit back down," Lou ordered. "This time you're going to listen to me."

Laurel didn't know if it was because she was a little frightened by her friend's sudden outburst or if something inside her recognized the truth of Lou's accusation. For whatever reason, she obeyed.

Allie slid closer to the recliner and placed a gentle hand on Lou's knee.

Lou stared down at her for a long moment before taking a deep breath and nodding. "I'm sorry. I was way out of line." She rubbed a hand over her face. "It's just that I saw how devastated you were after Chris died. It almost killed me to see you hurting so and knowing there was nothing I could do to help you. I'd almost given up on ever seeing you happy again and then Elaine came along and suddenly you started smiling."

Laurel fiddled with a loose thread on her shirttail and fought against the tears that burned her eyes.

Lou took Allie's hand and interlaced their fingers. "Elaine wasn't having an affair. I'm not saying she didn't think about it." She chuckled softly. "But, the truth is, when the opportunity knocked on her door, she ran like a scared rabbit. The woman isn't stupid. She knew she had a good thing at home, but something was broken and she didn't know how to fix it."

"Then why did she move out?" Laurel asked.

Lou pinched the bridge of her nose with her free hand. "You know. I shouldn't be the one telling you all this. You and Elaine need to sit down and talk. The bottom line is: she thinks you're having an affair, and you think she's having an affair. You're both too stubborn for your own good. Sometimes I worry that you two are just too much alike." She gestured at Laurel. "Now, do me a favor and go find her. I have a hot date. My sweetie and I are going to catch an early movie and then maybe grab a bite to eat. If you don't end up spending the night with Elaine, then you come back here to stay with us. That'll give us time to catch up."

CHAPTER TWENTY-TWO

After she left Lou and Allie, Laurel made a quick stop at the post office to retrieve her mail before she headed home. It felt good to be driving through familiar neighborhoods. When she pulled onto her street and spied Mrs. Blackburn's house, she almost wished the old woman would be out walking her poodle, Precious. She smiled when she remembered how she and Elaine had avoided being corralled by Mrs. Blackburn.

The empty driveway bothered her. During those last few months at the bookstore when everything started imploding, the simple act of finding Elaine's car in the driveway had given her a sense of comfort. Just knowing that Elaine was inside waiting for her had been enough to keep her going. As she sat in her car, it took her a moment to realize that a part of her had been hoping that Elaine would be here. Of course, that was a silly thought, she reminded herself. After all, she had left a note asking Elaine to move her stuff out. All sorts of random thoughts were shooting through her mind. Had the dinner with Myra been as innocent as Lou said? Lou wouldn't deliberately lie to her, but perhaps she was seeing what she wanted to see. *Or maybe I was.*

Laurel avoided the uncomfortable thought as she made her way to the front entrance, unlocked the door and stepped inside. The drawn shades made the interior dark and cool. Strangely enough nothing seemed different. She had expected to see empty spaces from where Elaine had removed her things. She frowned as she continued her tour. Had her note not been found? It took her a moment to realize that nothing looked different because every-thing she was seeing was hers. When Elaine moved in, she had brought very little with her—clothes, a few books and a couple of boxes of personal items. Since the house was already fully fur-nished, Elaine had decided to save herself the cost of moving and storing her furniture and had sold or given away all of her furni-ture in Houston.

A thin stab of guilt pierced Laurel. Maybe she should have insisted on making room for some of Elaine's things. It must have been hard for Elaine to leave everything behind. After only three weeks in Corpus, Laurel already missed being surrounded by familiar items. She made her way into the kitchen before she saw the first sign of anything being changed. The small ivy that had sat in the window was gone.

In the bedroom, she checked Elaine's closet and found it empty except for a few hangers arranged neatly on the rod. The dresser drawers and bathroom cabinets were empty of Elaine's things as well. She sat on the end of the bed. Elaine was really gone and they hadn't even bothered to say good-bye to each other.

As she glanced around the room at the antique chest of drawers with matching dark cherry wood dresser and bed, she realized that nothing really belonged to her either—or at least, she hadn't been the one to choose the furniture. All of it had belonged to Chris. She made a slow circuit back through the house and looked at it as if seeing it for the first time. There was very little in this house that was hers. At least ninety percent of the furnishings had belonged to Chris. The most troubling aspect was that she didn't even particularly care for the décor. Most of the furniture was heavy antique pieces that Chris had accumulated over the years. Laurel's own preference leaned toward more modern styles with sleeker lines. Suddenly she realized that she had been clinging to all of these things not out of love for them, but in an attempt to keep Chris alive by living her life. The house, the furniture and the bookstore were things from Chris's dreams, not her own. The realizations made her sway slightly. At what point had she stopped living her own life? Her hand flew to her mouth as a new thought occurred to her. Had Elaine resented having to live here surrounded by all of these ghosts of Chris's past? Could that have been part of the problem? She shook her head to clear it. Elaine hadn't left because of the furniture. Their problems went much deeper than that.

Lou was right. They needed to talk. She reached for the phone before remembering she had stopped the service. For the first time she cursed her decision to get rid of her cell phone. She grabbed her keys and headed back to the car. There was a convenience store a few blocks away. She would call Elaine and tell her how sorry she was and ask her to come home.

With keys in hand she started for the door, then stopped sharply. What was she doing? Was she seriously considering trying to patch things up with Elaine? If so, what about her decision to move to Corpus? True, it had been impulsive, but she had a job there. Salary-wise, it wasn't much, but Jim, Kate and Nina depended on her to be there each day. If she decided to move back here, she had promised Jim at least two weeks' notice and she would keep that promise. Was she even ready to come back to live in San Antonio?

She grabbed her head. "I'm losing my mind." She groaned. Why did everything seem so complicated? Then a new thought hit her. All along she had been thinking about how she felt, but what about Elaine? Maybe she had plans of her own. Laurel had no idea where Elaine was living. Had she already bought or rented a place?

A cold fear slithered into Lauren's thoughts. What if Elaine didn't want to patch things up? Maybe she had already decided to move on with her life.

She stepped into the living room and stood by the only piece of furniture that was hers, the red leather sofa. As she ran her hand over the back she smiled. Even this wasn't truly hers. It had originally belonged to her parents. A frown creased her forehead as her thoughts turned back to her problems. It was true that she had placed her own life on hold when Chris died . . . maybe even before then when she quit her job to help Chris with the bookstore. What did she want out of life now anyway? She knew it wasn't the bookstore, but she certainly didn't want to be a waitress the rest of her life either. She had sort of enjoyed working at the lawyer's office, but being tied to a desk for eight hours a day didn't sound very appealing. She suddenly recalled an eighth-grade teacher who had made the class write an essay on what their dream occupation would be. She chuckled when she recalled her essay. Her dream occupation at that point in time had been to become a stock car racer.

"Well I'm too old and chicken for that," she said. She sat on the sofa. Maybe it was time for her to start thinking about what she wanted to do with her life.

It was almost four before Laurel left her house. Despite wracking her brain for answers, she still wasn't any closer to a definitive answer for a new career, but there were a couple of things that were clearer. She had a tentative plan that would at least get her started in what she hoped was the right direction, but she would need help. From the house she drove to the convenience store and used her credit card to call Daniel.

"I need help," she said without preamble when her brother answered. If she hesitated she might not be able to ask for what she needed.

"What's wrong? Are you sick?"

"No. I need to borrow ten thousand dollars." She wasn't offended by the silence that followed. They were, after all, their father's children. One kept one's problems to oneself and found a way to work through them. She gave Daniel extra credit for his quick recovery.

"How fast do you need it? I can send it Western Union if you need it right now."

"No. I don't need it right this minute. I won't need it for a couple of weeks."

"That's okay. Give me your account number and the bank's routing number, and I'll do a wire transfer," he said. "The money should be available to you in a couple of days, just in case."

She pulled her checkbook from her bag and gave him the information. "I'll pay you back as soon as I can." She could hear the clicking of computer keys.

"I'm not worried about that." He hesitated slightly. "Are you sure you're okay?"

It was a bit of a struggle, but she made herself tell him that she had closed the store. She went on to explain how she wanted to lease the building, but to do so she would need to make some repairs. "That's why I need the loan. I own the building, but on my current income I don't think I could get an equity loan." She was pleased when he agreed with her that leasing the building sounded like a better financial plan. Since she was on a roll she made a clean sweep of it and rushed on to tell him about her breakup with Elaine and her recent relocation to Corpus.

"I'm really sorry to hear about your problems with Elaine," he said when she finally got it all out. "I liked her. I thought she was good for you."

His comment surprised her. "You never mentioned that before."

He gave a harsh laugh. "Personal conversations aren't highly rated in this family."

"Maybe it's time we changed that."

"Yeah, maybe it is," he agreed. "I just did an online request for the transfer of funds. The money should be in your account in a couple of days."

"Thanks. I really appreciate this. I should be able to pay you back soon."

"I told you not to worry about it. I know you'll pay me back when you can."

The conversation faltered. Laurel was hesitant to hang up. "How's Zane?" she asked.

An animation she wasn't accustomed to hearing crept into his voice. "He's unbelievable. The kid is a genius with anything electronic. He placed third in a nationwide science competition and was invited to the White House to meet the President. Judy and I went with him and—"

"Whoa," Laurel interrupted. "Back up a little bit. You and your ex-wife were in the same building."

"We've been sort of seeing each other again."

She shook her head in amazement. "That's a story I have to hear, but unfortunately, I don't think my credit card can handle it."

He laughed. "Get yourself settled, and maybe I'll fly down soon to see you and tell you all about it."

She agreed to do so and hung up. After digging some change from her pocket she called Angela Ramirez to tell her she had decided to take her advice and lease the building rather than sell it. They agreed that Laurel would have the store empty of merchandise and fixtures, replace the carpet and make any other minor repairs needed before the end of the year and that the property would be listed as available for lease after the first of January. She tried not to think about whether or not her old car could withstand the strain of weekly roundtrips from the coast to San Antonio that would be needed in order for her to work on the store.

With shaking hands she dialed a much more familiar number and prayed Elaine wouldn't hang up on her before she had a chance to apologize. There was so much she needed to say.

CHAPTER TWENTY-THREE

Elaine pulled the tail of her light green shirt from her jeans, then removed her jacket and dropped it on the bed. She'd just come from having dinner with the Harwells and once again she was stuffed. After a particularly hellish week at work, she had gotten up that morning and driven back to Rockport on the pretense of checking on Edgar and Vera. Three weeks had passed since Laurel had left. With each passing day, the hope of hearing from Laurel had dimmed. Elaine finally admitted that if Laurel was interested in seeing her, she would have called. The admission hadn't helped ease the pain she felt whenever she thought of her, which still proved to be quite often.

She'd found that keeping busy helped. She'd spent every evening this week looking at apartments and had finally found the perfect one, a small one-bedroom that was completely furnished. After conjuring up all sorts of excuses to herself, one of which was that she needed to check on Vera and Edgar, she had resisted signing the lease. At some level she knew she was trying to avoid making the final break. A tiny part of her still hoped Laurel would return and they could work things out.

She decided to go for a walk to make amends for her gluttony over Vera's excellent beef stew and corn bread. She changed into sweats and sneakers before she grabbed her key and started out. Just as she reached the door, her cell phone rang. The screen showed it was an out-of-area caller. She considered letting the call go to voice mail but changed her mind. It might be Lou or her mother. The walk was forgotten as soon as she heard Laurel's hello.

The sudden red hot anger that shot through Elaine frightened her. It took her a moment to collect herself enough to respond. When she did her voice sounded gruff.

"I know you're angry and I don't blame you," Laurel rushed on. "I shouldn't have run off like that."

"It wasn't your fault. I left first."

"Elaine, I'm . . . I—" She stopped. There was a long moment of silence before she continued. "Are you doing okay? Have you found an apartment?"

"No. I've been staying at the hotel. Where are you?" She knew it would be hard for Laurel to open up. To get her to do so would take a razor-thin balancing act.

"I'm at a phone booth near the house."

There was a brief hesitation and Elaine could almost see Laurel frowning and struggling to say what was on her mind. She held her breath and waited. If she pushed too hard Laurel would clam up. If she didn't push hard enough, Laurel could easily start discussing the weather.

"I was wondering if you'd like to have dinner with me tonight?" Laurel asked.

Elaine cursed her own lousy timing as she sat down heavily on the end of the bed. "I'm in Rockport."

"Oh." Silence again filled the line.

"I heard you'd decided to sell the store." Elaine decided it was probably best not to point out the fact that it hadn't been Laurel who had told her.

"I've changed my mind. I'm going to close the store but lease the building."

Elaine blinked. Part of her surprise was that Laurel had decided to keep the building but most came from the fact that she had actually shared her intention to do so. "That sounds like a great idea. I'm sure that location is a lot more desirable now that the mall has moved in." She bit her tongue before giving herself a swift mental kick. Laurel didn't need to be reminded of the mall with its bloodsucking mega bookstore. She quickly changed the subject. "I came down to Rockport because I thought you'd be here."

"Oh. I've been in Corpus."

"I thought you didn't like Corpus."

"It's okay. I prefer Rockport, but there are too many memories—" Laurel stopped short.

Elaine picked at a loose thread to a button on her jacket that was lying beside her. "I hope they're not all bad."

Laurel was slow in responding. "I have no bad memories of Rockport. That's the problem."

Elaine found herself hesitant to blurt out what she wanted. Why was she finding it so hard to simply tell Laurel that she wanted to come home and work things out? It dawned on her that she was afraid of being rejected, or worse, that Laurel was no longer interested in patching things up between them. But she had learned a long time ago that covering your head didn't necessarily make the bogeyman go away. She gathered her courage to ask. At least she'd know something one way or the other. She took a deep breath and hurried on before Laurel could speak. "If you're available I could meet you during the week. Work hasn't gotten too crazy yet."

There was a heart-stopping silence before Laurel replied, "I'm going back to Corpus tonight, but maybe we could get together the next time I'm in town."

Elaine pulled the thread and watched as it unraveled and the button fell. She felt like she had been sucker-punched. Laurel wasn't calling to try and work things out after all. She just wanted to get together, probably to make the split official. Elaine tried to answer but couldn't seem to find her voice.

"If you'd rather not, I understand," Laurel said softly.

"No! I'd like that. When do you think you'll be back?"

Again that slight hesitation before she answered. "Two weeks."

"That's the first weekend of December," Elaine said after some quick calculation. She sensed that Laurel was struggling with something but didn't know how to draw it out of her.

"That sounds about right."

Elaine swallowed her disappointment. "I'm not sure what my schedule will be like then. You know how crazy things get after Thanksgiving."

"That's right. Why don't I call you when I get into town and we can decide then?"

"Sure."

After they had said their good-byes, Elaine continued to sit on the bed, trying to interpret the call. The fact that Laurel had phoned should be seen as a positive sign. On the other hand, her returning to Corpus didn't bode well. Was she planning on living there, or was this an extended holiday? How could she afford that? A queasy sensation struck her. Perhaps it really *was* over between them. Maybe Laurel had already decided to move on with her life without Elaine. That might explain why she was going back to Corpus. Apparently, her new life was there.

The next thought made her nauseous. All this time she'd been worrying about Laurel leaving her for another woman. What if Laurel had simply walked away from her, from the relationship, because she was tired of it . . . tired of her?

Elaine told herself she wasn't going to cry, but that did little to deter the tears. When she was too exhausted to cry anymore, she kicked off her shoes and crawled beneath the covers, pulling them over her head. Maybe they wouldn't keep the bogeyman away, but they could close out the world for a while. She finally slept.

When she awoke the glowing dial on the small clock radio indicated it was almost four in the morning. Wide awake and needing to move, she packed her suitcase and wrote a short note to the Harwells thanking them for their hospitality and promised to return soon. After dropping the note and room key into the designated key slot, she headed home. It was obvious Laurel had moved on with her life and it was time for her to do the same. She would sign the lease for the apartment and move in as quickly as possible.

CHAPTER TWENTY-FOUR

After hanging up with Elaine, Laurel stood by the phone booth. The conversation hadn't gone exactly as she had hoped, but at least Elaine hadn't refused her invitation to get together. There was still a chance they could work things out between them. She wasn't willing to give up yet. If Elaine needed time, then she would get it. As long as there was a chance to make things right, Laurel could wait.

She left the phone booth and drove to the Lavender Page. The empty parking lot gave her a sense of sadness. She chased the feeling away by reminding herself that she had done her best for the store. As hard as it was for her to admit, she had to accept the fact that perhaps even Chris couldn't have saved the store in the face of the changes that had been gradually occurring since her death. It was a sign of progress that lesbian-themed literature could easily and in most cases safely be purchased in any of the larger mainstream bookstores.

She got out of her car and slowly made her way to the door. After letting herself in and turning on all the lights she browsed through the shelves, reacquainting herself with the all too familiar titles. As she scanned the books she began a mental list of things that needed to be done. The first thing to do was get the word out that a going-out-of-business sale would begin in early December. She would need to delay the sale at least that long in order to give Jim the promised two weeks' notice. Then she would return as much of the remaining merchandise as possible to the original distributors. That would be a time-consuming endeavor and by the time she paid the restocking fee and postage it would prove costly. Some of the self-help and informational books could be donated to various local gay and lesbian organizations.

After a quick review of the books, she went back to her office. She didn't want to think about how she was going to tell Jim she intended to quit. Her recent bout of impulsiveness and fickleness embarrassed her. A red blinking light caught her attention as she sat down to her desk. In all the confusion of leaving and closing the store, she had forgotten to cancel the phone service, and there were incoming messages waiting for her. As she played them back, she cursed her carelessness and the extra expense it caused. She tried to focus on the positive side. At least she wouldn't have to keep using her credit card at a convenience store pay phone.

When she checked the messages, most of the calls were from telemarketers. Only two calls were from potential customers searching for a particular book. The one that caught her attention was from a woman who introduced herself as Nancy Grady from the estate sale. It took Laurel a moment to recall the short brunette who had sold her the boxes of books. In the message she thanked Laurel for allowing her to post the rental flyer and wondered if she might impose on her to post another, this one being a help wanted ad.

Curious as to what the job might be, Laurel called the number Nancy had left and was surprised to hear the phone answered as Grady Landscaping Design. Laurel quickly introduced herself.

"I'm sorry to have bothered you," Nancy began. "When I called I didn't know you had closed the store. I didn't find out until I went by a couple of days later and saw the sign. I see you've returned. Were you just closed for vacation?"

"No. It'll be open for most of the month of December for a going-out-of-business sale, but I'll be leasing the building after that."

"That's too bad. It's a nice store. Allie showed me around when I came by a few weeks ago to drop off the flyer for the house."

"How did that go?" Laurel asked. "Did you find a renter?"

"Yes. It's working out really well. A young couple rented the top floor. They've only been together a few months and are absolutely adorable. They make me want to be twenty again."

Laurel groaned. "Oh, not me. I don't think I'd make it the second time around. I think I'll stick with being old."

"Come on, you're not that old," Nancy said with a teasing tone.

"There are days when I definitely feel older than others." Laurel quickly moved back to business. "If you still want to post another flyer and can wait, mail it to the store and I'll post it when I come back in a couple of weeks. I don't know how much good it'll do, but you're welcome to leave it."

"Thanks. I appreciate that."

"Just out of curiosity, what sort of job is it?"

"I think I mentioned that I'm a landscape designer and that I wanted to expand my business from Austin down here."

Laurel vaguely remembered the conversation. "Did you say you were closing the Austin location?"

"No. I'm going to open a second location. If business doesn't go well here, I'll still have the Austin location to fall back on. I need to hire someone to run the office here."

"What would they have to do?"

"Basically, they would need good general office skills—computer knowledge, some light bookkeeping, scheduling my appointments, good social skills since they would have some contact with clients and vendors and occasionally run errands."

Laurel thought for a moment before pursuing the matter. "I might be interested in the job myself."

Nancy was silent for a brief moment. "You're obviously qualified for the job, but are you sure you'd be happy with it? I mean, you've been self-employed for a long time. Do you think you'd be content to work in such a . . . a . . . back-office position?"

Laurel laughed aloud. "Oh, you have no idea how wonderful a 'back-office position' sounds. I'm more than over being self-employed. I want a job with some sanity and a steady paycheck."

"I can't promise things won't get a little insane sometimes, but knock on wood, I've never failed to make payroll."

"The only problem is I can't start until January," Laurel said. "I have to settle things here first."

"That won't be a problem. I've just started the process of opening the office here. I would like to have it operational by the first of the year, but I don't expect much of a rush in business before March. Spring is usually when people start thinking about landscaping." Her voice changed slightly as she slipped into what Laurel assumed was her business persona. "Since I've moved down here, I've made some contacts with a few of the local building contractors. Three of them have subcontracted me. One of the jobs is an apartment complex and the other two are private homes."

"It sounds like you've got your foot in the door."

"Yes and no. I prefer to deal with the homeowners directly. Most contractors aren't too concerned with real landscaping. All they're interested in is sod, one small fast-growing tree in the front, another in the back, a few boxwood hedges along the sidewalk or front of the house and, if I'm lucky, a window box of flowers."

"I guess there's not much room for creativity in that design."

"It's a pretty limited palette."

"So, can I apply for the position?" Laurel asked.

"Heck, you can have it, if you really want it."

"Don't you want a résumé or something?"

"I don't need it. I've seen how neat and well-run the store is."

"It doesn't make you nervous that it's closing?"

"It makes me sad that it's closing. Maybe it's because I own my own business, but I can see how much of your heart and soul you've poured into it. My guess would be that you've probably managed to keep it open a lot longer than most people would have. I've read about how the lesbian and feminist bookstores are struggling." She hesitated a moment. "Do you see the store's closing as some sort of failure on your part?"

The question caught Laurel off-guard. "I suppose I do," she finally replied. "I think Chris, the woman who opened the store, would have managed to handle the changes much better had she lived."

"Do you think she could have prevented the chain bookstore from moving into the mall?"

"No, of course not, but she would have been able to keep the old customers from drifting away."

Nancy made a soft murmur. Laurel couldn't interpret its meaning and Nancy didn't elaborate. Instead she changed the subject. "I have two people working for me in Austin. Brenda is the office manager and Jo is sort of a combined design apprentice and assistant. She's still in college working on her degree in landscaping design. If you take the position you'll be working with Brenda a lot. She'll be able to help you set the office up and get it running. In fact, I'll probably bring her down here for a few days to help you with that. After things are up and operational you'll pretty much be on your own. I'll be back and forth between here and Austin. My hope is that Jo will stay on with me once she graduates and eventually take over management of the Austin office."

Laurel started to ask about salary, but Nancy beat her to the subject.

"The position is a forty-hour work week, Monday through Friday. Clients can always reach me on my cell phone the rest of the time. I keep it on twenty-four-seven and I always answer it. The pay is eight dollars an hour with some medical benefits, and there's overtime pay for any time over the forty hours. If business is good, I try to offer a bonus at Christmas. Your bonus would be based on how the San Antonio office does. That may change later, but for now I don't think it's fair to Brenda and Jo to cut their bonuses because I opened this office. So their bonus will continue to be based solely on the Austin office's revenue." She paused long enough to catch her breath. "However, if by some miracle this office takes off, you won't have to share with them either."

Laurel knew the odds of that happening were pretty slim, but she kept quiet. "That sounds fair."

After hanging up with Nancy, Laurel sat at her desk. It looked as though her decision to move back to San Antonio was working out better than she had hoped. She called Lou and left a message on the machine, telling her that she had decided to go back to Corpus that night, but that she would return for good in two weeks. She wanted to get back to try and catch Jim at the pier tomorrow. She owed him an explanation and an apology for quitting so soon.

CHAPTER TWENTY-FIVE

On Sunday morning Laurel found Jim sitting in his usual spot on the pier. The mid-November day had dawned cooler than usual, but the bright sunlight promised warmer temperatures as the day lengthened. Laurel was glad she had pulled on a light-weight jacket before leaving the room.

"Hey, you finally decided to join me," Jim called out when he spotted her. He was dressed in his customary lime green Oyster Hut T-shirt with the requisite battered cap.

She shook her head. "I didn't come to fish. I still don't have my license."

He waved off her protest. "I told you I know the game warden. If he shows up, I'll take care of it."

Laurel leaned against the railing. "I guess I don't much feel like fishing today."

Jim peered at her intently before releasing a long-suffering sigh. "Are you here to tell me you're quitting already?"

"Yes. I'm sorry."

He nodded. "I figured you'd stay around a couple of months at least."

"When I took the job I didn't intend to quit so soon. I'm really sorry, but I need to leave. I'll stay on for two more weeks to give you a chance to find someone else."

He slowly reeled in his line and cast it back out before answering. "That would be good if you can, but if not, I understand. We'll get by. Business will be slower than usual until after the holidays. A lot of the regulars go off to visit family." He shook his head. "I know it ain't much of a job and the pay ain't enough for a body to get by on."

"It's not that," she said. "I shouldn't have left San Antonio. There was a lot going on in my life. I guess I sort of jumped the gun when I tried moving down here." She tucked her hands into her jacket pockets and glanced out over the water. "I always thought I wanted to live on the coast, but once I was here it didn't seem quite as special as it had before."

He jigged his line back in and recast. "Sometimes it ain't the place. It's the person we visit the place with that makes the time so special." He pulled his battered cap farther down on his head. "I met my wife when I was stationed in Puerto Rico. In my memories it was the most beautiful place on earth—almost magical. She got really sick right after I retired, and I insisted we move back there. In my mind I had this idea that if we could just get back there, everything would be as wonderful as it was when we first met." He shook his head. "But it wasn't magical. It was just an ordinary piece of land that couldn't turn back time or perform miracles."

Laurel looked out across the water. Her throat ached to talk, but it was hard to open up and voice her feelings. Jim didn't strike her as being homophobic, but how could she discuss something so personal with him? The longer she stood there the stronger the need became until the words started tumbling out. She felt powerless to stop them.

"I thought I wanted to turn back the clock." She swallowed

before gently clearing her throat. "That's all I thought about for years. In fact, I spent so much time thinking about the past that I let something really important slip away."

Jim nodded slowly. "Is it too late to try and get back what you lost?"

"Maybe. I'm not really sure."

Jim reeled his line in and traded the plastic worm out for a speck rig before releasing a long, curving cast. "Is that why you're leaving? Are you going back to try and fix things?"

A stiff breeze kicked up off the water. Laurel pulled her thin jacket tighter around her. "I need to let go of a few things first." She glanced at him then quickly looked away. "I guess I need to fix myself before I try to fix anything else."

Again he nodded. "That's sometimes the hardest thing to do."

Laurel had no response and the awkward silence that might have developed between them vanished when the rod in Jim's hand suddenly jerked and he began to reel. With little effort he pulled in a small speckled trout.

"What a waste of energy," he growled as he removed the fish from the hook and tossed it back into the water.

Laurel laughed. "Is that the only thing you've caught all morning?"

He squinted at her and nodded toward a spare rod. "I don't see you doing any better."

She picked up the rod and changed out the bait hook for a spec rig like the one he was using. Satisfied with the setup, she shook the rig at him and smiled. "Why don't I show you how this thing is supposed to work?"

The following morning, Laurel met Nina by the pool. It was too cold for Laurel to swim, but the cooler weather didn't seem to bother Nina.

"Where's your suit?" she called out as she swam over next to where Laurel stood.

"It's too cold." Laurel was dressed in jeans, a thick, burgundy sweater and her light jacket. Simply seeing Nina in the wet swimsuit made her shiver. "Aren't you freezing?"

"Not as long as I'm in the water, but you're right, getting out isn't much fun." She climbed out of the pool, grabbed a heavy terrycloth robe and wrapped it around herself before shoving her feet into a pair of slippers. "Come on, let's go into the kitchen. There's a small break room in the back where we can grab a cup of coffee." She motioned for Laurel to follow her. "If we're lucky, Reggie— he's the morning chef—will whip us up a plate of his fantastic blueberry pancakes."

Laurel felt a little uncomfortable slipping into the kitchen. "Are you sure it's all right for me to be back here?"

"Sure. As long as we don't get in anybody's way, they don't care." She led Laurel to a small room with half a dozen small wooden tables scattered around the area. Thankfully the place was empty. "Grab us a table and I'll be right back."

Laurel chose a table near the back. She had enjoyed her morning swims with Nina and would miss them. It helped that Nina didn't push her to talk. Other than that first day, they hadn't really talked much about themselves. Most of their time together had been spent swimming. When they did talk, it was usually about the restaurant or about books. Nina was an avid reader. Laurel had never even told her that she owned a bookstore, and she hadn't told her anything about Chris or Elaine.

She was thinking about Elaine when Nina returned several minutes later with two steaming mugs of coffee.

"How do you take your coffee?"

"Black," Laurel said.

"That's simple." Nina set a mug in front of her. "Reggie said he'd whip us up a couple of orders of his blueberry pancakes, but he's busy right now so it'll be a few minutes."

Laurel noticed Nina watching her as she sipped the coffee. "What?"

Nina shrugged. "I'm just waiting for you to start."

169

"Start what?"

"I assumed you wanted to talk. You came all the way over here when you didn't want to swim." Nina picked up her coffee and drank. "So what's going on?"

Laurel twisted her cup in small circles. "I gave Jim my two weeks' notice yesterday."

"I'm sorry to hear that. You were just starting to really get the hang of maneuvering those serving trays."

Laurel groaned. "I won't miss those things. I was always terrified I'd drop one when it was loaded with food."

"What did Jim say when you told him you were leaving?" Nina asked.

"You know Jim. He really was decent about it. In fact, he was a lot nicer about it than I would have been."

"If you don't mind my asking, why are you leaving? Did you find a better job?"

"Yes and no." Laurel wondered if it was her imagination or was it getting a little easier to talk about herself? "I'm going back to San Antonio. That's where I'm from." She wrapped her hands around the cup. The heat felt good. "My move down here was a little too spontaneous. It turned out that for me the idea of living on the coast was a lot more appealing than actually living here."

"What is there not to love about the coast?"

Laurel could have mentioned the never-ending mosquitoes, the humidity and the way sand seemed to make its way into every nook and cranny, but she resisted the impulse. "I'm just homesick."

"That I can understand." She leaned forward. "When I went to Hawaii with Rachel, I was sure that I'd be living in paradise. The feeling lasted for two or three weeks. After that, I'd catch myself comparing everything with home, and no matter how beautiful or lush the island was it could never compete with home. I tried to live in the moment and not make the comparison, but it was always there in the back of my mind."

Laurel recalled Jim's similar story about Puerto Rico. "I guess there really is no place like home."

Nina lifted her cup in salute. "Here's to home and family. May the journey to both always be short and met with opened arms."

Laurel raised her cup and tried to ignore the stab of sadness that Nina's toast had caused. Her own journey home was relatively short, but nobody would be waiting to meet her with opened arms. She wondered if there ever would be again.

CHAPTER TWENTY-SIX

The dim sound of traffic from the freeway drifted through the opened patio doors. Elaine dusted the wicker- and glass-topped coffee table again and placed the African violet she had purchased the previous afternoon in the center.

After returning from Rockport on Sunday morning, she had driven directly to the complex and signed the lease. The unit had been available for immediate move-in and the rent was reasonable despite the short six-month lease she'd insisted on. After only two days, she was finding the tiny space confining. Whenever she grew too discouraged with its dreariness, she reminded herself that the arrangement was only temporary. After the hectic rush of the holidays was over, she would start searching for the perfect house to buy. With Thanksgiving only two days away, things at work were already starting to hint at the bedlam that was about to descend. By mid-December it would escalate into complete madness. Plus, her mother had called to see if she and Laurel were planning on coming to Houston for Thanksgiving and/or Christmas. Elaine had assured her that she would take a flight into Houston on Wednesday night and be there for Thanksgiving, but she made excuses for Laurel, as she often had before. During the first couple of years of their relationship, Laurel had often accompanied her on trips home for either the holidays or various other family functions. Even though Laurel had gradually stopped attending, Elaine's mother never failed to include her in any invitation. Elaine didn't have the courage yet to tell her parents that she and Laurel were no longer living together. Luckily, her mother always called her cellular and therefore wouldn't discover the home phone had been disconnected. Her parents would be supportive, as they had in her two previous breakups, but that look of concern and worry would be in their eyes, and she didn't want to be the reason for it being there.

She glanced around at the strange rather drab furniture. Not owning anything other than her clothes and a few other personal items had made moving nothing more than two trips with a packed car between the hotel and apartment. The hardest part of the entire process had been the shopping all day yesterday for the multitude of everyday items she normally took for granted—towels, bed linens, kitchen items, groceries and so forth.

With nothing left to do she settled back on the overstuffed sofa and glanced at her watch. It was almost midnight, but she wasn't sleepy. Of course she'd be dragging at work tomorrow. She had never had problems sleeping when she was with Laurel. Restless, she went over and picked up one of the framed photos sitting on the fireplace mantle. It was a spontaneous shot of her and Laurel standing by a large rosebush in Lou's backyard. It had been taken at Lou's birthday party. They had wandered off by themselves. She ran a hand over the glass. They both looked so happy. Why couldn't they find that happiness again? When she thought about their planned get-together that following weekend, a spasm of excitement that bordered on pain gripped her stomach. Laurel hadn't mentioned why she wanted to meet, but Elaine's imagination had run a long gauntlet of possibilities that ranged from the "it's over and I never want to see you again" scenario to "I love you, please move back in." She tried not to dwell on either possibility. It was much more likely that Laurel simply wanted to talk to her about changing the wills they'd had drawn up a couple of years ago. The implications of that action didn't make her feel any better. She put the photo back on the mantle and went to take a bath. Maybe it would help her sleep.

"Good morning," Tom called out as Elaine walked into her office. "How was your Thanksgiving?"

"Probably the same as everyone else's," Elaine said as she set her partially opened umbrella inside a closet to dry. "I went to my parents' where I ate too much, slept all afternoon and sat through two overbooked flights before finally getting out of the Houston airport yesterday." She shook her head. "I don't know what possessed me to fly home when driving would have been so much easier." She plopped down in the chair next to his desk. "How was your holiday?"

He chuckled. "It sounds very similar to yours except we stayed in town and missed all the travel fun, although we did manage to create our own minor family drama."

She frowned. "What happened?"

"You know Sue decided she wanted to have Thanksgiving at our place this year." He rolled his eyes. "That was the first fiasco. Our apartment was nowhere large enough for a dinner with a guest list that included Sue's parents, paternal grandmother, her brother Albert and his wife, Pamela, and their twin boys, along with my mother." He rubbed his hands. "So here we are jammed in around our little table like proverbial sardines and right in the middle of dinner Sue drops her little bombshell."

Elaine leaned forward. "What?"

"She's pregnant."

"Congratulations." She jumped up and hugged him. She knew they had been trying to conceive for nearly a year now.

"Thanks."

"What a great thing—" She stopped. "Wait a minute. You said she 'dropped a bombshell.'"

He was nodding. "Have you forgotten Sue's fundamentalist family?"

"That's right." She grimaced. "Her parents almost had mutual strokes when you two moved in together."

"The moving-in scene was nothing compared to the 'a baby is on the way and they aren't married' scene. Believe me, I got a whole new perspective."

"Surely they must have realized that would happen eventually."

Tom rolled his eyes again. "Since I work as a 'secretary'"—he made little quotation signs with his fingers—"I think her family had convinced themselves that I'm gay and we were truly just roommates."

Elaine laughed aloud.

He held up a hand to stop her. "But that's still not the best part." He leaned forward in his chair. "The pinnacle of the evening came when little Joey, one of Sue's six-year-old demon nephews, dashed into the living room wearing one of the gold lamé g-strings I use in my act, as a mask." Tom was laughing so hard he could barely speak. "He and his equally diabolical twin were playing cowboys."

"Oh, my God," Elaine exclaimed as her face crunched up. "That's disgusting."

He waved off her protests. "It was clean, but you should have seen the expression on Pamela's face. You would have thought Satan himself had walked in and asked her for a lap dance." He stopped talking long enough to catch his breath and wipe the tears of laughter from his eyes. "Now keep in mind that for obvious reasons Sue had never told her family about my other job as a stripper. So, when Pamela went off the deep end and started ranting about my decadent underwear, Sue tried to explain that it's part of my costume."

"Ouch."

He nodded. "Exactly. As soon as they figured out what she was talking about, half of her family started packing up their gear to leave and the other half was trying to save my soul. And then dear Grandmother White, who is, as Sue's mother puts it, 'a little bit touched,' announced she wanted to see my act and started chanting for me to 'take it off.'"

Elaine's side was starting to ache from laughing so hard. When she finally gained some control over herself, she dug into her purse for a tissue and wiped her eyes. "God, I would've loved to have been a fly on the wall and seen that."

He leaned back in his chair. "I was hoping you might see it that way," he said, suddenly serious. "Because Sue and I have talked it over and we'd like you to be my best person at our wedding."

For a split-second all that registered with Elaine was "wedding." She was in the process of congratulating him when the rest of the request filtered through. She stopped and stared at him. "I'm sorry. What did you say?"

He smiled. "I said we'd like you to act as what would traditionally be my best man." Before she could respond he rushed on. "I know it's a little unconventional, but there's really no one else I'd rather have."

Elaine didn't know what to say. Her voice broke when she started to speak. She quickly swallowed and tried again. "I'm honored, but are you sure?"

He nodded. "I asked Mom, but she's way too traditional to defy convention. My father is dead and I'm an only child. I'm not nearly as close to the guys I know as I am you."

She started to protest, but he held up a hand to stop her.

"If it makes you too uncomfortable, I'll understand, but I'm really sincere in this."

After a long moment of him watching her closely she finally nodded. "All right, I'll do it, if you really want me to."

He flashed a brilliant smile. "You bet I do." He slapped his hand on the desk. "Just think of all the fun we'll have going to pick out our tuxedos together."

Elaine felt her jaw drop. "Tuxedos."

He looked at her and appeared crestfallen. "I suppose you're right. I should have realized you'd be more comfortable going with Sue." He perked up. "But don't worry, she'll help you choose a great tux. She has a real eye for clothes."

Elaine didn't know what to say. As she struggled to think of something she saw the glint of mischief in his eyes. "You're so mean. Just for that, I'm going to wear a tux. I can't wait to see what Sue's parents think about you having a dyke in your wedding party," she said as she stood and started toward her office. She smiled in triumph when she heard him gulp.

CHAPTER TWENTY-SEVEN

Since the Oyster Hut closed for the holiday, Laurel spent Thanksgiving Day doing her laundry and straightening her small room. Nina had invited her to join her family for dinner, but the thought of spending the day with strangers, no matter how well-intentioned the invitation, seemed worse than being alone. She had planned on treating herself to a nice dinner but ended up staying in her room watching television and eating a ham and cheese sandwich. When the walls threatened to close in, she reminded herself that she would only be there for eight more days and then she would go home. At some point during the day a small germ of a plan began to develop. For the next few days, she let it hover at the edge of her awareness, never really taking it out to examine it fully, but never letting it slip into obscurity either.

Her last days at the restaurant flew by unexpectedly fast. On Monday morning, she called the necessary numbers in San Antonio and rearranged for all her utilities to be turned back on.

Since it was a simple matter of flipping a switch somewhere, each number she called assured her that full service would be restored by Tuesday afternoon.

On Wednesday night she called Elaine and in a brief but friendly conversation they agreed to meet for dinner Saturday evening at eight. Laurel casually suggested the Crockett Street Bistro which was located downtown. One of her bookstore customers had told her about the place and had practically swooned every time she mentioned it. Laurel never dreamed she would ever want to go, but now it seemed like the perfect place. With the arrangement for dinner confirmed, a little more depth was added to Laurel's plan that had started developing on Thanksgiving Day. After hanging up she called the Crockett Street Bistro and asked to speak to André. Ten minutes and a promised twenty-dollar bribe later, she had reservations for Saturday night.

On Thursday, Kate finally hired someone to replace Laurel. The new guy would be starting on Monday, so Laurel never met him. On Friday night after the last shift Jim, Kate and Nina surprised her with a small party after the restaurant closed. Kate had made a chocolate cake that was so delicious it made Laurel's jaws ache. Jim provided a tray of boiled shrimp and crab cakes, and Nina whipped up a batch of luscious margaritas. Touched by their consideration, Laurel promised she would drop by to see them anytime she came to Corpus. Jim wouldn't let her leave until she agreed to get her fishing license and come back soon to fish with him. Throughout the week, The Plan, as she now thought of it, slowly continued to evolve.

As soon as she got back to the motel she packed her car before going to bed and trying to sleep. It quickly proved to be a useless endeavor. She finally gave up and turned the television on, hoping it would lull her to sleep, but that too failed. When the eastern sky started to lighten, she slipped the room key into the drop-off slot and crawled into her car. As she traveled the nearly deserted road toward San Antonio, The Plan continued to grow. By the time she pulled into a small roadside diner for breakfast all of the pieces had fallen into place. She felt better than she had in a long time. Mainly because she knew exactly what she needed to do to attract Elaine's attention and win back her love. She had messed up before, but she was determined to make things right. If she managed to win Elaine back she vowed to never again take her love for granted.

After consuming a leisurely and hearty breakfast of eggs and hash browns she drove on to San Antonio. Before going home she stopped by the post office to pick up her mail and to reestablish her regular mail delivery.

As soon as she arrived home she did a quick check to ensure all the utilities had been reconnected. When she found everything was operational, she went to the back of the house to the room that had been Chris's office and looked beneath the bonnet of the rolltop desk and located the Rolodex. On one of the cards she found the name of Lewis Wayne, one of the antiques dealers Chris had done business with. She explained what she wanted, and he agreed to meet her at the house at noon.

She unpacked her car then drove to a nearby grocery store and purchased a few basic items. From there she stopped at a liquor store and picked up several empty boxes. After returning home and putting away her few groceries, she went to the bedroom and began to empty the numerous drawers of the dresser and then those on the matching chest of drawers.

By the time Lewis Wayne arrived she had filled all the boxes she had picked up from the liquor store and had resorted to dumping things into small piles wherever she could find room.

Lewis looked around the house and gave a soft whistle. "It looks like you've been doing some serious cleaning."

"It's not cleaning yet. Right now, I'm just dumping everything together."

He nodded. "Let's see what you've got."

As they walked through the rooms he quoted her prices on several chairs, four side tables, the full bedroom suite, the dining table and six matching chairs, an armoire and an elaborate coffee table.

The only pieces she refused to sell were Chris's rolltop desk and the accompanying chair. Those she would never part with. It was almost two when he left with a promise to return the next afternoon with a large truck to pick up the furniture and a nice check to bolster Laurel's bank account.

After he left, Laurel started going through the things she had indiscriminately stuffed into boxes, and sorted them into three piles: keep, Goodwill and toss.

At four she stopped and took a long hot shower. Despite the lack of sleep from the previous night and the long hours she had put in today, she hummed with energy. After getting out of the shower, it took her over half an hour to whip her normally wild hair into soft curls that fell gently behind her ears. Then she dug to the back of her closet and pulled out a black dress with a flattering empire waist and a crossover V neck that provided a tasteful yet provocative glimpse of cleavage. She had bought the dress for a wedding the previous year, but something had come up at the store and she hadn't been able to attend. So Elaine had never seen her in the dress. Since the dress struck her at mid-calf, she chose a pair of tall, black suede boots with silver-studded accents, side zippers and comfortable two-inch heels. Almost satisfied with what she saw in the mirror, she removed her everyday small hoop earrings and replaced them with her mother's diamond studs. Finally, she added the beautiful solitaire pendant with the princess-cut diamond that her grandfather had given her grandmother on their wedding day.

By the time she was ready to leave, little fingers of doubt were crawling down her spine. She chased them away by studiously going over The Plan one step at a time. For the maximum effect she hoped to achieve, she had to time her arrival at the bistro perfectly. If everything went as she envisioned, tonight she would work on reestablishing contact and, hopefully, she would be able to plant the seed for the next step.

CHAPTER TWENTY-EIGHT

Elaine pulled into the parking lot of the Crockett Street Bistro. The clock on the car's dash told her it was five minutes until eight, but she wasn't in a hurry. Laurel was always at least ten minutes late. She checked her hair twice before stepping out of the car. Despite the cooler than usual evening temperatures, she was feeling overly warm and regretted wearing the lightweight black wool jacket and matching slacks. She had chosen this particular suit because every time she wore it someone would make a comment on how nice it looked on her. As she made her way across the parking lot, she caught herself arranging her hair. *Stop preening*, she told herself. From the looks of the outside of the place, she could have worn jeans and a jacket. She was certain Laurel would. It was rare when she wasn't in either jeans or shorts.

As soon as she stepped inside she was glad she hadn't worn jeans. Despite its rather modest outward appearance, the inside was very chic with an ambiance that screamed expensive. Each table was covered with a crisp white linen cloth and held a candle and a small crystal vase containing a single red rosebud. The tables were spaced far enough apart to allow for intimate conversations, and the soft music and subtle lighting created the perfect setting for such.

An elegantly clad maitre d' materialized seemingly out of thin air. Somewhat startled by his sudden appearance Elaine stepped back and bumped into the closed door.

"You have a reservation."

She felt certain his comment was meant as a directive. It most definitely wasn't a question. She considered waiting outside to warn Laurel. This wasn't the sort of place Laurel would like. She probably hadn't even realized they would need a reservation. He was waiting for her to answer. Oh, well, she could always tell Laurel she had tried. "Yes, it would probably be under Laurel Becker." To her dismay his attitude instantly changed from guarded reserve to complete admiration.

"Of course, right this way." He escorted her to a table and held the chair.

Elaine felt a little disoriented. Had Laurel been here before? This certainly wasn't the normal burger and fries type of place Laurel normally chose. Elaine had been to several formal dining affairs, but the intimacy of this place intimidated her. This was the sort of place you brought a date when you wanted to impress or, more likely to seduce. Her face burned. Was Laurel planning to seduce her? Was there more going on here than dinner? She was torn by the warring feelings of hope and dread.

"Ms. Becker requested this specific table," he said in a suave accent that Elaine felt certain came and went at the same time as his shift did.

She glanced up and realized why Laurel had requested this particular table. It could be clearly seen from the doorway. She immediately relaxed. This location was the most public one in the place. Laurel certainly wouldn't have chosen this spot if she had plans for any hanky-panky. She apparently liked the food here or else thought Elaine would.

The maitre d' called a pale young man over. "This is Steven. He will be your waiter tonight."

Steven took Elaine's wine order and both men disappeared into the recesses of the room. As Elaine's eyes adjusted to the soft lighting, she gradually became aware of the plaintive cries of a violin. She couldn't help but smile when she thought about how Laurel would react to all this.

Suddenly a glass of Chardonnay appeared on the table in front of her. She barely caught Steven's form melting back into the shadows. Elaine picked up the glass and was about to taste it when the door opened and in the dim glow at the doorway she saw a tall elegant woman step in. Elaine watched for the woman's reaction as the maitre d' materialized from the shadows. She was slightly embarrassed that the woman hadn't seemed at all fazed by his sudden manifestation when she herself had practically fallen on her ass trying to get away from him. Unable to take her eyes off the woman, Elaine saw her slip something to him.

Probably an exorbitant tip to secure a table, she thought.

As the two turned to make their way across the floor, Elaine nearly dropped her glass of wine. Long after her brain processed the identity of the woman, she wasn't ready to accept it. She cursed the dim lighting and squinted. Could that really be Laurel? She continued to stare stupidly even after Laurel was seated across from her.

"Did you have any trouble finding the place?" Laurel asked as if there was nothing unusual going on.

"Uh . . . uh . . . no." Elaine cringed. She sounded like an idiot, but thankfully Laurel didn't seem to notice.

"I've heard a lot about this place, but I've never been here. Have you?" Laurel asked. As she picked up a glass of wine that Elaine hadn't even noticed being ordered, much less arriving, a tiny glint of light caught Elaine's attention. Even in the dim light she could easily make out the small diamond pendant that rested softly in the delicate valley between Laurel's breasts. The slightest movement caused the tiny sparkles of reflected light to dance.

She was unable to tear her gaze away from the silken skin, and she knew exactly how soft it would feel beneath her fingertips, her lips and her tongue. How many times had she—

"Elaine."

Her attention snapped back when she realized that the waiter, Steven, was standing beside her holding a menu out. She felt her face begin to burn as beads of sweat popped out along her hairline. Her hands shook as she took the menu and tried to pretend to study it, but her gaze kept creeping back to the spot where the pendant lay.

"Are you all right?" Laurel asked gently after Steven had disappeared.

It took Elaine a couple of tries before she was finally able to speak. "Of course I am. You look very nice." Her throat felt so dry it ached. She sipped her wine, trying to alleviate the discomfort, but then Laurel leaned toward her, providing her with an unimpeded view of the tops of her full breasts that grew even fuller as she leaned forward. It took all of Elaine's willpower to stop her fingers from reaching across to caress the soft white skin.

"Thanks for agreeing to come tonight. I've missed talking to you." Laurel sat back and began to study the menu without waiting for Elaine to respond. "I know you love pork and I've heard the pork medallions with Madeira are wonderful. I think I'm going to try the lobster with roasted butternut squash." She closed her menu and set it aside. "So how have you been?"

Elaine tore her gaze away from Laurel's breasts and nodded. "Fine." *Say something, you idiot.* "Uh . . . work is starting to get a little crazy."

"It's the holidays. You'll sail through with flying colors like you always do." She sipped her wine. "How's Tom?"

Elaine grabbed onto the question as a drowning rat would a board. She started telling Laurel about Tom's Thanksgiving fiasco. At some point in the story, Steven arrived to take their food order. His appearance made such a small ripple that the mood of the story wasn't diminished in the slightest. By the time Elaine had fin-

185

ished the tale they were both laughing and the tension between them was gone.

Their food arrived and it was every bit as good as Laurel had suggested it would be. "The pork is wonderful," Elaine said.

"Here, try the lobster."

Before she could protest, Laurel was offering her a tempting-looking bite. The intimacy of taking the bite from Laurel's fork unnerved her. She tried to concentrate on the food, but the damn pendant pulled her back.

"Can I taste yours?" Laurel asked.

"My what?" Elaine croaked as Laurel leaned forward, providing that wonderful view again.

Laurel's gaze seemed to slowly travel down Elaine's front. She could almost feel her skin burning beneath Laurel's scrutiny. "Your meat, of course. What else would I want to taste?" Laurel's dark eyes mesmerized her.

It took all of her willpower to tear her gaze away. She tried to focus on cutting the meat. Her hand shook as she cut a thin strip of pork and held it out. She wanted to hand the fork to Laurel, but she obviously didn't intend to take it. Elaine could only stare and wiggle in misery as Laurel's hand closed around hers and her full lips closed around the succulent pork and ever so delicately pulled it into her mouth. Long after the tiny sliver of pork was savored, Elaine's attention was still riveted on Laurel's mouth. She remembered with excruciating clarity the mind-numbing pleasure those lips and that tongue were capable of producing. Her body began to tremble from the pent-up lust. If she didn't get her mind off Laurel's body and do so quickly, she was afraid she would climb across the table and take her right there in front of the magically appearing and disappearing staff and other diners.

Once again it was Tom who came to her rescue. "Tom asked me to be his best man or best woman or whatever it's called," she blurted.

The statement seemed to take Laurel by surprise. Elaine rushed on to fill her in on the details of the wedding. As they talked

Elaine's hormones settled down into an almost normal level, giving her a small sense of hope that her chair would at least be dry when she stood up.

That hope was dashed when Steven suddenly appeared with a dessert tray. Laurel insisted Elaine try a decadent-looking slice of chocolate cake, while she chose a small pastry filled with a creamy pudding. As soon as Laurel held out a spoon and asked, "Would you like to taste my pudding?" Elaine gave up all hopes of the chair ever drying.

When they finally left the bistro Elaine moved to Laurel's side with the intention of walking her to her car. As soon as she stepped next to her she was engulfed by Laurel's tantalizing scent. She leaned in to savor the all-too-familiar bouquet, and as she did her gaze settled on the ivory skin just below Laurel's ear. She ached to kiss it. She was actually leaning in to do so when she caught herself.

What am I doing? Laurel had made it pretty obvious that tonight was just a dinner between old friends. *Then why did she go to all the trouble with the dress and restaurant?* a tiny voice probed. *I need to get out of here before I make a complete fool of myself and drive her even further away.*

"I had a good time," Elaine said and stepped away. She thought she saw a flicker of something in Laurel's eyes. It happened so quickly there was no time to determine if it was disappointment or relief.

"Me, too," Laurel said as she turned to face her.

The movement caused the pendant to catch the full moonlight. Elaine closed her eyes and turned away before opening them. She knew that if she didn't get away at that very moment, she wouldn't be able to stop herself from reaching out and caressing the soft skin this time. She took the coward's way out and ran.

CHAPTER TWENTY-NINE

Laurel drove home from the bistro with mixed feelings. There had been times when she was certain that Elaine had noticed her. There had even been a moment when their gazes had met across the table, and Laurel could almost feel Elaine's desire, but the moment passed with no acknowledgment. In fact, Elaine hadn't said anything that would indicate that she still had any interest in her. The closest she had come was when she had mentioned that Laurel looked nice.

She blinked back tears. They had spent most of the night talking about either the food or Tom. When it was time to leave, Laurel had hoped Elaine might at least try to kiss her, but instead Elaine had practically run to her car and sped off before Laurel had even managed to get her old clunker started. There had been no mention of them getting together again or even the offer of a call later in the week.

"So much for the stupid plan," she grumbled as she pulled into her empty driveway. Once inside she changed into sweats and went back to sorting the piles of stuff that she continued to collect from around the house. It was almost two in the morning before she finally gave up trying to figure out what had gone wrong with her plan. Too tired to think anymore, she stretched out on the sofa and instantly fell asleep.

She woke up the next morning with a stiff neck and a new determination to get on with life, because she wasn't ready to write off Elaine Alexander by a long shot. A hot shower and a cup of coffee kick-started her day. By the time Lewis Wayne arrived with a crew to pick up the furniture, Laurel had finished sorting the piles of castoffs and was loading the Goodwill pile into her car.

"You're still at it, I see," Lewis said as his crew began to remove dollies and protective pads from the back of the truck.

"It's way past due," Laurel assured him.

While the men loaded the furniture Lewis had purchased from her, she started walking through each room and making a detailed inventory of the remaining, albeit less valuable pieces of furniture that she wanted to get rid of. After the last of his take was loaded, Lewis found her. "We're finished, unless I can get you to change your mind and sell me that desk."

She smiled. "No. I think I'll keep it."

"I can't blame you. It's a beautiful piece." He tore a check from the book and handed it to her. "If you ever change your mind, give me a call. I'll give you top dollar for it."

"I'll do that," she promised.

After they had left, Laurel took the items in her car to a Goodwill drop-off point and helped the young boy unload them. As soon as they were finished he handed her a form. "Here's your receipt."

She looked at the blank spaces. "Shouldn't you fill this out?"

He shook his head. "Naw, just write in whatever you want. Nobody cares."

She wanted to tell him that someone should care, but it seemed pointless and a waste of time. Besides, maybe he was right. She tossed the form on the front seat and drove to the bookstore where she worked on sending out e-mails and updating the store's Web site to let her former customers know that the Lavender Page would be having a going-out-of-business sale. Afterward she made a large sign and hung it in the front window announcing the sale. With everything on her list checked off, she sat at the office desk and waited for the anticipated sense of melancholy she expected the projected closing to bring. When it failed to appear, she knew she was doing the right thing.

The following morning on her way to the Lavender Page, Laurel stopped by the bank to deposit the check Lewis Wayne had given her and to get change for the cash drawer. It seemed strange to open up without Allie around. She made a mental note to call her and Lou to invite them to dinner. She had been a pretty decent cook at one time, and even though she hadn't done much cooking in the past couple of years, she assumed she still remembered how.

It was already after lunch before her first customer came in. It was Lou.

"I should have known you'd be the first to arrive," she said as she hugged her friend.

"You know I can't pass up a chance to buy books."

Laurel shook her head. "Unfortunately, I still don't have anything new for you."

Lou dismissed the objection. "That's okay. I'm here to Christmas shop." She pulled a list from her pocket and proceeded to spend the next two hours browsing the shelves and checking names off her list. When she finally tucked the paper back into her pocket, there was a large stack of items waiting to be tallied. "I hope you're still taking credit cards," she said.

Laurel nodded. "They were always my bread and butter. I couldn't live without them and neither could the store."

Lou stood looking at the card in her hand. "It's funny how we can get so dependent on something."

"Are you talking about that credit card or something else?" Laurel teased and smiled when her friend's face turned red.

"You don't think I'm an old fool do you? I mean, there's more years between me and Allie than either of us care to think about."

"Do you love her?"

Lou nodded shyly.

"Does she love you?"

Again Lou nodded.

"Then what else do you need to worry about?"

"I'm so much older. I don't know how many years I have left."

"Heck, Lou. None of us knows that. Chris was younger than you. Sometimes age has nothing to do with it."

"Yeah, I guess you're right. Still I wonder sometimes if I'm being unfair to Allie. Maybe she should be out there looking for someone closer to her own age."

Laurel put an arm around Lou's shoulder and squeezed her gently. "I think Allie is right where she wants to be." She stopped suddenly. "Where is she anyway?"

"She's working. The temp agency called her this morning. She normally just works a few days at each place. The job sort of stinks now, but they told her they would work with her to find her jobs that will fit her schedule once she starts to school."

"So she has definitely decided to go back to school?"

"She starts at UTSA in January. She had to jump through a few hoops to get all her ducks lined up, but she did it," Lou explained and Laurel chuckled to herself at the mixed metaphor. "After she gets her bachelor's degree she wants to go on for her master's."

"Good for her."

Lou looked up at her. "You know she would never have done this if you hadn't decided to close the store. I think she had some sort of weird sense of responsibility to stay with you."

Laurel sighed. "I was wrong to try and hold on to it for so long. It seemed like the right thing to do while I was doing it, but now I can look back and see that it only caused a lot of pain." Lou shook her head furiously. "No, ma'am, I won't agree to that. You helped

191

a lot of people with this store. Okay, so maybe you hung on a little longer than you should have, but you never stopped helping people."

Tears stung Laurel's eyes. "Thanks for saying that. It helps."

Lou rubbed a hand over her face roughly. "Well, are you going to ring this stuff up, or leave me standing here all day? I've got things to do, you know."

Word about the sale spread quickly and by Wednesday afternoon the store was doing a fairly steady business. Like Lou, a lot of the women were taking advantage of the sale to do some early Christmas shopping.

Each night she left the store tired, but as soon as she got home she would change into some old clothes and work for a couple of more hours on the house. It was slow going, but she was beginning to see a difference. Since she had sold the bedroom suite, she was sleeping with the mattress and box spring sitting on the floor. The entire house looked as though a tornado had blown through it, but she didn't care. She knew eventually she'd get everything back into place. She had all the time in the world to finish it and no one to answer to about the mess.

She spent a lot of time thinking about Elaine but warned herself not to rush anything. Despite their last meeting, she was convinced that things would eventually fall into place for them. She simply couldn't imagine a future without Elaine by her side.

CHAPTER THIRTY

It was only a little after ten Friday night when Elaine dropped down on the green floral sofa in her office and slipped her shoes off. If she could just lie down for a moment and rest her feet then maybe she would survive. She had barely gotten comfortable when Tom came in. There was a small tear in his shirt sleeve and the legs of his slacks looked wet.

"What happened to you?" she asked.

"Some jackass crammed rolls of toilet paper and wads of paper towels in the commodes in the restroom by the banquet hall and then flushed them all. I've spent the last twenty minutes unclogging them and mopping water up from the floor."

"Why were you doing it? Where's maintenance and house-keeping?"

Tom slid to the floor and rested his head against the end of the sofa. "Let me see. Half of the maintenance crew is out with the flu. The remaining members were in the lobby stairwell trying to get a kid's head from between the banisters."

"How did the kid get stuck? Those spindles are really close together."

Tom shrugged. "I have no idea. It's the night of the weirdoes."

"And housekeeping," Elaine prompted. "Where were they?"

"One crew was at the restroom by the Milam Room doing exactly the same thing I was doing, and the second one was over in the Bowie Room cleaning up the mess that was made when the overly tipsy father of the groom fell on the wedding cake."

Elaine raised her head. "How did he fall on the wedding cake?"

"Who knows? Myra said something about him dancing on the table or something." Tom's cell phone started chirping. "God, please let that be a telemarketer."

Elaine gave a tired chuckle that died in her throat when her own phone started ringing. She sat up and reached for her cell. When she answered she had to ask the caller to repeat the problem twice, because she couldn't believe she'd heard it correctly the first time. "I'll be right there."

Tom was already up and moving.

"What have you got?" she asked.

"It's the insurance company Christmas party. Someone found a goldfish doing the backstroke in the Champagne fountain."

They walked out the door together.

"Where are you off to?" he asked.

"The ice sculpture intended for the Knights of Columbus dance just arrived."

"What's wrong? Did they drop it?"

"No. It seems we've had a minor mix-up in delivery. Rather than the dove bearing the branch of peace, we've gotten Venus baring everything."

"Have fun," Tom called as they sped off in different directions.

It was after two in the morning before Tom and Elaine were finally able to call it a night.

"I'll never understand it," Tom said as he resumed his earlier spot on the floor by the sofa.

"Understand what?" Elaine was too tired to lie down. She knew she'd never get up if she did. She sat on the end of the sofa instead.

"What happens to normally sane, responsible people when they come to a hotel? Why do they suddenly turn into fourteen-year-old adolescent males?"

"Do you think it might have something to do with the massive amounts of liquor they consume?" she asked, not bothering to hide her sarcasm. She cringed every time she booked an event with an open bar. Thankfully, due to company budget cuts, those events were slowly disappearing.

He sighed. "Sometimes I feel like I was born about a hundred years too late."

"How's that?" she mumbled.

"I wish there was still some semblance of . . . of . . ."

She glanced over at him, surprised. She couldn't remember him ever being at a loss for words.

" . . . that old-fashioned ingrained sense of courtesy and respect for others." He dropped his head back against the sofa arm. "Don't mind me. I'm just exhausted and smell like Tidy Bowl."

Elaine tried to lighten the mood. "What happened with the goldfish?"

"They weren't goldfish after all, but those sucker thingies that people put in their aquariums to keep them clean. It seems the back-office employees from the insurance company wanted to express their opinions of the sales reps."

"Ouch. Monday morning ought to prove interesting for them."

"What happened to Venus?" Tom asked.

"I had her taken over to the big freezer in the kitchen. It was going to take too long to straighten out the delivery mix-up so I had a couple of large floral arrangements brought in and gave the Grand Poobah or whatever he's called a bottle of Chivas."

"Do you ever wonder why we keep doing this year after year?"

She chuckled. "Where else can you legally have all this fun and get paid for doing it?"

He pushed himself to his feet. "If you don't need me for anything else, I think I'm going to go home and try to sleep for a few hours."

Elaine stood. "I'll see you tomorrow afternoon around one so we can start gearing up for round two." As she walked to her car she thought about Laurel and wondered how things were going with the store. It had been a week since they'd had dinner together and she lost track of the number of times she had reached for the phone to call her. Each time she did, the image of that pendant resting against Laurel's soft breasts came back to haunt her, and Elaine didn't trust herself not to blurt out her true feelings. What would Laurel's reaction have been if she had leaned over and kissed her when they were having dinner? Elaine shook her head. "You can't be stupid about this," she mumbled to herself. There had to be a way for her to show Laurel how much she still cared, without pushing her.

Suddenly, something Tom said earlier made the proverbial light come on. Sometimes an old standard was exactly what was needed. She would court Laurel. It would give them a chance to spend time together and get to know each other again, while at the same time giving Laurel the space she needed to get things straightened out in her life.

A wave of energy shot through her, the earlier exhaustion forgotten. She would start today by sending Laurel some flowers, and in a couple of days she would casually drop by the store. Elaine was smiling as she drove out of the parking garage and headed home.

For the first time in weeks, Elaine slept soundly through the remainder of the night. It was a little after nine when she awoke and placed the call to the florist before she even started her coffee. She assumed Laurel would be at the store and had the mixed bouquet delivered there. Roses had been her first choice, but she worried they might suggest more than friendship and she didn't want to scare Laurel off, but she couldn't resist ordering the larger arrangement. The small one just didn't seem to be enough. She paid extra to ensure it was delivered that morning.

After hanging up she put on a pot of coffee and took a quick shower. She caught herself humming and checking her watch as she dressed. How long would it take the flowers to arrive? Would Laurel call her right away? A sudden thought brought on a small frown. Laurel might not call her at all. She might just drop a thank-you card in the mail. *Then I'll call her and thank her for her thank-you card*, she thought. She shook her head when she realized how ridiculous she would sound.

She poured a cup of coffee and sat down at the tiny kitchen table where she could see the clock on the stove. After staring at the clock for several minutes she got up. If she continued doing this she would drive herself crazy. She didn't have to be back at the hotel until one, so there was still time for her to run a couple of errands. The refrigerator was practically empty and she was almost out of coffee. She grabbed a pen and paper and started a grocery list. On a second sheet she started a Christmas shopping list. She wrote Laurel's name at the top of the page and stared at it. What could she buy her? It had to be something special, but at the same time it couldn't seem as though it was overly expensive or that she had spent an excessive amount of time searching for it. She would have to walk a very fine line and balance the two measures carefully.

CHAPTER THIRTY-ONE

Laurel was running a credit card for a customer when the door opened. She looked up to see a young man carrying a rather large bouquet of flowers.

"I've got a delivery for Laurel Becker," he said.

"I'm Laurel."

He placed the flowers on the counter. "These are a special delivery, so I'll need you to sign for them." He handed her one of those electronic signature devices.

"You certainly made an impression on someone," the woman said as soon as the guy left.

Laurel moved the flowers aside so she could complete the customer's transaction.

"Aren't you even curious about who they're from?" the woman asked.

Not nearly as much as you are, Laurel thought. "I already know who sent them," she said and deliberately gave the woman a knowing smile.

The woman didn't bother to hide her disappointment as she signed the credit card slip and gathered up her bag. "I guess I should have waited to buy this. I'm sure you'll be offering a larger discount next week."

"Maybe, but then again the book might have been gone by next week." Laurel didn't bother hiding her disdain for the customer's crass comment and felt a slight vindication when the woman blushed. "Thanks for dropping by, and happy holidays."

As soon as the woman was out the door, Laurel snatched the card off the bouquet. She knew they had to be from Elaine. Who else would be sending her flowers? Her hands shook as she fumbled to remove the card from the tiny envelope. The message read: *Dinner was lovely. Hope to see you soon. Elaine.*

She read the message several more times, searching for any hidden meaning that might be there. Did Elaine really want to see her again? If so, why hadn't she called? Laurel had been waiting all week for a call from her. She reminded herself how crazy things would be for Elaine with the holidays. She probably hadn't had time to call, but she'd found time to order the flowers. A small buzz of excitement ran through her. Elaine had been thinking about her. She grabbed the phone and started dialing Elaine's cell phone. A little voice in her head warned her to not seem overly anxious. She overrode its protests. After all, it would be rude to not call and thank her.

Elaine answered on the second ring.

Laurel wondered if she had been waiting for her call but knew it was more likely that she had been on standby for any disaster that might take place at the hotel. As soon as she heard Elaine's voice her hands began to shake. "I wanted to call and thank you for the flowers. They're beautiful."

"Oh. They've arrived already?"

Laurel frowned. Hadn't the messenger said they'd been sent special delivery?

Elaine spoke again before she could respond. "I'm glad you like them. I really enjoyed dinner. I've been meaning to call you, but work has been a little crazy."

"Remember to not put PETA next to the South Texas Wild Game Hunters."

Elaine laughed. "You won't ever forget that, will you?" It had been a major foul-up that had occurred during Elaine's first year in San Antonio. "I still don't know how those two groups managed to be booked in adjoining rooms."

"I remember it made the local news."

"I'll never forget it. I had gone over to check on something and was there when several of the PETA members walked in. Gosh, I can still remember the look of horror on their faces when they saw those tables covered with mounted deer heads and dozens of other stuffed animals."

"I know you found it just as offensive."

"Yes, but I couldn't tell them that. I thought they were going to start a riot. The PETA members stormed out and ended up calling for a boycott of the entire hotel chain. They kept a handful of pick-eters in front of the hotel for a week." She gave a short giggle that made Laurel's heart catch. "It's a wonder I wasn't fired."

Silence ensued and Laurel struggled to think of something to say that would keep Elaine on the line, but everything she thought of seemed asinine.

"I guess I should go," Elaine said. "I have to get back to the office to make sure everything is moving smoothly for tonight."

"Sure, I understand. Thanks again for the flowers."

"Thanks for inviting me to dinner."

Neither of them seemed to want to be the first to hang up. Then suddenly they both spoke at the same time.

"You first," Laurel said with a nervous laugh.

"Oh, I was just going to suggest that maybe I could drop by the store during the week. I could bring you lunch or something."

"I'd like that." *Slow down*, the little voice whispered. "I mean, it would be nice. I'm here by myself and it's hard to get away. I usu-ally just bring my lunch, but you know how I get tired of sand-wiches." She clamped her hand over her mouth to stop herself from rambling on.

"How about Monday? I'll call you before I leave to see what you're in the mood for."

I'm in the mood for you! Laurel wanted to scream. Instead, she removed the hand from her mouth and forced herself to calmly agree.

After hanging up, she kept herself busy straightening the books on the already perfectly aligned shelves. It was only Saturday. Monday would be a long wait. When the phone rang again, she snatched it up, hoping it would be Elaine. She swallowed her disappointment when she realized the caller was Adam Sanchez, the owner of the small mystery bookstore.

"Did I call at a bad time?" he asked.

"No. I was just putting away some books," she lied.

"Oh." He hesitated. "I heard you were closing."

She sighed, and in keeping with her new resolution to not hold so much of herself from others, she decided to tell him the truth. "Yeah, I'm tired of fighting for every dollar. I'm not getting any younger and I need to start thinking about my future."

"I probably should do the same," he said wearily.

"I don't know. I think you're doing a lot better than I was. Your client base is much larger than mine."

"I still can't compete with the big guys' discounts."

"But you do well with your reading groups, and everyone seems to love your mystery nights." Once a quarter, he would host a whodunit party. Laurel had attended a couple and both times there had been a large crowd in attendance. "Hey, listen. Don't let my closing get to you. I should have closed the store years ago. I was just too stubborn to do it." She took a deep breath. "Adam, the truth is I never loved doing this the way you do. So don't give up just because I finally came to my senses."

"What are you going to do?" he asked. "Do you think you'll be able to find a job right away?"

"I already have a job waiting for me."

"Really?"

"Actually, you're sort of responsible for it," she said and went

201

on to explain how the estate sale he had referred her to had resulted in her landing a job.

"Wow," he said when she had finished. "Isn't it weird how these things come about?"

She was about to reply when he interrupted.

"Hey, I've got to go. I've got customers. Give me a call or stop by and we'll go to lunch or something."

Laurel agreed, then hung up and picked up the card from the flowers. As she read the message yet again, she wondered how often, if ever, Elaine thought about her and their time together. There were so many things Laurel would do differently if given the chance. She prayed she would eventually be given that chance.

CHAPTER THIRTY-TWO

On Monday morning, Elaine tried to make herself wait until ten before she called, but by nine thirty she could no longer restrain her longing to speak to Laurel. She felt it was a good sign that Laurel answered after the first ring.

"I know it's a little early to be thinking about lunch, but I was going out anyway and thought I'd call before I left," Elaine explained. It was a lame excuse for calling since she would have the cell phone with her, but it was the best she could come up with.

"I'm glad you called," Laurel said. "I got so busy this morning I didn't take time to grab breakfast."

Elaine pounced on the opportunity. "Why don't I stop by that little taco place on McCullough that you like so much and pick up some *carne guisada* tacos."

"Oh, gosh, that sounds good. You know how I love their *carne guisada*, but what about your errand?"

"I can do that later. It's not pressing. I was just going to get it out of the way while I had a few minutes to spare." *Don't sound so busy*, she warned herself. "It's really nothing anyway. It's just some little . . . thing." *Shut up! You sound like a moron.*

"Okay, if you're sure."

"Of course I'm sure. I'll go get the tacos now." Elaine was actually already locking her apartment door. "I should be there in about thirty minutes."

"Good. I'll put on a fresh pot of coffee."

Elaine practically ran to her car after hanging up. As she was backing out a horrible thought hit her. What if they were out of *carne guisada*? God, if they were she'd probably go postal on them.

When she reached the popular restaurant there was a line of customers waiting to be seated. She ignored the nasty comments and complaints and pushed her way to the front. She snagged a passing waiter. "I need an order to go," she told him.

"Someone will be right with you," he promised as he disappeared into the kitchen. True to his word, a moment later a woman appeared and took Elaine's order for half a dozen tacos. She knew it was way too many, but she didn't care. The woman warned her it would be at least fifteen minutes before they would be ready. Elaine had no choice but to nod. As she moved aside to get out of the way she spotted the bakery next door. Laurel loved their cinnamon rolls. Without delay, she dashed out the door and purchased a bagful of pastries before rushing back to wait for the tacos.

In no time at all she was hauling the two stuffed bags into the Lavender Page. She almost cried when she walked in and found Allie and Lou there. She tried to cover her disappointment by holding the bags up. "I knew there would be other people here, so I brought extras."

Laurel herded everyone into her office where Allie helped her clear off the worktable.

Elaine smiled when she saw the floral arrangement sitting on the corner of Laurel's desk.

"Do I smell doughnuts?" Lou asked.

"It's better than doughnuts," Elaine said as she sat the bags down. "Those are cinnamon rolls from Leticia's."

"Oh, save me one," Laurel said as she started passing the tacos out. "You really did bring extra," she said, looking to Elaine. "Did you guys plan this?"

"How could we? We haven't talked to Elaine in ages," Lou said, giving Elaine a knowing look.

"Hey," Elaine said. "The phone line runs in both directions."

"True, true," Lou agreed.

"I wasn't sure you two were up to visitors yet," Elaine teased and was rewarded by blushes from both Lou and Allie.

"I'll go get the coffee," Allie said and rushed out amid gales of laughter.

The teasing and chatter slowed down as they all dug into the food with obvious gusto. Elaine hadn't realized how hungry she was until she bit into the taco. She was glad she had purchased the extra food and, despite the fact that she had originally resented Allie and Lou being there, she soon forgot about it and enjoyed their company.

After finishing the tacos they started in on the pastries and Laurel made another pot of coffee. While they ate, Allie told them all about her adventures in enrolling in college and Laurel even told them about the people she had met in Corpus. When she told them about Nina and Rachel, the conversation turned to the injustice of the military's stance on gays and lesbians. They kept talking until the bell in front rang to indicate a customer. Allie jumped up, but Laurel made her sit back down.

"You're a guest. Sit down. I'll handle it."

Elaine watched Laurel until she disappeared around the corner.

"So what's the deal with you two?" Lou asked as soon as Laurel was out of earshot.

Elaine shrugged. "Nothing's going on. I just came by to say hi."

"And you just happened to bring food," Lou persisted.

"It's nothing," Elaine said. "I had some errands to run and was going to be in the neighborhood so I called her this morning and mentioned stopping by later with lunch." She looked at Allie. "You remember how hard it was to get away when you were here alone."

Allie nodded, but she did so with a knowing smile.

"I'm telling you it's nothing," Elaine said.

Before they could harass her more, the bell sounded again and Laurel returned. "It was just someone trying to sell me a raffle ticket for some church's fundraiser."

"That used to chap my butt," Allie said. "The way those old biddies would walk by, pointing and whispering, but the minute they had something to sell or needed a donation, here they came with both hands out."

Lou patted Allie's arm. "Don't get started." She stood up. "We've got to run. I promised I'd drop by the community center and help them paint."

"What are they painting?" Laurel asked.

"It's a mural depicting the AIDS Quilt," Allie said. "You two should come by when you have a chance. It's really beautiful."

"Lou, I didn't know you painted," Elaine said.

Lou shrugged. "I putter."

"She does more than putter," Allie insisted. "The next time you come over, I'll show you some of her so-called puttering—"

"That reminds me," Lou interrupted. "We're having a little get-together next weekend. I was supposed to mail out the invitations, but of course I've fiddle-farted around and haven't gotten it done. So, I'll just tell you two. Be there on Saturday night around seven."

"I'm sorry," Elaine said. She hadn't missed the surprised look Allie had thrown Lou's way when she mentioned the party. "I can't. I'm working every Friday and Saturday night until after New Year's."

"What about Sunday afternoon?" Lou asked.

"No, I'm free Sunday."

"Good, then we'll see you around one on Sunday."

Laurel laughed. "Wait a minute. Did you just change the date of your party?"

Lou shrugged. "I told you I didn't mail the invitations. We can make it any date we like. Can't we?" she turned to Allie and smiled.

Allie kissed her on the cheek. "Yes. We can."

After they left, Laurel and Elaine returned to the office.

"What do you think about Lou's party?" Elaine asked.

Laurel chuckled. "I think she's playing matchmaker."

"Would that bother you?" Elaine bit her tongue. Why had she asked that?

Laurel looked at her for a long moment. "No. I don't think it would." She slipped her hands into her jeans pockets. "What about you? Would you mind?"

The food she had eaten seemed to congeal into a heavy ball in the pit of her stomach. Were they moving too fast? "I don't think it would."

A small frown appeared between Laurel's eyes. "You don't *think* so?"

Elaine shook her head. "No. It wouldn't bother me at all."

Laurel was about to say something else when the front bell dinged. Elaine's phone began to ring at almost the same time. They looked at each other and smiled for a second before turning away to deal with the matters at hand.

Elaine's call was from the hotel. There was a problem with the seating arrangement in the banquet room. The client, a small software company, was holding an awards ceremony there late that afternoon and had called wanting to change the seating arrangement, but the requested changes weren't working due to the room's configuration. Elaine told them she would be right there.

When she walked out of the office Laurel was talking to a customer. Elaine waved and mouthed "see you later."

Laurel gave her a slight nod and a smile that would stay with her for the next several hours.

CHAPTER THIRTY-THREE

Laurel spent the rest of the afternoon thinking about Elaine's admission of not minding Lou's matchmaking. Maybe things were going better than she'd thought. The dinner at the bistro had felt awkward at times, but she'd never gotten the impression that Elaine didn't want to be there, and they had gotten along fine today. Of course, Lou and Allie had been there. She thought about calling Elaine and inviting her to dinner during the week, but the cleaning rampage she'd started left the house a mess. Plus she no longer had a dining table. They could eat in the kitchen, but that didn't solve the mess problem. She couldn't afford to eat out again. The price of the meal at the bistro had cost her a small fortune. She went back into the office and sat down to think. It was almost a week until Lou's party and she didn't want to wait that long before seeing Elaine again. Then the idea came to her. She hadn't yet seen Elaine's new apartment. Maybe she could find a way to wangle herself an invitation to see it.

She was still mulling over the problem when the front bell rang. She walked out expecting to find a customer. Instead she found Angela Ramirez and a razor-thin woman dressed in a designer suit. The woman was walking around the store nodding.

"Laurel, this is Shirley McIntyre," Angela said.

Shirley McIntyre stuck out her hand. Laurel had to bite her tongue to keep from crying out when the woman wrung her hand with a Neanderthal handshake.

"I'm sorry to barge in on you like this," Angela said. "We were in the area and Ms. McIntyre insisted on seeing the building."

Laurel got the impression that Shirley McIntyre was a woman who normally got what she wanted. "It's no problem."

Angela smiled her gratitude.

"This place is perfect," McIntyre boomed in a voice as strong as her handshake. She turned to Laurel. "How soon can you be out?"

"The building will be available the first of January," Laurel said.

"I didn't ask about available. I asked how soon you can be out. I want to open another printing shop and this spot is perfect, but I want it operational by January one. I need you out of here by the eighteenth." McIntyre's odd rapid-fire twang slapped the air like the admonishments of a Midland preacher on speed.

Laurel blinked and tried to hide her astonishment. "That's next Monday. I can't possibly be out by then."

"Can't or won't?" McIntyre demanded. Her hands flew to her hips.

Angela started to step forward, but Laurel held up a hand to stop her. "I'm sorry. That's impossible."

"Nothing's impossible if you set your mind to it," the strange woman boomed. "Now, here's the deal. I'll sign a five-year lease at the rate Angela quoted me earlier."

Laurel started to protest again, but McIntyre rode right on over her.

"If you're out of here by the eighteenth, I'll pay you a full month's rent for December."

Laurel didn't really like this pushy woman. "Five years is a long time—"

Once more McIntyre cut her off. "Okay, okay. You got me by the short hairs."

Laurel tried not to grimace. That would be one of the last places she would want to have a hold of this obnoxious woman.

"I'll agree to three years at your current rate, with a two percent increase for years four and five and a three percent increase for the sixth and seventh year."

"Seven years is a long time," Laurel replied. She didn't miss the stunned look in Angela's eyes at McIntyre's offer.

"If you're worried about me skipping out on you, Angela can include a clause with something to the effect that if I do opt out early I'll pay you a year's rent or some such." She waved a dismissive hand. "We're wasting time. All this other stuff can be worked out later." She leaned toward Laurel slightly. "Well, do we have a deal or not?"

Laurel looked at Angela, who nodded slightly. "The deal certainly sounds good," Laurel began, "but even if I could get rid of all this, there's no way I could ever get all the repairs made in time."

McIntyre's head shot up. "Repairs? What repairs?" She began peering at the walls.

"I told Angela I'd replace the carpet and paint."

McIntyre made a rude, sputtering noise. "Hellfire, I don't want a carpet in here. Didn't you hear me say I'm putting a print shop in here?"

"Ms. McIntyre owns several print shops across central and south Texas," Angela explained. "She's interested in opening a second shop here in San Antonio."

"So you'd take the building as is?" Laurel asked.

"Yeah. Just get rid of all these books and shelves." She stopped and pointed to the shelves on the side wall. "Are those shelves attached to the wall?"

"Yes."

"Then leave those. I can use them to display some of our products." She looked around. "Everything else has to go."

210

"Would you mind if I spoke to Angela alone for a moment?" Laurel asked.

McIntyre waved her off. "Chatter all you want. I'll be outside." She was pulling a phone out of her pocket before she reached the door.

As soon as the door closed behind her, Angela exhaled sharply. "I'm really sorry about this. I was taking her to see another property. When we drove by she saw the realty sign from the road and insisted we stop." The original for-sale sign had never been taken down. "I can't apologize enough. Even about the sign. I thought it had been taken down."

"That's okay. Do you think she's for real?"

Angela nodded. "Oh, she's definitely for real. I helped her locate the other property she leases here. She may be way over the top, but she's a heck of a businesswoman."

"Do you think I should do it?"

"If you're serious about leasing the place, you certainly won't get a better deal. I'll make sure the increases and everything else she offered are stated in the contract."

Laurel glanced around the room. "I don't know where I'd put all this stuff."

"Could you put it in storage for a while?"

"Sure, but I'd never be able to get rid of it there."

Angela pushed a stray lock of hair behind her ear. "I don't want to pressure you, but a deal like this won't come around again." When Laurel didn't respond she tried again. "Laurel, I quoted her sixteen dollars a square foot annual gross. If memory serves, you told me this building is slightly more than twenty-two hundred square feet."

"Twenty-two thirty," Laurel muttered, already doing the math.

"That's just shy of three thousand a month."

Laurel thought about the stack of bills lying on her desk. Combined, they totaled a little over eleven thousand dollars. Plus, there was the ten thousand dollars she owed Daniel. If she took McIntyre's offer she could use the first month's rent and Daniel's loan to pay off all the store's creditors. Then she could use the monthly rental income to repay Daniel. By spring she could be debt-free. "Tell her I'll do it," she said.

Angela practically ran out to tell her client the news.

Laurel realized there was only one way she'd ever be able to meet McIntyre's deadline and, she wasn't sure if she could do it. She was going to have to ask for help.

CHAPTER THIRTY-FOUR

It was only a little after six when Laurel unloaded the final stack of packing boxes the following morning. After Angela and Shirley McIntyre had left the previous afternoon, Laurel had driven to a nearby moving center and purchased as many boxes as her car would hold. She used the time to build up her courage to make the calls. It wasn't that she didn't think her friends would come to help, of that she had no doubt. It was just hard for her to ask. She had called Elaine first, then Lou and Allie and finally Adam Sanchez. As soon as she explained her dilemma to each of them they had all promised to be at the store by six thirty the following morning.

She went back to the car to get the bag filled with rolls of packing tape she'd also purchased from the center. Elaine's Honda was pulling in the parking lot as she walked out. Laurel timidly went over to the car.

"Thanks for coming," she said as Elaine stepped out.

Elaine gazed at her for a long moment before replying, "Thanks for asking. I know how hard it must have been for you."

Laurel glanced down at her feet. She didn't want Elaine to see the tears.

"The food went over so well yesterday, I thought I'd treat everyone again today," Elaine said as she started handing the bags out to Laurel.

"My gosh. How much did you buy?" There were a total of four large bags. "Elaine, there's enough food here for a small army."

"You know, with everyone working, I just thought we'd eat more."

Laurel laughed. "If we eat all this, we'll be too full to work." She shook her head. "Come on inside. I was getting ready to put on a pot of coffee."

Before they reached the door Lou and Allie arrived in Allie's truck. Laurel waved at them. "I can't believe you bought all this food." She stopped talking as another car pulled in. "That looks like Gilda's car."

"Yeah," Elaine said and smiled. "I think Allie might have called her."

Laurel looked at Elaine and then the bags of food. "My gosh, who else did she call?"

Elaine shrugged and urged her into the store. "Who knows?" She winked suddenly as they set the bags on the counter. "But I'll bet we have to call out for pizza for lunch."

Laurel felt her knees weaken. She wasn't sure she could handle all this sharing.

"Hey." Elaine took her by the shoulders. "Listen to me. Just remember that anyone who shows up here today is doing so of their own free will. They want to be here to help you."

"Why?"

Elaine smiled and shook her head. "You really don't know, do you?"

Laurel nodded numbly.

"They're coming to help you, just as you've helped them over the years." Without warning Elaine softly kissed her. "Now, you'd better get that coffee going. I'll go out and see if Lou and Allie need any help."

Within ten minutes the store was transformed into a bustling center of activity. Shortly after Elaine, Allie, Lou and Gilda came in, Adam appeared, then Tom and finally, to Laurel's complete surprise, Cindy, the clerk she'd had to fire.

Laurel walked to the door to meet her. "Thanks for coming," she said as she gave Cindy a hug.

"Is it okay that I'm here?"

"Of course it is. I'm sorry I was such a bitch to you."

Cindy shrugged. "I deserved it. I didn't do a very good job."

"Are you two going to dilly-dally around all day?" Lou called. "I thought there was work to be done."

"We're coming," Laurel replied as they headed back to join the group.

Elaine and Lou went to work setting up the folding tables Lou had brought over. They started an assembly line on them. Cindy and Gilda put the packing boxes together, Allie, Lou, Laurel and Elaine packed them, and Tom and Adam hauled the boxes out to Tom's and Allie's trucks on a dolly. They all ate as they worked and Laurel made sure the coffeepot was never empty.

Adam had to leave at nine to go open his own store, but he promised to return as soon as his salesclerk arrived at eleven. Elaine took Adam's place in helping Tom carry the boxes out.

Laurel was kept so busy she barely had time to think about the kiss Elaine had given her, but each time their eyes met, she felt the heat all the way to her toes.

"The trucks are full," Tom announced.

Laurel was in the middle of helping Lou empty a large display case filled with rainbow paraphernalia. They had been working hard for three hours and the store was a wreck. She glanced around and felt a stab of panic. Suddenly Elaine was by her side.

"Why don't you stay here," Elaine suggested. "I'll ride over with Tom and Allie to help them unload the boxes at the house."

Laurel quickly agreed and gave Elaine the house key.

"Where do you want the boxes stacked?" Elaine asked.

"Start with the guest room and then fill up the back wall of the office." She rubbed her arm. "If you still need space, I guess you can put them in the family room. Just leave me a path to walk through there."

Elaine squeezed her arm gently. "Don't let it get to you. It's not as bad as it looks. We'll figure out how to get rid of everything soon."

Laurel surveyed the store as she thought about all the stuff scattered throughout the house. "I should probably warn you that I've been trying to organize some things at the house and it's sort of a mess."

Elaine shrugged it off. "Don't worry about it. We'll be back as soon as we can."

Laurel watched her leave. She liked the way Elaine had said "we" when she talked about finding a solution for all the merchandise. She caught Lou watching her with an amused look on her face. "What's wrong with you?" she asked with a grin.

"Not a thing," Lou called cheerfully. "In fact, I'd say things are better than they've been in a long time."

Laurel saw Gilda and Cindy glance at each other and shrug. *They probably think we're all senile*, she thought. She grabbed another box and got back to work.

Adam returned in a van he had borrowed from a friend. Since the other group had the dolly, he helped pack boxes.

They had just finished when Elaine phoned to let them know they were on their way back. Laurel called and ordered pizzas, then went back to packing. As soon as the others returned, Elaine pulled Laurel into the office.

"Why didn't you call me?" Elaine insisted.

Laurel heard the edge of anger in Elaine's voice. "What are you talking about?"

"You sold your furniture. You didn't have to do that. You know I would have helped you if you would've let me know." Her voice cracked. "Damn it, Laurel, do you have any idea how awful I felt when I saw what you had to do?"

Laurel put a hand on her arm and stopped her. "Wait a minute.

I sold the furniture because I wanted to. Not because I had to." She took a deep breath and tried to think of how she could explain what she did and why. "I don't know what happened. It was like I just woke up one day and realized that for the past several years I've been trying to live for Chris. I never even liked that dark, heavy furniture, but I kept it because she did. That's why I kept the store so long, for her." She turned to look Elaine in the eye. "I'm sorry about everything I've put you through. I can only imagine how hard it must have been for you to always have Chris's shadow hovering in the background."

Elaine shook her head. "Don't make it sound like it was all bad. We had some good times, didn't we?"

Before Laurel could reply Lou called from the front and interrupted them. "We're taking a break in here if anyone wants to join us."

Laurel rolled her eyes. "I swear that woman has the absolute worst timing in the world. Let's go before she sends someone back here for us."

They walked out together.

"What a mess," Lou said as she slid to the floor and leaned back against the counter.

"I had no idea there was so much stuff in here," Gilda said as she plopped down beside Lou.

"Yeah, I'm exhausted," Cindy said when she came in.

"Exhausted," Lou challenged. "You're too young to be exhausted. When I was your age I could party all night and work all day without ever getting exhausted."

"And look where it got you," Laurel teased as she rumpled Lou's hair.

"I think she's doing just fine." Allie stretched out beside Lou. Tom and Adam moved some boxes out of the way and joined them.

"What's left to pack?" Elaine asked as she and Laurel sat down with the rest of the group.

Laurel glanced over her shoulder. "Well, let me see. We've fin-

ished all the non-book items and the used books section is empty."
She did a quick visual survey. "We still have the romance, mystery,
self-help and biographies sections to do."

Allie groaned. "Which just happen to be the four largest sections."

Adam cleared his throat softly. "Maybe now would be a good
time to get everyone's opinion on something I've been thinking
about ever since I heard you were closing," he said, glancing
around at the group.

They all turned to him.

"I've been thinking about maybe buying your stock of mysteries and adding a gay and lesbian section to my shop." He turned to
Laurel. "What do you think?"

Laurel nodded. "I think it would be great, but a better question
might be how would your current customers feel about it?"

He rubbed his chin. "I've given it some thought and I don't
think it would bother the majority of them at all. There might be
a few who would get bent out of shape over it, but not enough to
make a difference."

"I love the idea," Lou replied. "I hate the thought of having to
order my books through the mail. I'm a very tactile person. I like
to see the book and touch it before I buy it." She shrugged. "Heck,
for me, shopping for the book is half the fun, and I'd much rather
support an independent store."

"We had a lot of mystery readers," Gilda replied. "I know quite
a few of them already go to your shop."

"It sounds like a good deal for everyone," Elaine said.

Adam turned to Laurel. "You figure out a price and we'll see
what we can do," he said.

Laurel shook her head. "What would you think about taking all
of them on a sixty-forty commission? That way, if it doesn't work,
you won't be stuck with a lot of useless inventory."

Adam nodded and smiled. "No up-front money. I like that."

They all laughed. Just then the door opened and the pizza

delivery guy came in with a stack of pizzas. "Whew, what happened here?"

"We've got a going-out-of-business sale going," Lou chirped. "Can we interest you in a few books?"

He shook his head. "Naw, I don't like to read books. I'd rather wait for the movie."

Laurel saw Lou take in the skinny kid's enormous shirt, low-riding baggy shorts and the green and purple sneakers. Before Lou could open her mouth to respond, Laurel jumped up to pay him. Within minutes the only noise to be heard was the crunching of pizza crust.

Shortly after lunch Elaine and Tom had to leave in order to have time to get ready for work. They had been able to take off the morning because they were working such late hours, but they had to be at the hotel no later than three in case something went wrong during a setup. Elaine had told Laurel that the hotel conference and banquet rooms were all booked straight through until January second.

After Tom and Elaine left, the remaining group worked on packing the mysteries and getting them loaded into Adam's van. Laurel thanked them all before sending them home to rest. She offered to drive over and help Adam unload the boxes from the van, but he assured her he would have plenty of help.

CHAPTER THIRTY-FIVE

It was after midnight when Elaine and Tom sat down in Elaine's office.

"God, I can't remember when I've been so tired." Elaine groaned as she stretched her legs out in front of the sofa.

From his usual spot on the floor, Tom leaned his head back against the sofa arm. "At least it was a calm night for a change."

"Tom, I really appreciate you helping Laurel today." Elaine had simply mentioned to him that she was going and as soon as he heard what was happening, he had volunteered to pitch in.

"I was glad to help." He turned slightly to look up at her. "How are things coming along with you two?"

She shrugged and thought about the conversation they'd had in Laurel's office earlier that day. "It's hard to say. We're taking it slow. But, I'm confident that everything will work itself out with time."

"I hope so. Make sure you bring her to the wedding."

"You know you never told me when it's going to be."

"We haven't set a date yet. Sue's parents would prefer that it happen yesterday. I want to wait until March so that my taking vacation won't be an issue and Sue wants to be a June bride, which could prove to be extremely interesting when you consider she's already three months pregnant."

Elaine gave a tired chuckle. "Can you imagine going into labor at your wedding?"

"Worse, can you imagine the look on her parents' faces when their daughter waddles down the aisle nine months pregnant?" He grew serious. "I'm afraid that when it comes time for the wedding they're going to go fundamentalist on her and not show up. She tries to pretend like it wouldn't bother her, but I know better."

"It's hard to imagine that Sue could have such uptight parents. I mean, she's so easygoing and open." She lightly swatted his shoulder. "I know what we'll do. Let's plan on you and Sue and Laurel and me going to Hawaii and we'll have a double ceremony. Her parents will be so grateful that their daughter is straight, they'll forget all about the pregnancy." Her knees protested with tiny pops as she stood.

He slowly came to his feet. "You know, I sort of like that idea. The only problem is that we can't both be on vacation at the same time."

"Yeah, right. That is a problem." She hobbled toward her desk to get her bag. "Okay, I've got the solution. Just before it's time for the wedding, I'll fire you and then we can both go."

"On second thought, I think I'll just take my chances with Sue's parents."

"I knew I could make you feel better."

When Elaine pulled out of the parking lot ten minutes later, she turned toward Laurel's house rather than her own apartment. She didn't think about what she was doing or why, she simply followed a gut instinct. The fact that there was still a light on inside the house only encouraged her. As she rang the doorbell a few flurries of doubt tried to push their way in, but she shoved them away.

The curtain on the window near the door moved slightly as Laurel checked to see who was on the porch. Elaine moved over so Laurel could get a better view of her. A moment later, the door swung open.

"What's wrong?" Laurel asked as soon as she opened the door and stepped back.

Elaine had made up her mind. There were times when it was better to wait, and then there were times when it was better to take action. She felt the time for action had arrived. She prayed her instincts weren't off when she stepped into the room, pulled Laurel into her arms and kissed her deeply.

There was a slight hesitation on Laurel's part, but when Elaine's tongue gently slipped between her lips, she responded with an urgency that took Elaine by surprise. Elaine kicked the door closed with her foot and pulled Laurel to her. As the kiss deepened and grew more frantic, Elaine slipped her hands beneath Laurel's yellow terrycloth robe. She pushed Laurel against the hallway wall, and moved her lips across the silky softness of Laurel's throat. With deliberate slowness she continued her journey downward to first one hardened nipple and then the other. With the tip of her tongue, she traced each nipple before sucking it between her lips and teasing it with her teeth. She lost track of who the sighs of pleasure were coming from. Her own heart felt as though it would burst from her chest when her lips trailed a line of kisses across Laurel's stomach. Already she could smell the warm secret scent of her quest. Soon she would reach her goal and revel in the sweet sounds of pleasure that Laurel made. She tried to hold back, but the feel of the curly hair against her chin was driving her crazy. Her breaking point came when Laurel spread her legs and slowly slid down the wall then lay back on the carpet. Almost crazy with desire, she used her hands to fully open Laurel to her probing tongue. Only then did she allow herself to become lost in her own pleasure.

An hour later, they lay on the floor in an exhausted heap. Elaine experienced the first real stabs of doubt and prayed her rash decision wouldn't turn into a disaster. "I guess I should have called first," she said.

Laurel rubbed her face across Elaine's shoulder and chuckled. "It's probably a good thing you didn't."

"Would you have told me not to come over?"

"I don't know. I've been telling myself to take things slow between us, but I was certainly singing a different tune a minute ago."

"You know I love you." Elaine decided she might as well go all the way.

Laurel raised her head and kissed her softly. "Yeah, I know, and I love you, too."

"So why are we making things so hard on ourselves?"

"Elaine, I want to ask a favor. It might not make sense to you right now and maybe it never will, but . . . it's . . . it's something I have to do."

Elaine feared she knew what was coming, but there was no way to stop it. "Sure," she answered, bracing herself.

"Stop that," Laurel demanded.

"What?"

"You went all tense, like you were about to be put before a firing squad."

"I'm sorry." Elaine tried to relax. It wasn't easy.

"I'd like for us to date for a while. There are so many things that I need to do for myself. I still don't know what I want to do about this house, and I don't know how the new job will go."

"I didn't know you'd already found a job."

"There's been so much going on, I guess I forgot to tell you." Laurel quickly reminded her who Nancy Grady was, how they met and how the job offer had come about.

Elaine pushed down a streak of jealousy. "I understand."

Laurel sat up and pulled her robe back on. "Do you like this house?"

Elaine attempted to put her clothes back into some semblance of modesty. "Sure."

"No. I mean honestly. Do you like it? Did you like living here?"

"I never minded the house. There were a lot of ghosts from your past here, but I tried to place myself in your shoes." She glanced at Laurel. "Sometimes it was hard."

Laurel took her hand. "If we ever decided to live together again, would you be okay living here or would you prefer to live somewhere else?"

Elaine hoped she wasn't slitting her own throat, but it was time to be honest. "I think it might be best if we found a place of our own. We could choose a house together, someplace where we could build our own memories." She gently squeezed Laurel's hand. "I don't ever want to take the memories of Chris away from you, but if we get back together I'd like to be first in your life." She leaned over and kissed Laurel's forehead. "I should go. I promised to help a friend tomorrow and she wants me there at the crack of dawn," she teased.

"She sounds like an awfully demanding woman."

"That's all right. I sort of like demanding women."

CHAPTER THIRTY-SIX

Laurel was late getting to the store that morning. Lou and Elaine were already there waiting for her. It would only be the three of them today, so at least she was spared some level of embarrassment.

"I'm sorry I'm late," she called as she raced across the parking lot. "I forgot to set the alarm and overslept."

"I guess you were so tired you got distracted," Elaine said innocently as she held Laurel's bags while she unlocked the door.

Laurel tried to send her an evil scowl but couldn't maintain it and ended up laughing.

"Oh, Christ," Lou muttered. "Now we won't get anything done."

"What are you mumbling about back there?" Laurel asked.

Lou thumped Elaine as she pushed past her into the store.

"Ouch. What was that for?"

"General principle," Lou replied. "I'm going to have to stand around here and watch you two make moony eyes at each other all day."

"Moony eyes." Laurel giggled. "As though we haven't had to put up with you making moony eyes at Allie for months."

"I did not."

"Yes, you did," Laurel and Elaine chimed in at the same time.

"Are we here to work or chatter like old hens?" Lou groused.

"Sounds like somebody could use some moony eyes," Elaine whispered loudly and barely managed to duck out of the way as Lou threw an empty tape roll at her.

They started packing boxes and stacking them in Allie's truck. Allie had gotten a last-minute call to work, so she and Lou had swapped out vehicles. Tom was going to cover for Elaine and call her only if something he couldn't handle popped up. The three women worked together smoothly and before they realized it the final book was being packed away.

"That's the last of them," Lou said as Laurel taped the box closed.

Elaine picked up the remaining three empty boxes. "You were pretty close in estimating the number of boxes you'd need."

"Hey, as many boxes as I've packed to haul to off-site events, I'm surprised I'm off by that many," Laurel said. A sudden sense of sadness filled her when she looked around at the empty shelves. "I'm glad Chris never had to see this."

Lou patted Laurel's shoulder. "I think she would have said the old girl had a good run." She looked around the room. "Above all else, Chris was a realist. She would have been proud of how you've kept the store going, but she would have also approved of your decision to close."

"I always felt like I was letting her down."

"You shouldn't have. You did your best. Now it's time to move on."

Laurel nodded. "Let's go. I'll come back later and clean up this mess. There are still a few things I need to take care of here anyway."

They all drove to Laurel's in their respective vehicles. As soon as the boxes were unloaded, Lou gave a rather hasty good-bye and left.

"She's such a sweetie. I know she's probably juggling two or three other things while she's helping me," Laurel said as they watched her drive away.

"I guess it's something she needs to do, her way of letting go of the store," Elaine said. "You know you aren't the only person losing it."

Laurel nodded. "I keep forgetting that. I'm just now starting to realize how selfish I've been all these years. After Chris died I tried to gather it all in and it became *my* store. I never saw how much others loved it and depended on it."

"You did what you had to do. I can't imagine going through what you did."

"Can you stay for a while?" Laurel asked.

Elaine glanced at her watch and then took Laurel's hand. "It's almost four. I wish I could, but Tom has been covering for me all day. I should go home, get cleaned up and go in to help him. I swear I think this is the worst year yet. It seems like all the crazies booked with us this year."

Laurel chuckled. "You say that every year."

"Do I really?"

"Yes."

They stood in silence for a long moment.

Laurel finally broke it. "When will I see you again?"

"How about breakfast tomorrow? After that I can't make any promises that I'll be able to get away from the office."

Laurel grabbed Elaine's hand. "Are we going to get through this?" Tears burned her eyes.

Elaine hugged her tightly. "Yes, I think with time everything will settle into place."

"What if they don't? I mean, what if it turns out that we love each other, but we can't live together?"

"In that case, I'll rent a room from Mrs. Blackburn and Precious so I can sneak over and visit you every day."

227

"You must really love me to go to such extremes," Laurel said as she pulled back and chuckled.

Elaine kissed her lightly. "I do love you." She kissed her again. "I have to go." She turned to leave. "Why don't you come over to the apartment tomorrow for breakfast? I'll whip us up an omelet."

"That sounds good, but I don't know where you live."

Elaine seemed shocked. "Well, we can't have a torrid affair if you can't find me." She pulled a pad from her pocket and jotted down the address.

Laurel stood in the doorway until Elaine drove off. When she stepped back into the house, it seemed emptier than it had a moment ago. She grabbed her keys and drove back to the store to start cleaning. The work helped take her mind off missing Elaine. When she finally made her way in to clean the office, she groaned. They had been so busy packing the merchandise that all the stuff in the office had been forgotten. On the corner of the desk was the stack of bills that needed to be paid. She smiled and grabbed her checkbook. She wouldn't wait on Shirley McIntyre's check. She'd use Daniel's loan and the money she had gotten from selling the furniture to pay off the bills.

When she sealed the last envelope she stamped her feet in glee. She wasn't completely out of debt because she still owed Daniel, and her credit card carried a hefty balance, but the Lavender Page was at last debt-free. She spent the next couple of hours sorting through files, packing the ones she needed to keep and carrying garbage bags filled with catalogs and old paperwork to the Dumpster.

It was after ten when Laurel crammed the last box of papers into her car and went back inside to shut off the lights and lock up. When she stepped inside she noticed for the first time the sense of emptiness. She walked over to the counter and ran her hand along the top. How many times had she cleaned and polished its top? How many times had Chris cleaned it? She continued around the room, touching the empty shelves and display racks. The store seemed so much bigger now that it was practically empty.

Tomorrow she would call a place that bought and sold furniture and fixtures for retailers. She would sell the stand-alone shelves, display racks, display case, worktables and maybe the folding chairs she had used for readings and special events. She hadn't made her mind up if she'd let the desk go or not. It had been Chris's, but she already had the roll top desk at the house. Maybe she should let this one go. She started to sit down at the desk when the phone rang, startling her. She considered ignoring it but changed her mind. Tomorrow she would have it disconnected, so for the last time she picked it up.

"Lavender Page." The words almost stuck in her throat.

"Are you okay?"

"Elaine." Merely saying her name made her feel better.

"What's wrong?"

"I thought I'd come over and start cleaning. I needed to clear out the office and do a few last-minute things." She glanced at the stack of bills by her bag and again experienced a sense of relief in being able to pay them off.

"If this is a bad time, I could call back later."

"No. I guess I'm just sitting here feeling sorry for myself."

"Closing the store is a big step. It's been your life for a long time."

And it cost me dearly, Laurel wanted to say, but she couldn't. She tried to lighten the mood. "You're not trying to weasel out of making me breakfast, are you?"

"No. In fact, I was calling because by some miracle things were really quiet at the hotel again tonight. I was wondering, if you're not too busy, if perhaps you'd like to drop by my apartment and spend the night."

Elaine's low voice in her ear sent a ripple of desire dancing through Laurel.

"That way," Elaine continued, "you'll be there tomorrow morning and can show me what ingredients you'd like in your omelet."

"Yes, that certainly sounds like a sensible suggestion. I need to run home first and pick up some clothes."

229

"Why? I wasn't planning on you staying in the ones you're wearing for very long."

"Now you have my attention. I could be at your apartment in less than twenty minutes."

"Good. I'm already here waiting on you."

Laurel giggled. "What are you wearing?" she teased.

"Nothing but a smile."

Laurel nearly dropped the phone. After a couple of deep breaths to regroup, she grabbed the stack of bills and crammed them into her bag. "Forget what I said earlier. I'll be there in fifteen minutes."

A long throaty intake of breath filled her ear.

"Elaine Alexander, don't you dare start without me!"

CHAPTER THIRTY-SEVEN

Elaine and Laurel parked on the street for Lou's party on Sunday afternoon.

"We must be the first ones here," Elaine said. "There aren't any cars except theirs in the driveway. You don't think people stayed home because of the weather, do you?" An unexpected cold front had moved in during the night and they were both wearing their heavy coats. Since truly frigid weather was a rarity in San Antonio, whenever it occurred people tended to stay home and huddle under blankets or crowd around the fireplace, since it might be the only time they got to use it all year.

Laurel shook her head. "No. I told you. I think we're being hoodwinked and Miss Lou is playing matchmaker."

"If so, she's a little late." Elaine squeezed Laurel's hand. They had spent almost every night together since she'd invited Laurel over for omelets.

"I don't think she's going to be too disappointed. Come on, let's go inside. I'm freezing."

Allie and a blast of warm aromatic air met them at the door. "Hey, I didn't hear the cars. Why didn't you park in the driveway?"

"We didn't want to get blocked in."

Allie frowned as she waved them into the small hallway and closed the front door. "Blocked in? What do you mean?"

"The other guests," Laurel said pointedly.

"Oh . . . oh . . . yeah . . . the other guests." Allie looked over her shoulder as she took their coats and hung them in the hall closet.

As they stepped into the living room, Lou came out of the kitchen with Dooley at her heels.

"They were just asking about the other guests," Allie said.

Lou plastered on her best Cheshire Cat grin. "I sort of forgot to mail the invitations." She shrugged. "Then we got so busy with the store, I forgot to call anyone else."

"So, it's just us," Laurel said, trying to keep the smile off her face.

"I guess so," Lou chirped.

"You're so full of bull." Elaine laughed. "You never intended to invite anyone else."

Lou tried to look offended, prompting Allie to roll her eyes. "You guys are so-o-o weird."

"That's why you love me," Lou said.

Allie shook her head and smiled. "Yeah, it's sort of sick, isn't it?" She gave Lou a loud kiss. "Come on into the kitchen. Due to the weather, the menu has changed from grilled steaks to beef stew."

"It smells wonderful," Laurel said as she pressed a hand to her grumbling stomach. She glanced at Elaine and found her watching her. They had missed breakfast that morning. The memory of why made her cheeks burn. When Elaine gave her a knowing smile, Laurel almost tripped over her own feet.

Elaine put out a hand to steady her. "It's the perfect day for stew."

As they walked through the living room, Laurel noticed several large plastic boxes stacked against the wall. "What are all the boxes for?"

"Those are filled with Christmas decorations," Lou said. "We figured that with everything going on, you two probably hadn't even thought about a tree this year, and we thought it might be nice if you shared ours."

Laurel was touched by their consideration. "That sounds like fun." She turned to Elaine in time to catch her brushing a quick hand over her eyes.

"You're absolutely right," Elaine said. "It hadn't crossed my mind."

"With all the mess at the house, I wouldn't have room for one," Laurel added.

"What are you going to do with that stuff?" Allie asked.

"Well, you know Adam took all the mysteries on consignment. That got me to thinking, and I got online and found a listing for all the gay and lesbian shops in Texas and I started calling them. On like the third call, I got this guy in Austin who owns a bookstore there and is thinking about opening another one in Houston. He's driving down next week to look at everything. He says he might take it all, if the price is right." She held up her hand. "And trust me, I'm certain that we'll eventually be able to settle on a price."

"That was a great idea," Allie said as they all sat down at the kitchen table. Dooley dropped down near Allie's feet.

Elaine nodded. "She even managed to sell all the fixtures and extra furniture to Sommers. They sell items for stores."

"You've been busy," Lou said as she removed a pan from the oven and dumped the contents into a large wicker bowl that had been lined with a kitchen towel. "These are Allie's sausage and jalapeño bread sticks. They're perfect with the stew."

Allie placed a stack of bowls on the table.

Lou removed the lid from a large pot on the stove. "Grab a bowl and start dipping. You know there's nothing formal around here."

"I'm going to feed Dooley in his room," Allie said as she coaxed the basset hound from beneath the table.

Elaine and Laurel filled their bowls and within minutes the four were crowded around the table wolfing down the savory stew.

After they ate, they sat around the table chatting and laughing away the afternoon.

"Where's this tree we were going to decorate?" Elaine asked.

Lou and Allie jumped up.

"We'll be right back," Lou called as the two ran outside.

Elaine leaned back in her chair. "I'm stuffed. That stew was delicious."

"I ate too much," Laurel said as she stood and walked to the kitchen window. "Where did they go? They're going to freeze out there." She didn't hear Elaine come up behind her and was a little startled when Elaine's arms slid around her waist.

"They're so happy. They probably won't even notice it's cold," Elaine said as she nuzzled Laurel's neck.

Laurel turned to face her. "Could you ever be that happy again?"

Elaine smiled. "What makes you think I'm not already?" She kissed her.

"All right, all right," Lou called out. "We were only gone for a couple of minutes."

They turned to find Lou and Allie pushing a flat dolly on which sat a tall Christmas tree that had already been secured in a large bucket.

"I didn't realize you meant a live tree," Elaine said, rubbing her hands together. "I love live trees."

Lou twisted the dolly around and deftly slipped the container off. "I have an artificial one that I normally use, but we thought we'd get a live tree this year."

They all worked together to get the tree settled into the perfect spot before tearing into the plastic containers of decorations. Lou and Elaine got themselves so entwined in the yards and yards of lights that it took all four of them to get them untangled.

"I can't believe you just dumped them in the box without rolling them," Elaine said as Laurel helped straighten out a particularly long strand.

"It was all almost Valentine's Day," Lou grumbled. "I had to get the blasted tree down in a hurry."

Allie stepped over the containers and started toward the

kitchen. "I'm going to get the eggnog. You two are taking this way too seriously."

"Yeah," Laurel said. "We're supposed to be having fun."

Lou tossed her a jumbled nest of lights. "Okay, Ms. Sunshine. Let me see you unravel those."

Laurel stared at the mess in her hands before tossing them back into a box. "You know, I think there are already plenty of lights on the tree."

"Oh, yeah, now there are plenty of lights," Lou said, causing the group to break into laughter.

Allie returned with mugs of eggnog, and gradually the tree began to fill with the glittering shimmer of Christmas ornaments. Everyone was laughing and joking when Laurel pulled an ornament from the box that made her gasp.

The other three turned to look at her. Lou seemed to recognize it immediately and sighed. "Damn, Laurel, I'm sorry. I'd forgotten that was in there."

Elaine leaned closer to see what it was and immediately stepped back.

Laurel sat staring at the small round photo-frame ornament that held a photo of her and Chris. The only sound was the loud ticking of the grandfather clock in the hallway. She glanced up at Elaine. "I'm sorry. It just took me by surprise."

Elaine knelt down beside her.

"I'll put it back in the box," Lou said, reaching for the frame.

Elaine stopped her. "No." She held out her hand for the ornament. "May I?"

Laurel reluctantly handed it to her.

Elaine gazed at it for a minute before speaking. "I hope the four of us will be able to share many, many more nights like tonight. I have to confess that for a long time I was jealous of Chris and the strong feelings she could evoke from those who loved her. In the past few weeks I've come to realize that it wasn't Chris that was bothering me so much as it was my own insecurities. Someone I loved was hurting." She looked at Laurel. "And I didn't know how to help her." She glanced down at the ornament and then back at Laurel. "No one is without a past. It makes us who we are. Laurel, I love you for who you are and I know you love me too." She turned and hung the ornament on the tree. "I'm okay with this."

The silence grew deeper until Laurel finally reached over and removed the ornament. "I'm not." She ran a thumb across the photo. "I didn't think I could ever love anyone after Chris, and then you came along and showed me how wrong I was. I won't ever forget her, but you're my life now." She handed the ornament to Lou and took Elaine's hand.

For a long moment no one spoke. Allie finally broke the silence by jumping up and rushing to the stereo. "I can't believe we forgot to put the Christmas music on."

Dooley banished the awkward moment when he hopped off his favorite chair and, without ceremony, plopped his ponderous body beneath the tree and began to howl. Soon they were all laughing and singing along.

CHAPTER THIRTY-EIGHT

Christmas morning found Laurel in the middle of Elaine's bed surrounded by discarded wrapping paper and boxes.

"I have one more thing for you." Laurel hesitantly pulled a thin, flat, simply wrapped item from beneath her pillow.

"You kept one back, did you?" Elaine said as she reached for the gift.

Laurel continued to hold onto the present. She was suddenly nervous about giving it to Elaine. What if it was too soon? They really hadn't discussed moving back in together. "It's really nothing," she said, regretting her impulsive act. "Maybe I'll wait to give you this one."

Elaine frowned slightly before reaching into her robe pocket and removing a smaller packet. She cleared her throat gently as she handed the item to Laurel. "This isn't really a gift either, but now seems like a good time to give it to you. Once you open this, it's going to need a little bit of an explanation."

Confused, Laurel took the gift. It was small, extremely thin and lightweight. "I can't imagine what it is." She tore it open and found a small stack of paint sample cards. She glanced from them to Elaine and back.

Elaine placed a hand on Laurel's knee. "I just picked those out to have something to wrap. My point being, maybe we could do a few changes to the house and make it ours." Laurel started to speak, but Elaine stopped her and rushed on. "It's your house, so if you don't want to paint it or anything, I understand."

"I like the idea."

Elaine smiled. "Good. Since you've already invested so much into the house, I think it's only fair that I buy the materials. We'll select everything together and if you're up to it, we'll do as much of the work as we can ourselves."

Laurel stared at the cards a moment longer before she began to laugh.

"What?" Elaine asked.

When Laurel saw the anxious look on her lover's face, she handed over the gift she'd held back. "I guess now is the time to open this."

Elaine took it and tore it open. It was a brochure from a real-tor's office. It took a moment for the item to make sense. When it did it was her turn to laugh.

"I thought you might feel more comfortable if I sold the house and we bought one together," Laurel explained. "Some place where there's no history except ours."

"It doesn't matter to me where we live, as long as we're together." Elaine leaned forward and kissed her.

As the kiss deepened, Laurel realized that the year wouldn't be ending on the sad note she had anticipated. In fact, things had never seemed brighter.

Publications from
BELLA BOOKS, INC.
The best in contemporary lesbian fiction

P.O. Box 10543, Tallahassee, FL 32302
Phone: 800-729-4992
www.bellabooks.com

OUT OF THE FIRE by Beth Moore. Author Ann Covington feels at the top of the world when told her book is being made into a movie. Then in walks Casey Duncan the actress who is playing the lead in her movie. Will Casey turn Ann's world upside down?
1-59493-088-0 $13.95

STAKE THROUGH THE HEART: NEW EXPLOITS OF TWILIGHT LESBIANS by Karin Kallmaker, Julia Watts, Barbara Johnson and Therese Szymanski. The playful quartet that penned the acclaimed *Once Upon A Dyke* are dimming the lights for journeys into worlds of breathless seduction.
1-59493-071-6 $15.95

THE HOUSE ON SANDSTONE by KG MacGregor. Carly Griffin returns home to Leland and finds that her old high school friend Justine is awakening more than just old memories.
1-59493-076-7 $13.95

WILD NIGHTS: MOSTLY TRUE STORIES OF WOMEN LOVING WOMEN edited by Therese Szymanski. 264 pp. 23 new stories from today's hottest erotic writers are sure to give you your wildest night ever!
1-59493-069-4 $15.95

COYOTE SKY by Gerri Hill. 248 pp. Sheriff Lee Foxx is trying to cope with the realization that she has fallen in love for the first time. And fallen for author Kate Winters, who is technically unavailable. Will Lee fight to keep Kate in Coyote?
1-59493-065-1 $13.95

VOICES OF THE HEART by Frankie J. Jones. 264 pp. A series of events force Erin to swear off love as she tries to break away from the woman of her dreams. Will Erin ever find the key to her future happiness?
1-59493-068-6 $13.95

SHELTER FROM THE STORM by Peggy J. Herring. 296 pp. A story about family and getting reacquainted with one's past that shows that sometimes you don't appreciate what you have until you almost lose it.
1-59493-064-3 $13.95

WRITING MY LOVE by Claire McNab. 192 pp. Romance writer Vonny Smith believes she will be able to woo her editor Diana through her writing . . .
1-59493-063-5 $13.95

PAID IN FULL by Ann Roberts. 200 pp. Ari Adams will need to choose between the debts of the past and the promise of a happy future.
1-59493-059-7 $13.95

ROMANCING THE ZONE by Kenna White. 272 pp. Liz's world begins to crumble when a secret from her past returns to Ashton . . .
1-59493-060-0 $13.95

SIGN ON THE LINE by Jaime Clevenger. 204 pp. Alexis Getty, a flirtatious delivery driver is committed to finding the rightful owner of a mysterious package.
1-59493-052-X $13.95

END OF WATCH by Clare Baxter. 256 pp. LAPD Lieutenant L.A Franco Frank follows the lone clue down the unlit steps of memory to a final, unthinkable resolution.
1-59493-064-4 $13.95

BEHIND THE PINE CURTAIN by Gerri Hill. 280 pp. Jacqueline returns home after her father's death and comes face-to-face with her first crush.
1-59493-057-0 $13.95

PIPELINE by Brenda Adcock. 240 pp. Joanna faces a lost love returning and pulling her into a seamy underground corporation that kills for money.
1-59493-062-7 $13.95

18TH & CASTRO by Karin Kallmaker. 200 pp. First-time couplings and couples who know how to mix lust and love make 18th & Castro the hottest address in the city by the bay. 1-59493-066-X $13.95

JUST THIS ONCE by KG MacGregor. 200 pp. Mindful of the obligations back home that she must honor, Wynne Connelly struggles to resist the fascination and allure that a particular woman she meets on her business trip represents.
1-59493-087-2 $13.95

ANTICIPATION by Terri Breneman. 240 pp. Two women struggle to remain professional as they work together to find a serial killer. 1-59493-055-4 $13.95

OBSESSION by Jackie Calhoun. 240 pp. Lindsey's life is turned upside down when Sarah comes into the family nursery in search of perennials. 1-59493-058-9 $13.95

BENEATH THE WILLOW by Kenna White. 240 pp. A torch that still burns brightly even after twenty-five years threatens to consume two childhood friends.
1-59493-053-8 $13.95

SISTER LOST, SISTER FOUND by Jeanne G'fellers. 224 pp. The highly anticipated sequel to No Sister of Mine. 1-59493-056-2 $13.95

THE WEEKEND VISITOR by Jessica Thomas. 240 pp. In this latest Alex Peres mystery, Alex is asked to investigate an assault on a local woman but finds that her client may have more secrets than she lets on. 1-59493-054-6 $13.95

THE KILLING ROOM by Gerri Hill. 392 pp. How can two women forget and go their separate ways? 1-59493-050-3 $12.95

PASSIONATE KISSES by Megan Carter. 240 pp. Will two old friends run from love?
1-59493-051-1 $12.95

ALWAYS AND FOREVER by Lyn Denison. 224 pp. The girl next door turns Shannon's world upside down. 1-59493-049-X $12.95

BACK TALK by Saxon Bennett. 200 pp. Can a talk show host find love after heartbreak?
1-59493-028-7 $12.95

THE PERFECT VALENTINE: EROTIC LESBIAN VALENTINE STORIES edited by Barbara Johnson and Therese Szymanski—from Bella After Dark. 328 pp. Stories from the hottest writers around. 1-59493-061-9 $14.95

MURDER AT RANDOM by Claire McNab. 200 pp. The Sixth Denise Cleever Thriller. Denise realizes the fate of thousands is in her hands.
1-59493-047-3 $12.95

THE TIDES OF PASSION by Diana Tremain Braund. 240 pp. Will Susan be able to hold it all together and find the one woman who touches her soul?
1-59493-048-1 $12.95

JUST LIKE THAT by Karin Kallmaker. 240 pp. Disliking each other—and everything they stand for—even before they meet, Toni and Syrah find feelings can change, just like that.
1-59493-025-2 $12.95

WHEN FIRST WE PRACTICE by Therese Szymanski. 200 pp. Brett and Allie are once again caught in the middle of murder and intrigue.
1-59493-045-7 $12.95

REUNION by Jane Frances. 240 pp. Cathy Braithwaite seems to have it all: good looks, money and a thriving accounting practice . . .
1-59493-046-5 $12.95

BELL, BOOK & DYKE: NEW EXPLOITS OF MAGICAL LESBIANS by Kallmaker, Watts, Johnson and Szymanski. 360 pp. Reluctant witches, tempting spells and skyclad beauties—delve into the mysteries of love, lust and power in this quartet of novellas.
1-59493-023-6 $14.95

ARTIST'S DREAM by Gerri Hill. 320 pp. When Cassie meets Luke Winston, she can no longer deny her attraction to women . . .
1-59493-042-2 $12.95

NO EVIDENCE by Nancy Sanra. 240 pp. Private Investigator Tally McGinnis once again returns to the horror-filled world of a serial killer.
1-59493-043-04 $12.95

WHEN LOVE FINDS A HOME by Megan Carter. 280 pp. What will it take for Anna and Rona to find their way back to each other again?
1-59493-041-4 $12.95

MEMORIES TO DIE FOR by Adrian Gold. 240 pp. Rachel attempts to avoid her attraction to the charms of Anna Sigurdson . . .
1-59493-038-4 $12.95

SILENT HEART by Claire McNab. 280 pp. Exotic lesbian romance.
1-59493-044-9 $12.95

MIDNIGHT RAIN by Peggy J. Herring. 240 pp. Bridget McBee is determined to find the woman who saved her life.
1-59493-021-X $12.95

THE MISSING PAGE A Brenda Strange Mystery by Patty G. Henderson. 240 pp. Brenda investigates her client's murder . . .
1-59493-004-X $12.95

WHISPERS ON THE WIND by Frankie J. Jones. 240 pp. Dixon thinks she and her best friend, Elizabeth Colter, would make the perfect couple . . .
1-59493-037-6 $12.95

CALL OF THE DARK: EROTIC LESBIAN TALES OF THE SUPERNATURAL edited by Therese Szymanski—from Bella After Dark. 320 pp.
1-59493-040-6 $14.95

A TIME TO CAST AWAY A Helen Black Mystery by Pat Welch. 240 pp. Helen stops by Alice's apartment—only to find the woman dead . . .
1-59493-036-8 $12.95

DESERT OF THE HEART by Jane Rule. 224 pp. The book that launched the most popular lesbian movie of all time is back.
1-1-59493-035-X $12.95

THE NEXT WORLD by Ursula Steck. 240 pp. Anna's friend Mido is threatened and eventually disappears . . .   1-59493-024-4 $12.95

CALL SHOTGUN by Jaime Clevenger. 240 pp. Kelly gets pulled back into the world of private investigation . . .   1-59493-016-3 $12.95

52 PICKUP by Bonnie J. Morris and E.B. Casey. 240 pp. 52 hot, romantic tales—one for every Saturday night of the year.   1-59493-026-0 $12.95

GOLD FEVER by Lyn Denison. 240 pp. Kate's first love, Ashley, returns to their home town, where Kate now lives . . .   1-1-59493-039-2 $12.95

RISKY INVESTMENT by Beth Moore. 240 pp. Lynn's best friend and roommate needs her to pretend Chris is his fiancé. But nothing is ever easy.

                                    1-59493-019-8 $12.95

HUNTER'S WAY by Gerri Hill. 240 pp. Homicide detective Tori Hunter is forced to team up with the hot-tempered Samantha Kennedy.   1-59493-018-X $12.95

CAR POOL by Karin Kallmaker. 240 pp. Soft shoulders, merging traffic and slippery when wet . . . Anthea and Shay find love in the car pool.   1-59493-013-9 $12.95

NO SISTER OF MINE by Jeanne G'Fellers. 240 pp. Telepathic women fight to coexist with a patriarchal society that wishes their eradication.

                                    1-59493-017-1 $12.95

ON THE WINGS OF LOVE by Megan Carter. 240 pp. Stacie's reporting career is on the rocks. She has to interview bestselling author Cheryl, or else!

                                    1-59493-027-9 $12.95

WICKED GOOD TIME by Diana Tremain Braund. 224 pp. Does Christina need Miki as a protector . . . or want her as a lover?   1-59493-031-7 $12.95

THOSE WHO WAIT by Peggy J. Herring. 240 pp. Two brilliant sisters—in love with the same woman!   1-59493-032-5 $12.95

ABBY'S PASSION by Jackie Calhoun. 240 pp. Abby's bipolar sister helps turn her world upside down, so she must decide what's most important.

                                    1-59493-014-7 $12.95

PICTURE PERFECT by Jane Vollbrecht. 240 pp. Kate is reintroduced to Casey, the daughter of an old friend. Can they withstand Kate's career? 1-59493-015-5 $12.95

PAPERBACK ROMANCE by Karin Kallmaker. 240 pp. Carolyn falls for tall, dark and . . . female . . . in this classic lesbian romance.   1-59493-033-3 $12.95

DAWN OF CHANGE by Gerri Hill. 240 pp. Susan ran away to find peace in remote Kings Canyon—then she met Shawn . . .   1-59493-011-2 $12.95

DOWN THE RABBIT HOLE by Lynne Jamneck. 240 pp. Is a killer holding a grudge against FBI Agent Samantha Skellar?   1-59493-012-0 $12.95

SEASONS OF THE HEART by Jackie Calhoun. 240 pp. Overwhelmed, Sara saw only one way out—leaving . . .   1-59493-030-9 $12.95

TURNING THE TABLES by Jessica Thomas. 240 pp. The 2nd Alex Peres Mystery. *From ghosties and ghoulies and long leggity beasties* . . .   1-59493-009-0 $12.95

FOR EVERY SEASON by Frankie Jones. 240 pp. Andi, who is investigating a 65-year-old murder, meets Janice, a charming district attorney . . . 1-59493-010-4 $12.95